Phoebe bit her lip.

Nick's torso was lean and solid-looking, his arms defined. And then her gaze landed on the upper part of his chest. She was in her nightgown, staring at his naked chest as he mixed some sort of chocolate concoction. In the middle of the night. This entire scenario really shouldn't be happening.

But it was...

His stare still holding hers, he raised her hand. Then he placed her finger, dripping chocolate batter, to his lips. He slid her finger into his mouth and licked, swirled his tongue around her skin, sucking off every last drop. Her breathing was fast, and her nipples were pebbling beneath her nightgown. She moved to turn but he reached out and grabbed her, stopping her.

"I thought you wanted a taste."

Every nerve in her body was thrumming with desire. For her smug chef.

She was losing her mind. Because she did want a taste. Of more than just chocolate...

Bound to Please

Also by Lilli Feisty

Bound to Please
Dare to Surrender

Deliciously Sinful

LILLI FEISTY

FOREVER

NEW YORK BOSTON

Forever
Hachette Book Group
237 Park Avenue
New York, NY 10017
www.HachetteBookGroup.com

Forever is an imprint of Grand Central Publishing.
The Forever name and logo are trademarks of Hachette Book Group, Inc.

The publisher is not responsible for websites (or their content) that are not owned by the publisher.

Printed in the United States of America

First Edition: December 2011

10 9 8 7 6 5 4 3 2 1

ATTENTION CORPORATIONS AND ORGANIZATIONS:

Most Hachette Book Group books are available at quantity discounts with bulk purchase for educational, business, or sales promotional use. For information, please call or write:

Special Markets Department, Hachette Book Group
237 Park Avenue, New York, NY 10017
Telephone: 1-800-222-6747 Fax: 1-800-477-5925

To Brian. How's that novel coming along?

Acknowledgments

I need to give a big thank-you to my agent, Roberta Brown, and the editors at Grand Central Publishing, Alex Logan and Amy Pierpont. Thank you for being wonderful, talented, and supportive while I wrote this book. Alex, your comments always get me through revisions and make me LOL.

I would also like to thank my amazing friends who have been by my side during a very challenging year. J. and G., we'll always have quicksand. BRCU, thank you for being my surrogate family. Jerry Fucking Snyder and Kristen Amazing, home is wherever I'm with you. Melanie, I love our domestic partnership. Paul, you are the best car husband a girl could ever have. Leutzy, I want to be you when I grow up.

Reno, you rock.

Deliciously Sinful

Prologue

When Phoebe Mayle touched her forehead, it was sticky with blood. She looked at her fingertips and red stains spotted her skin. The front end of her car was smashed into a fallen redwood tree, and steam was rising from under the hood to mingle with the earsplitting downpour of rain that was hitting the roof of her car like a shower of nails. If she'd broken any bones, she couldn't feel it. She didn't feel anything except the way her entire body was shaking from the shock of the impact.

The windshield was cracked, but the rearview mirror was intact. Her quivering hands were barely able to tilt the mirror so she could inspect the wound on her forehead. She gasped at her reflection. There was a gash that was dripping blood, and both of her eyes were already turning the shade of an eggplant. Otherwise, she didn't appear to have any major injuries. No, her current worry was the fact that she had just totaled her car, and now she was stranded miles from help. She might have a concussion, and the temperature was dropping steadily. Who knew how long it would take for a rescue team to navigate the road and find her?

She wasn't quite sure what had happened. The last

thing she remembered was the tree falling directly in front of her car. Luckily she'd been driving slowly because of the weather, or the damage would have been a lot worse. As it was, she'd blacked out when her head hit the steering wheel, and she wasn't sure how long she'd been out. Now she tried to gather her wits and figure out a plan.

Good luck with that.

From what she could see through the curtain of rain, several trees had fallen, mudslides were coating large portions of the cracked road, and the nearest house was probably a good ten miles away.

This is all your fault. Everyone had told her not to go out to the farm in this weather, but she had insisted on going. Insisted because she was a control freak who was trying to prove a point. And the point was that she could do it all, with or without a certain person named Nick Avalon, who'd left her high and dry when she needed him most.

She should have done so many things differently.

You can't do everything.

Ah, yes. Finally. *Finally*, she could admit that to herself. Sitting there, staring at her bloody hand, she didn't have any choice but to realize that she simply wasn't able to control every aspect of her life—or those around her.

Great time for such amazing self-realizations. She was caught in a downpour that made it incredibly stupid to start walking anywhere, and—by the looks of the nearest hill—she was fairly certain a mudslide was about to occur in the near future, covering what shelter she had.

And why are you here? Because you couldn't let Nick Avalon get the better of you. You had to risk your life for some quail eggs just to prove you were as capable as he was?

So here she was. Shivering in a wrecked car deep in a redwood forest, in the middle of what used to be a road, with no food, water, or even rain gear.

This never would have happened before she'd met Nick. She'd started adopting his ways; she'd become just a bit too carefree and she'd started taking risks.

All her life, she'd avoided hazardous situations. So what had she done? Fallen for the charms of the most hazardous situation on the West Coast.

"Nick. Avalon." She said the words aloud in a bitter tone.

She would bet he was sunning himself in L.A., getting ready for a new job at some fancy restaurant, surrounded by hot young Hollywood starlets. Smoking a cigarette and drinking tequila.

Frustration overwhelmed her, and she screamed. Loud. And screamed again.

Out of all the days in her life, the one day she wished she could take back was the day Nick Avalon drove into her town.

Chapter One

Four Months Earlier

Blowing a frizzy strand of hair out of her eye, Phoebe Mayle looked at the bowl of organic, vegan, carob brownies she was mixing. It looked like brown glue. It was her third attempt that day. And looked like it was going to be her third failure.

You're making brownies, not Pavlova.

What was she doing wrong? She'd followed the recipe down to the last half teaspoon of vanilla. Glancing at the calendar hanging on the wall, she sighed. The summer bake-off was in a few months, and these brownies had won the contest for ten years running.

Unless a fairy godmother came down and waved a magic spatula over the mixture, there was no way the Green Leaf was going to take first place this summer.

Great. The entire town would know that since Phoebe had taken over the café, one of the oldest establishments in Redbolt, California, everything was going downhill. Customers would dwindle until only "Grandpa Dave"— the town's oldest resident—would come in for his daily cup of tea (which, Phoebe was convinced, the old man would do until the day he died), the place would close, and her aunt and uncle would be turning in their graves.

Take a deep breath. You can do this! They're just brownies. Wiping her hands on her apron, Phoebe looked out the café window. Indeed, a monstrous, shiny yellow SUV had pulled up out front, and though she couldn't see the driver due to the late-afternoon sun reflecting off the windshield, she knew it could be only one person.

"Thanks," Phoebe said sarcastically.

Jesse said, "Pheebs, I can't believe you hired some guy from L.A. to come and run the café."

She'd known the girl since she was born, and had had the pleasure of watching Jesse grow into a young woman. A few years ago her niece had started growing the dreadlocks that were now piled high on her head and wrapped in a colorful scarf. True to the nature of the family's long-standing belief in personal expression, Phoebe's brother-in-law had heartily approved when his daughter had quit washing her hair.

Phoebe reached behind her back and untied her apron. "Do I have chocolate on my face?"

"No," Jesse said innocently.

Rolling her eyes, Phoebe picked up a stainless-steel frying pan and looked at her distorted reflection. She wasn't surprised to find a brown smudge of chocolate on the bridge of her nose. Using the tip of a towel, she wiped it off. Scraped it off, actually; chocolate crumbs fell off her face and onto the floor.

"And I still don't understand why you couldn't have found someone local."

"I tried. Come on, Jesse. You know there isn't anyone around here qualified to maintain Sally and Dan's standards."

"What about you?"

Phoebe must have looked surprised because Jesse replied, "Well...you could learn, right?"

Phoebe picked up the product of her previous attempt at the organic brownies and tossed it at Jesse, who jumped aside before the lump hit her right in the chest. "Hey! Watch it. I don't want to die from a fatal brownie wound to the chest!"

The hard square landed across the café with a hard thud. "That's why. Everything I make turns out like crap. Not to mention, I just don't have the time. I have a whole other business to run, remember?" A business that had been suffering ever since she'd inherited the Green Leaf Café from her deceased relatives.

"I really thought I could handle it. I mean, I have all the recipes. Why can't I just make them work?" She glanced at the myriad reviews tacked to the wall. All photocopies from food magazines, travel guides, and newspapers. All praising the simple, organic cuisine produced by the Green Leaf Café. All written before Phoebe had taken over the place.

Luckily, no critic had visited recently. Phoebe really didn't want to be responsible for denting the café's stellar reputation as the best gourmet bistro north of San Francisco. A six-hour drive north, to be precise.

"Hey," Jesse said gently. "It's okay. I didn't mean to give you grief. We all know you're trying really hard."

Phoebe blew a strand of hair away from her eye. "And the cook-off is right around the corner."

Jesse smiled, but she was biting her lip as she did so. "Yeah!" she said with enthusiasm. A lot of enthusiasm, way more than any cook-off deserved.

"Are you, um..." Jesse glanced at the plate of rock-hard brownies. "Are you sure you want to enter the brownies this year?"

"Well, what choice do I have?" Phoebe picked up another brown lump of brownie and bounced it on her palm. The rough edges pricked her skin. "Dan and Sally have been winning that cook-off with their brownies for the last ten years. I know it seems silly, but I really want to get the ribbon this year. For them." And also for herself. She needed to prove that she could *do* this. That she could run the business as well as the family who entrusted her to do so. Winning the cook-off the first year Dan and Sally weren't there to enter themselves—well, it all seemed monumentally important.

"Everything is going to be okay," Jesse said.

She tossed the rest of the brownies into a garbage can. "It's my own fault. I never should have committed to running this place." But she had to. Phoebe believed in tradition, in family. In obligation. "I had no idea my organic farming business would become so popular."

"Hey," Jesse said, "you rock."

"I don't know about that. But so many local markets and restaurants are placing orders. I even got one out of Berkeley yesterday."

"Wow. So things are booming, then?"

Phoebe nodded slowly. "Yeah. They are."

"That's great; it really is. I know that farm is your true passion."

"Maybe..." But it shouldn't be. *This* should be; this café. Her family's reputation. Making brownies and winning the cook-off and being responsible and successful.

"Is that a freakin' *Hummer*?"

Phoebe glanced up at the teenager who'd spoken the

words. "That must be our new chef," Phoebe said. "Thank God."

Jesse, her eighteen-year-old waitress and niece, leaned against the counter, eyeing the Hummer with a frown.

Jesse turned toward the window and crossed her arms over her chest. "He's getting out of the monster."

It was early spring, and now the bright sun reflected off the so-shiny-it-hurt-your-eyes yellow-painted metal of the huge vehicle her newly hired chef had arrived in. The windows were tinted dark, so she couldn't make out any images from inside the vehicle.

This would be the first time she'd actually meet the person she'd hired to take over the kitchen at the Green Leaf Café.

Her heart sped up a bit and she wiped her damp palms on her apron. She hoped she had chosen wisely. She realized hiring Nick Avalon was a risk. She knew he'd been fired from his last job. She knew he had a bit of a reputation as a bad boy. But she'd also done extensive research of his history as a chef, and he'd had what was definitely the most impressive résumé of any she'd received. Magazines like *Bon Appétit* had done articles on him and featured his recipes. He'd made a few guest chef appearances on popular Food Network television shows. And he'd worked at restaurants so popular even Phoebe had heard of them.

Still. In essence, she'd hired a stranger to help carry on her family business. Their legacy.

It's okay. You're a smart businesswoman. You know what you're doing.

And she'd spoken with him on the phone. He had a nice voice and seemed friendly enough. And he was British, which she couldn't help but find a bit engaging. Heck, he could have called her a *daft cow*, and it probably would have sounded charming.

Had she made a mistake? Well, there was nothing she could do about it now. Only time would tell.

She watched as the Hummer door swung open. Then two shiny black sneakers, the likes of which Redbolt had surely never seen before, hit the pavement. Ascending over said sneakers were the hems of black jeans covering long, long legs. A tight black T-shirt clung to a lean torso.

But it wasn't his clothing that had "attitude problem" written all over it. No, it was his face—the way his mouth turned down and his nose lifted up, and the way his eyebrows slashed over blue eyes framed by inky lashes.

He had short black hair, and his dark aviator sunglasses didn't hide the air of disdain that emanated off him as he shut the door of his SUV and glanced up and down the town's main street.

Phoebe bit her lip. When she'd described the town, she may have slightly exaggerated its attributes. She watched him gazing at the "colorful shops" and "various entertainment options" that she'd portrayed in her ad. The shopping options included an organic baby clothing store, a bead store, a small art gallery, a hookah lounge, a hardware store, and a few other establishments selling an array of tie-dyed clothing. As for entertainment, Redbolt did boast two small bars and one theater. Unfortunately, the movies generally played a month or so later than anywhere else in the country.

Okay, so it wasn't exactly Hollywood. He'd have to deal with it.

She watched as Nick Avalon shook his head, took a

deep breath, and came toward the front door. Phoebe ignored the flutters in her belly. Why should *she* be nervous? She was the boss, right? He was the one who should be suffering anxiety.

Right?

She was a modern, confident woman who ran two businesses, one of which was booming, the other of which was, well...

She narrowed her gaze on the man walking through the door. The man who would be, in large part, responsible for continuing her family's legacy.

Dear Universe: Please let this man be the right choice; please, pu-lease *let me have made the right choice.* If the universe cared about her at all, maybe it was listening to her plea. Or Carl Sagan was full of crap, and the universe was some kind of lie that hippies and hipsters used to fulfill their spiritual needs. Either way, she hoped she hadn't made a mistake.

He pushed through the door and stopped. "So this is what nowhere looks like," he said as the door quietly closed behind him.

But she still heard the door shut. And that was because the café was entirely silent. Everyone—her staff, her patrons, the flies on the wall—was looking at this man who obviously didn't belong here. He looked like he belonged in a magazine as a model of what every man in L.A. should aspire to in terms of appearance. (She knew this because sometimes she secretly watched reality television, including the exceedingly popular cooking series *Satan's Pantry*.)

Without removing his sunglasses, he glanced around the bistro. His stance was easy, nonchalant, and confident.

He didn't look impressed.

Oh no. Maybe her love of the television series had influenced her decision to hire Nick Avalon. He definitely had a devilish air about him.

But he was far, far away from the set of *Satan's Pantry*. Phoebe held out her hand. "You must be Nick."

Slowly, he pulled the aviators off his face. When his gaze fell on hers, she nearly gasped. Instead, she bit her lip as she took him in.

Eyes as blue as the morning glories taking over her front yard arrested her. His black hair only emphasized the striking color of his eyes, and the way he was looking at her—staring, really—made those flutters in her belly spread to her chest.

Because that look of disapproval was aimed straight at her.

Phoebe steadied herself. She would *not* be intimidated by some fancy-pants from Los Angeles. She continued to hold out her hand. "I'm Phoebe. The owner."

He shook her hand, and she refrained from cringing at his hard grasp. And tried not to jerk away as a shiver of heat rushed up her arm. That would be showing fear, and she had to convey nothing but absolute confidence. Right away, she knew that showing any sign of weakness to this...this...predator could be deadly.

"Pleasure." He took another long glance around the café.

She'd interviewed him on the phone, so his British accent wasn't surprising. However, it was a bit shocking how the smooth, relaxed intonation of his tone made her want to get a bit closer to his mouth.

Where had that crazy thought come from? Maybe she

was low on blood sugar. Too bad the brownies were the texture of bricks, or she would have popped one into her mouth. But she really didn't need a broken tooth right now.

He said, "So. Here we are, then. The Green Leaf *Café*." He ground the last word out of his mouth; then he nodded, but it was more to himself, as if he was processing the fact that everything was real. That he was there. *Here.*

Phoebe straightened. "I'm sure it's not quite like what you're accustomed to."

"No. No, not really what I'm used to."

"But I'm also sure you'll find things here are more modern than you might imagine. We have a state-of-the-art kitchen that was remodeled just last year. And our wine cellar holds one of the finest selections in the area."

"Is that so? The whole area of Redbolt?"

He glanced across the counter to the prep area. Okay, compared to those showcased on the TV show *Satan's Pantry*, it might be small. But it was efficient, and the appliances were of professional quality.

None of which helped Phoebe make a decent batch of brownies.

"Anyway," she said, "welcome to the Green Leaf Café. I hope you'll be happy as our new chef."

She thought she saw a shudder go through him, but she wasn't sure.

Then he actually shivered, as if he'd just caught a chill, or seen a ghost.

She raised her chin. How dare he walk in and give her such attitude? He was lucky she'd hired him. Lucky! The café might be small, and rural, and rustic—but that was certainly no reason to give it, or her, disrespect.

"Mr. Avalon—"

"What is *that*?"

His gaze fell on the brown lump of brownie on the floor in the corner. He glanced at her and cocked a brow. Then he strode over and picked it up. He started juggling the brown lump between his palms.

Darn it to heck. She began to feel her face flush. "It's, um, er..." She bit her lip and straightened her spine. "A brownie."

He dropped the nugget into one palm and stared at it. "All right, then." He glanced up and that brow cocked at her again. There was a little scar on the very edge of his eyebrow, and she wanted to know where it came from.

One of his bosses probably whopped him in the head with a frying pan.

"And it's here why? Brownie fight?" he said, his accent dissolving the sarcasm she knew cannoned the sentence. "Is that considered a spectator sport, or more participatory?"

He started juggling the brownie again and she marched over and caught it mid-toss. "Just trying out a new recipe." She wasn't sure why she lied, but for some reason she didn't want to seem anything less than one hundred percent capable of doing anything. Including making brownies.

She turned toward Jesse. "So, I think that new organic butter we used must have been bad."

Jesse looked confused, so Phoebe widened her eyes and tried to convey a secret signal that would get her niece to go along with Phoebe's ploy.

Finally Jesse nodded. And furrowed her brow. And crossed her arms in front of her chest. "Yes. The butter. Definitely bad. Very, very, um...bad."

Oh, God. This wasn't going well. Phoebe threw the brownie into the garbage. Time to change the subject. "Nick, this is my niece, Jesse. She works here."

"Wow. Isn't this just a sweet little family endeavor?"

Phoebe looked him straight in the eyes. "Yes. It is."

He paused, and she barely caught the look of surprise that flashed across his face. Did he think she wouldn't talk back to him? That she'd put up with his snide remarks?

Well, ha, ha, ha. Boy, was he wrong.

Obviously, she was going to have to establish herself as the boss from the get-go.

Fine. She was fine with that. She could do this.

Even if something about him made her nerves buzz with nervous energy. Even if his direct stare was unnerving. Even if, for some reason, she felt herself responding to Nick as a woman, when she should be reacting like his superior.

Get a grip. You can do this.

"Now. If you'll come with me, I'll show you around the café."

His smile dripped sugar as he made a sweeping hand gesture. "After you, Miss Mayle."

Chapter Two

So what do the kids call this kind of music, anyway? Death by synthesizer?" Phoebe asked.

Pausing, Nick Avalon clenched the wooden spoon in his hand. He was caramelizing onions for a quiche. Not a vegan one, not a vegetarian one. A real quiche, with ham and cheese and eggs and butter. Lots of rich, creamy, calorific butter. Butter he'd procured from a British import store an hour north of where he currently resided. Which was exactly nowhere.

Eleven more months, he told himself. Eleven months, three weeks, and—he glanced at the clock—seven hours until he could return from exile. It was a time frame he'd set for himself, one he'd decided on before he'd accepted this job. Not that he'd ever mentioned to his boss the fact that he didn't plan on staying in Hippieville longer than one year. If he could last that long.

The decor of the café was hideous. Rustic tables that looked as if they'd been collected at various yard sales made up the dining area. The wooden floor was scratched up and needed a good refinishing. In fact, the floor should be replaced with stained concrete. And the random assortment of chairs needed to be traded for something more modern. And something that actually matched.

"This music is called house trance, and I like it," he said through gritted teeth. And he did. It had a beat, something he could feel hard and deep in his soul. Unlike that slow, uninspiring, outdated crap that his manager always snuck onto the sound system.

"House trance? Do they play that at the raves you go to?"

Pausing, he closed his eyes. "I wouldn't call them raves." In fact, he tended to listen to music alone, so he could be free to feel the beat of something and lose himself, but he wasn't about to admit that to her.

"Then why?"

"Why what?"

"Why listen to music without words?"

"It takes me away from distraction." Hoping she'd get the point, he returned to his onions. He wasn't about to explain himself; he preferred music without words. Words sidetracked him. He needed a rhythm that blended. He needed to feel the pulse in his soul, his gut. Nick could tenderize a piece of meat to perfection. All he needed was a mallet and a thumping bass line.

Today he'd managed to slip his own CD, burned by a DJ back in West Hollywood, into the stereo. And listening to the music, for just a few minutes, he'd been able to nearly forget he was working in a café in Butt-Fuck, Nowhere.

His boss, Ms. Phoebe Mayle, had actually left him alone long enough to think about what he was doing. Cooking.

Now she put an unpolished fingertip to her lip. "Oh, I'm sure you love this type of music. I hear it's quite popular with the hip, cool twenty-somethings. How old are you again?"

She knew damn well he was thirty-five. He gave her his best scowl. He was notorious for that look, a look that had been known to make sous-chefs recoil in fear. A look that could send any waitstaffer running to the restroom in tears. Nick's stare was intimidating, menacing—scary.

Well, it had been back in Los Angeles.

Here in Redbolt, California, a million miles away from civilization, no one seemed to comprehend the fact that he was *Nick Avalon*, one of the country's most *recognized* chefs. Hell, before he'd been "let go," there'd even been talk about his getting his own TV show.

That seemed a lifetime ago, even though only a few days had passed since he'd moved. Now here he was, working for a woman who was currently gazing at him with a snotty look, as if he were some sort of factory-line cook at a chain restaurant. But he wasn't about to give her, or anyone else, their own way.

Food was his art. His expression. His love. Anyone who thought otherwise could fuck off.

"Pardon me," he said after a deep breath. "Go ahead and put on that hippie crap everyone around here seems to prefer."

She smirked. He hated it when she did that. Her little nose got all scrunched up, and the pale skin around her big green eyes got all crinkly. As if she didn't give a crap that he actually knew what he was doing. And she didn't know this music helped him cook. Helped him forget.

She shrugged. "Well, I suppose this music suits you. It's so . . . *trendy* and *cool*."

He just stared at her and let the acerbic tone of her voice drip off him like melted butter.

Of course, she went on. "But you're not in some hip nightclub right now. You're in the Green Leaf Café. And we have a slightly more relaxed atmosphere than those fancy Los Angeles places you're used to."

He clenched the wooden spoon in his hand. Like he could ever forget where he was. He was used to running kitchens that turned out more than two hundred plates per night. Last month, he'd been known for his escargot. Now, a quiche Lorraine was not only some sort of exotic specialty, but also it was practically forbidden, what with the egg and cream and *ham* and all.

Casually, Phoebe reached into his sauté pan, plucked out an amber-colored onion, and popped it into her mouth. She grimaced.

He shouldn't care. Why should he be concerned about what she thought? She had inherited a café from her aunt and uncle, and they obviously hadn't passed on any of their "gourmet" knowledge to their niece. Granted, she appeared to have a decent palate, but she was utterly devoid of skill at actually creating cuisine of any sort.

Basically, the woman couldn't boil a pot of water if her life depended on it.

Still, he couldn't deny she knew how to grow some amazingly tasty produce. At least she had that going for her.

And so he waited for her reaction. Hating the fact that he had a flashback to Paris, heartbeat racing, waiting for a response, just like back in culinary school waiting for his instructor's reaction.

"It's good," she said. Finally. After swallowing.

Good? This recipe had been featured on the cover of *Gourmet* magazine, and all she could say was that it was good?

Tearing his gaze away from her throat, Nick leaned against the counter. "Thanks, love. So glad you liked it." He heard the sarcasm dripping from his voice. Again, he reminded himself that her opinion didn't matter to him. He'd gone to Le Cordon Bleu in Paris, for fuck's sake. She'd probably never left Humboldt County.

"Sorry, it was hot. But good. Really good. Different, but good."

"Good. Yes, you said that. Repeatedly."

"It's true." Her eyes were wide as she said it, and he may have caught a flash of actual appreciation. Okay, so maybe he was being overly sensitive. "You're a hard woman to please, aren't you?"

Her green eyes widened in surprise. "No, I don't think so." She paused and then said, "Why do you say that?"

He shrugged. "Just an observation." *Whatever.*

"Right," he continued. "Well, you just took it right out of the pan. Things that are cooked at high temperatures tend to be hot." Why was he going on like a defensive idiot?

She shrugged. "Sorry. It's just the things you cook smell so..."

"Yeah?" he said nonchalantly. And then, "They smell so *what*?"

"Delicious."

He grunted and looked away. "Well, what did you expect?"

Grinning, she plucked out another onion. "Just because something smells good doesn't mean it tastes good."

"Really? You grow broccoli. Broccoli doesn't exactly smell like roses. It smells like gas."

"Right! When it's growing it doesn't smell very nice. But when you cook it correctly—like the way it should be prepared for our veggie tofu stir-fry—the scent can certainly be lovely."

Whenever she talked about her farm, her entire demeanor changed. Carrots made her passionate. When she went on about her honeybees, her eyes sparkled. And now she was radiating as she preached about the attributes of broccoli.

As if he didn't know about vegetables. "I know how to cook broccoli."

"I'm sure you do."

Was she humoring him? "I *can*," he bit out.

"*I said*, I believe you. But can you make it without smothering it in some fancy, heavy sauce?"

"Yes." He quirked his head to the side. "But why would I?"

"Exactly."

She made his brain hurt. "Listen. I know what I'm doing."

Her expression softened, just a bit. "I know you know what you're doing. I know we are lucky to have you."

He barked a laugh at her sentiment.

"I mean it. We are lucky to have someone like you in our kitchen. I just think, maybe, you could think about the fact that you're not in L.A. anymore. This community is a bit more simple."

"Trust me. That's one thing I have no doubt about."

"That doesn't mean we're not sophisticated. So maybe you can just learn to change a little. Adapt to what we do here, which is to try to live with a few less complications. I mean, I've seen *Satan's Pantry*. I know how intense it must be."

He ground his teeth so hard his inner ear cringed. *Satan's Pantry*. He hated that show.

So close. He'd been so close to being chosen as the host of the now insanely popular reality television series that takes place in a restaurant known for its celebrity drop-ins.

So close to having everything he'd wanted.

And he'd fucked it up.

For some unfathomable reason, she reached out and touched his shoulder. Warily, he met her gaze. "What?"

She shrugged. "I don't know. You just looked like you needed..."

"I don't need anything." He shook her hand off his shoulder. "I *know* what I'm *doing*." How many times did he need to hammer it into her frizzy little head? He hadn't been the best chef in London, Chicago, and then Los Angeles for nothing. He'd worked hard. He was good at what he did. He rarely fucked up.

Yeah, you never fuck up. That's why you're here, idiot.

Whatever. Being fired from the best restaurant in L.A. had absolutely nothing to do with his skill as a chef. Nope. Getting fired from his job had to do with lame bullshit. How was he supposed to know that chick he'd taken home from some club was actually the daughter of *Satan's Pantry*'s producer?

Whatever. He was an amazing chef. And, more important, he knew how to run a kitchen.

And yet this Phoebe person didn't seem to care. At all. Sure, she could try to pretend to be all open and caring and helpful, but he'd seen that temper of hers enough times to know it was all an act. The woman was a control freak *extraordinaire*.

She crossed her arms over her chest. He couldn't help it. His gaze dropped to the two perky mounds of her breasts. Real ones. It wasn't normal for a woman to have such amazing, natural breasts. And Nick should know. He'd sampled a smorgasbord of silicone back home.

She snapped her fingers in front of his face, and his gaze shot back up.

"All I'm saying is, this isn't the big city. People around here like simple food."

Simple. If he heard that bloody word one more time, he thought he'd poke himself in the ear with a metal skewer.

As if he didn't know everything about this fucking town was *simple*. In fact, it could just be called Simple Town, and maybe no one would feel the urge to constantly hammer the concept into the head of everyone who happened to pass through.

However, her breasts were anything but simple.

Damn it.

Don't look down; don't look down. Anyway, he really didn't need to. He knew she wore a brownish T-shirt that was not low-cut enough, a long skirt, and practical sandals.

And her body rocked the plain outfit.

He shook his head. "*I get it.* You can stop saying that now. And you think quiche is so fancy? It's one of the first things you learn in cooking school."

"Did I say I thought it was fancy?"

"No, but—"

"But what?" She had a wide, annoying mouth that

quirked a lot, usually morphing into a smug grin. "You're the one who keeps going on about quiche. Not me."

He watched as she leaned closer and lowered her voice. "Do you have some sort of egg fetish I should know about?" She nodded, trying to look dead serious, but he saw her eyes were twinkling. "Because we treat our chicken products with respect around here. Just so you know."

Nick was rarely speechless, but now—now he just stared at this woman. This woman with her frizzy, kinky deep-brown hair, her clean face, and her freckles. Yes, freckles. She had them. Scattered all over her face, like he might sprinkle shaved chocolate across a meringue tart.

"Are you actually joking with me?"

She pulled back. "Yes. Why?"

"I've just never seen it. Your sense of humor, that is."

She looked affronted. "I have a perfectly good sense of humor."

"When you're not telling me off with that temper of yours."

"I do not have a temper."

"Right. Of course you don't. That's why you threw an onion at me when I accidentally used heavy cream in the vegan mushroom soufflé."

"Nick Avalon, I do not for one second think that was an accident! You're smart enough to know exactly what ingredients you're using!"

After flashing a scowl in his direction, she turned on one sandal and walked away. He watched her walk. If he were to think about it, he'd wonder if she had a nice ass under that long, full skirt. He'd think her waist was sweetly small beneath the orange tank top she wore tucked into that skirt. He'd think that belt made of rope she wore low on her hips accentuated the curve of her waist.

He'd think he'd like to twist his fingers into that obnoxiously out-of-control hair and tug until she gasped—

But he wasn't going to think or wonder about any of that. He was going to think about the fact that he was here for one year. And in one year, he'd be back in Southern California where he belonged. Where his objective wasn't satisfying a small community of people who preferred vegan brownies and tofu nut loaf over *gâteau chocolat* and foi gras *en tourrine*. He'd think about when he could return from exile, and when he could make real food again. Cuisine he'd spent years perfecting and that had helped him earn a reputation as one of the best in the business.

"I don't think I can do it." Phoebe blew a kink of hair out of her eye and leaned against the storage room wall. "I don't think I can deal with him." Crossing her arms over her chest, she jerked her head toward the door leading to the kitchen. "He's just so..."

Jesse heaved a case of canned organic tomatoes onto a pile of wooden crates. They were in the stockroom of the restaurant, prepping inventory for the evening dinner crowd. "So what?" Jesse asked. "He's so what?"

"I don't know."

"Hot?"

"Obnoxious."

"Well," Jesse said with a grin that was much too wicked for any teenager to possess, "at least you picked a hot guy to run the kitchen."

"I have no idea what you're talking about." Even if every time she was around Nick Avalon her heart did funny things, it wasn't because he was hot. It was because he annoyed the living daylights out of her. "Anyway, he's not my type."

"Auntie Phoebe, no one is your type."

"That is not true." It was just that maybe her niece didn't know her type.

She shrugged. Logistics. She'd figure it out. She could do anything she set her mind to.

Except, apparently, make brownies.

"When was the last time you, you know...did the clam dip?"

Phoebe gasped. "What?"

Jesse waggled her eyebrows. "You know. Dipped your spoon in the batter? Churned the butter?"

"Jesse!" Phoebe straightened her skirt. "That is most definitely not only a totally inappropriate question, but also none of your business." Hadn't she asked herself a similar question just the other night?

"You can't answer because you probably can't even remember."

Phoebe snapped her attention back to reality. "I can, too."

Jesse hopped up onto the stack of crates and sat back. "Then spill. Was it Bear?"

"No. We're just friends now."

"I'm sorry, Pheebs. I shouldn't have brought Bear up."

"It's okay. Really. You know we're still friends."

"Okay, then if not Bear, who?"

"Who what?"

"Filled the hole in your doughnut."

"That is none of your business!" Phoebe felt a flush creep up her neck and took a few deep breaths. This was *so* not an appropriate conversation to be having with her niece. "And it certainly wasn't Bear." But she wished it had been. Just the thought of Bear O'Malley made her happy. Tall, strong, and gorgeous. Phoebe had known the man since high school. Although he kept a house here, he was rarely in town because he traveled the world as an agricultural consultant to third-world countries.

The fact that she could be by his side doing all of that never made her sad. Not at all.

Still...

Bear. Altruistic, kindhearted, and a bit of a daredevil. He was everything Nick Avalon was not, but Bear never stayed around.

"Are you sure you're just friends with him? Because every time someone says his name, you get that dreamy look on your face."

"Believe me, I'm sure. I'm only going to say it one more time. We're just friends." And that was true. Even if Bear *had* shown any interest in her recently, which other than some innocent flirting, he *hadn't*—she would never go there. It would hurt too much when he left.

"Anyway, like I said. If I had a type, *which I don't*, Nick Avalon would certainly not be it. No way, nohow."

"Then tell me, aunt of mine. What type of guy is Nick?" Jesse pushed an escaped dreadlock back into the tie-dyed scarf wrapped around her head.

"He's the kind of guy who thinks he can say whatever he wants, no matter how offensive. He's the kind of guy who drives an expensive and obnoxious off-road vehicle, but has probably never driven it off the pavement of a city. He's the kind of guy who has no respect for women. He's the kind of guy who makes me want to tear my hair out!" Phoebe realized she was breathing as if she'd just sprinted down the street, and she calmed herself down. Jesse was looking at her as though she'd gone off the deep end.

When she was breathing normally again, she said, "And I hate his hair." She did. She despised his spiky black hair, his blue eyes that shot right through her, and his long, lean body that made her seriously wonder what his skin would feel like touching hers.

She hated that type.

Jesse said, "Okay. I get it. Nick Avalon is not your type. But you know half the girls in this town are in love with him, right?"

"He's only been here a couple of weeks! How could anyone be in love with him?" Phoebe rolled her eyes. "Anyway, even if that's true, it's just because he's new and different."

Jessie heaved a smitten sigh. "And that accent. Oh my God, that accent."

"It's just a British accent. What's the big deal?"

Yeah, that's not what you were thinking when you spoke with him on the phone that first interview, was it?

And darn it to heck. Why did her heart skip whenever he called her something irritating like *bumpkin*? She shuddered. *Bumpkin?* Really?

Phoebe retrieved a box of soy milk for the vegan ice cream that had to be made for their lactose-free clients. "Anyway, it's just the fact that Nick's not from the area that makes the locals interested."

Jesse tossed another crate of tomatoes onto the stack.

"He's definitely not like the usual guys you find around here."

Phoebe yanked out another carton of soy milk. "I've never met anyone so arrogant in my entire life. And everything's a battle with him. I mean, I'm the boss!" She stabbed herself in the chest with her index finger. "He should listen to *me* instead of trying to turn the Green Leaf into some version of a chic Los Angeles restaurant."

"I ate his lamb."

Phoebe blinked. "What?"

"The other night, after everyone had left." Jesse lowered her voice. "Don't tell my dad. He'd freak if he knew I ate even one bite of a dead animal. But oh my *God*, Phoebe. Nick Avalon knows what he's doing when it comes to cooking meat. Did I tell you I had his duck the other night, too?"

"Stop!" Phoebe raised her hand. "I don't want to hear any more. You used to confess when you snuck out at night to go down to the river. Why does this seem worse somehow?"

"Because you know my dad's a militant freak about vegetarian eating?"

"He is not." Phoebe felt the need to stick up for her brother-in-law, who was one of the sweetest, nicest people she had the pleasure of knowing. "He's always let you make your own choices about what you consume."

"Yeah," Jesse scoffed. "But you know how he'd always look so sad if I ate chicken or something. Like I was disappointing him."

"You never disappoint your father, Jesse." Steve wasn't just Phoebe's brother-in law; he was her best friend.

Judy, his wife and Phoebe's sister, had died five years

ago. At the time, Phoebe had been living with her aunt and uncle in their huge Victorian house, and Steve and Jesse had eventually moved in as well. Just when Steve seemed to finally be getting past the death of his wife, Phoebe's aunt had passed away. And then Uncle Dan had followed within a year. Now there was a sadness about Steve that hovered like a dark cloud.

Shaking the thoughts away, she focused on what her niece was saying.

"Pheebs," Jesse said. "Even *you* have to admit Nick is really cute."

Phoebe pushed herself off the wall. "What do you mean, *even* I?"

"You're picky."

"I am not! I'm just...particular."

"Particularly picky."

"Not true."

"You can't even remember the last time you had your muffin buttered."

Phoebe looked away, thinking. "I can too remember when I last had my muffin buttered." What was she saying? "I'm not going to talk about that with you!"

"Exactly. So what's wrong with Nick?"

"What?" Phoebe demanded. "W-what are you talking about? Even if I were interested, which I'm not, he hates me." She shook her head. What was Jesse thinking? "And we work together!"

Jesse shook her head. "He doesn't hate you."

"Do you have a dreadlock in your eye? Because you obviously have some clouded vision."

"I don't think I'm the one with limited sight here."

"You have no idea what you're talking about."

"I may be young, but I"—she tapped her temple—"I see things."

Phoebe laughed. "Oh, do you now? And I'm supposed to take love advice from a teenager?"

"Yeah. In fact, I smell things, too. Like something burning. Like, *now*."

Just then, the distinct scent of something that was indeed burning filtered into Phoebe's nose. "What's he done now?" Dropping the cartons of soy milk, she burst through the storage door, ran down the hallway, and headed straight for the kitchen. Where she found Nick Avalon surrounded by a cloud of smoke. Smoke and a group of her staff, who were watching him with expressions of awe.

"What's going on here?" she demanded.

He took a sip of his ever-present glass of golden liquid. He usually licked a wedge of lime after each sip and, as he did so now, she couldn't help it. Her gaze drifted to that luscious mouth of his, and she watched him lick the tart fruit.

When she glanced back up, he was watching her with a devilish gleam in his eyes.

Damn. Had he known she'd been distracted by that gorgeous mouth of his? She tucked a strand of hair behind her ear and sharpened her gaze. "Nick. I asked what is going on here."

"Just showing the kids how to flambé bananas."

She picked up a few bunches of cauliflower from the counter and dropped them into the sink. Then her gaze fell on the three other members of her staff, all teenagers she'd known their entire lives, who were currently staring at Nick as if he were some sort of god.

Well, she supposed in his mind, he was. Even Jesse, who'd followed her out of the storage room, seemed to be enamored with Nick.

"That's not on the menu," she said, pointing at the pan.

He took another sip from his small glass. "I know. But it should be." And licked the lime. His lips were shiny with the tequila.

Shiny and smirky and kissable.

Jeez. She needed a date with her vibrator to kill these urges about Nick.

"Those bananas were for the bread you're meant to be baking."

He raised one of his perfectly shaped black eyebrows. "I'm sure you can get more bananas."

"That's not the point."

"Then what *is* your point?"

She felt everything inside her constrict with irritation. "Why did I hire you again?"

His glance flickered to the far wall and to the montage of reviews. "Because you actually want this place to succeed." He looked back at her, and she didn't miss that annoying, troublemaking twinkle in his eyes. "How are those brownies coming along? I hear they're quite the hit at the bumpkin cook-off."

Damn him, why did he have to go there? In the privacy of her home kitchen, she'd attempted that damn brownie recipe about ten more times, and it hadn't improved one bit. In fact, she thought the brownies had actually become progressively worse.

It was then that she noticed every one in the café had gone still. Her staff was watching Nick and her bicker as if it were a tennis match.

She turned and started to walk away. When she noticed he wasn't following her, she jerked her head. "Come here." Then she continued stalking, her skirt flowing around her ankles in angry swooshes of gauzy fabric.

After he'd sauntered into the storage room, she kicked the door shut. "Stop that," she growled.

"What?" He crossed his arms over his chest, causing the short sleeves of his black T-shirt to tighten around biceps that made Phoebe's mouth water.

She swallowed. Then, pointing a finger at him, she said, "Don't give me that innocent look. You know exactly what I'm talking about."

"You mean the bananas?"

And it was then that she realized he held a wooden spoon in his hand. With an evil glint in his eye, he uncrossed his arms and held it out to her.

Like some sort of horrible Pavlovian food whore, her mouth began to water. She backed up. "Get that away from me."

He stepped forward. "Come on. Taste. I promise it's better than banana bread."

"That's not the point." Then her back hit the wall. Nowhere to go. He was coming at her with his wooden spoonful of mouthwatering, and no doubt delicious, glistening banana slices.

She clenched her clammy hands. "I don't want to argue with you in front of my staff."

"What's there to argue about?" He held the spoon just under her nose. She tried to hold her breath, but she couldn't help it; she had to breathe, right? And *oh my God*. The bananas smelled amazing. She licked her lips.

He watched her lick her lips. His blue eyes were dark, unreadable.

"Taste." When he said the word, his voice was raspy.

"Don't tempt me with your flambéed bananas!"

His eyes sparkled with humor at her words. She inhaled, realizing it was the first time she'd seen real humor in his eyes. It softened her, just a bit.

"Go on," he coaxed. "You won't regret tasting my banana."

"Stop it." But her mouth opened. Why did it do that?

He slid the spoon over her lips, and her tongue slipped out to allow him to tilt the sweet caramelized banana into her mouth. Her eyes drifted shut. He kept the spoon in her mouth, too good and too long.

In that second, that moment of silence in which all she could do was taste and listen to their breathing, heat rushed through her body. Her nipples hardened. She could smell the bite of tequila on his breath, he was that close to her.

She pushed him away, ignoring the way his body felt beneath the palms of her hands, warm and solid. She cleared her throat. "That doesn't taste that bad. But it's not on the menu."

"You always stick to the menu, bumpkin? No special orders for you?"

"Shut up." She wiped her hands on her skirt. "Go make the bread. And stop trying to show me up in front of my staff." Then she walked out of the storage room, slamming the door behind her.

Chapter Three

Later that night, Nick sat on his front porch, staring at ...

Nothing. Because that was pretty much all he was surrounded by. Trees, trees, and more trees. Nowhere to go, nothing to do. And certainly no one to go anywhere with.

He took a deep drag from his cigarette and sipped his tequila. His leg bounced restlessly, the heel of his trainer tapping a fast beat on the wooden porch. All this quietness drove him crazy. Normally he'd be in the kitchen until at least 1:00 a.m., or he'd be at a club. Back at home, he was very rarely alone, and this wasn't something he was adjusting to well. Not well at all.

The cabin wasn't helping. It was nice, he supposed, by cabin standards. Fortunately, he didn't know much about cabin standards. This one was small but functional, with a decent kitchen. A living room with an overstuffed sofa and matching chairs. A nice TV and even a decent stereo.

He looked through the tree branches to where a small light glistened in the distance. *She* was there. It was Phoebe's house. Part of the deal in coming here included residing in her guesthouse. Although at least an acre separated the residences, he somehow always felt her presence. And on the other side of her house was her "farm."

Which consisted of about ten acres of seasonal produce. She was, after all, a farmer. She smelled like the earth. It shouldn't smell good to him.

Why did it?

Stop thinking! He picked up his cell phone and dialed.

"Nick?" a female voice answered.

"Hey, Sherry. What's up?"

"Just trying to explain to my son why he can't combine cabernet with sushi." Nick heard some shuffling, the low voice of her son in the background, and then Sherry's screech. He yanked the phone away from his ear as she yelled, "I don't care if it's considered avant-garde! It's just bad taste." More phone shuffling and then a deep sigh came through the phone. When she spoke, her voice was overly calm. "Sorry, Nick. Shawn is driving me nuts. If you ever have a child, pray he doesn't go into the food or wine industry."

Nick shuddered. "I don't think you have to worry about that."

"Right, right," Sherry said. "Nick Avalon. Perpetual bachelor and ladies' man."

"You got it, sweetheart."

"One day, Avalon. One day."

"What?"

"Some girl is gonna crack that stone heart of yours."

"Not likely." He took another sip of tequila. He would have preferred to chase it with a lime, but he was too lazy to get up and get one.

"Anyway. How are things going up there in the center of clean living?"

"Bloody horrid. Can you tell me again how I ended up here?"

"Let's see. You drank too much at work. Showed up late far too many times. Tortured your staff, and what was that last thing? Oh, right. You publicly humiliated a Hollywood legend over a crème brûlée."

"He sent it back!"

"And?"

"It was perfect."

"Right. Because everything Nick Avalon does is perfection."

"Damn near." It was true.

"Must be nice to be you, Mr. Avalon."

Nick gritted his teeth. Sherry was the only person in the world who could get away with talking to him like this. Somehow, they'd become best friends. Years ago, she'd been his wine distributor, and he'd taken her with him to every restaurant he worked at. He'd hit on her, of course. But she'd brushed him off, saying he was way too much of a bad boy for her.

She was the only girl in L.A. who'd rejected him. Which was probably a good thing because she had turned out to be one of his only true friends. L.A. was good for many things: parties, women, and entertainment. Finding people a bloke could count on wasn't on the list, but that was just fine with Nick. Early in life, he'd learned to count on only himself.

He took another deep drag off his cigarette.

"You should really quit those things."

"So you've said. Right around a million times."

"They're bad for you."

"You'd fit in perfectly here, you know."

Sherry laughed. "Are you trying to say I'm some sort of a hippie?"

"No. Well, you kinda are. I mean, with all your yoga and Pilates and those disgusting smoothies."

"That's not being a hippie. That's being health-conscious. You should try it."

"Not my style." He downed the rest of his tequila.

"Right. Partying all night and sleeping with starlets is more your thing."

"Not anymore. Sadly."

Sherry chuckled. "What? No hot, young, barely legal groupies up there?"

"Hardly." He thought of Phoebe, with her bright green eyes, frizzy brown hair, and attitude problem. "I think the most excitement I'm going to have anytime soon will involve my hand and an X-rated video."

"Aw, poor Nick. Reduced to living like a normal single man."

"Well, Sherry, I'm glad you think my situation is so amusing, because I sure as hell don't." He lit another cigarette.

Her voice softened. "Is it really that bad?"

"Yes." He blew out a lungful of smoke. "It's worse. You don't understand. These people—most don't eat meat. Quite a few are *vegan*." He spit the word out as if it tasted bad. "I mean, what's the point of living if you forgo luxuries such as cheese? The owner has no taste for anything new or different. And she's bossy. She doesn't listen to a thing I say. She's always hovering over my shoulder, as if I don't know what I'm doing." He brought the cigarette back to his mouth. "Did I mention she's bossy?"

"She sounds just awful." But he could tell Sherry was biting back a smile.

"She is." But Phoebe hadn't looked awful earlier, when

he'd been spooning caramelized bananas into her mouth. Her eyes had gone glassy, and her breathing had quickened. He'd found himself drawn to her luscious mouth, leaning toward her, as if he was going to touch his lips to hers—

It was a damn good thing that she'd pushed him away.

Wait? *She'd* pushed *him* away? That hadn't happened since...Sherry.

He shifted on the hard wooden porch swing. "She's incredibly annoying. She has no idea what she's doing."

"Well, didn't she inherit the business?"

"Yeah. From her aunt and uncle."

"Does she have another job?"

Nick brought the cigarette to his lips. "I guess so. Some organic farming business. And that's another thing. She always expects me to cook whatever random vegetables she brings me and make them into something amazing."

"And this is a challenge for you?"

"Hell no. But I can only cook so much cabbage and carrots before I want to slice my hands off."

"Ah. Local cooking. It's actually all the rage."

"Not where I come from."

"Nick?"

"What?"

"Don't take this the wrong way, but regional cuisine is popular here as well. You just don't know it because you've been so caught up in your own world."

The words stung. He hadn't been caught up in his own world. He'd been a professional, a traditionalist. He wasn't prone to fads and he liked himself more for it. Everyone else could sod off with their passing trends.

To this day, Julia Child sold more cookbooks than any modern chef. Her classic recipes using basic things like dairy were as popular now as they were twenty years ago.

He exhaled a breath of smoke. "It is a fad. What people really want are delicacies, things they can't make at home. That's what I do." It's what he loved to do.

"I know, Nick. And you're damn good at it."

He grunted at the compliment. "That's not the point. The point is, I don't bow to trends. Not in Los Angeles, and definitely not here."

"Anyway," Sherry said. "So, back to your boss."

"Phoebe?"

"Yes. Phoebe. So she's an organic farmer who knows nothing about running a restaurant and is driving you crazy."

"Pretty much." He poured another few ounces of tequila into his glass.

"Is she cute?"

"What? Why?" He shifted in his chair. "And *no*." But even as he said the word, he could envision her green eyes and imagine the way her nose crinkled up when she was annoyed with him. And he longed to bury his nose in the crook of her neck and inhale her scent. Honey. She smelled like honey.

"No," he repeated. "She's not cute at all."

He could practically hear Sherry shrug. "You just have a funny tone in your voice when you talk about her."

"That tone you hear is my infinite irritation at being stuck in a place I hate, working for a woman who has no palate whatsoever, and spending way too much time sitting on my front porch when I should be out getting laid."

Sherry ignored his tirade. "So. She's an organic farmer."

"Yes." Shifting, he took another deep drag of smoke.

"That would explain why she isn't exactly an expert in the field. She's been concentrating on other things. What's the name of her business? Maybe I've heard of it." Sherry specialized in organic California wine and was the lead distributor in Southern California.

"I have no idea," Nick said.

"Well, find out."

Nick grunted. "Why does it matter?"

"Because you're going to be working with her for the next eleven months. You may as well at least try to make the best of things. Why don't you think of it as a learning opportunity?"

"I already know how to cook vegetables."

"Maybe this is your chance to get back to basics, to re-learn your craft."

He clenched his hand around his tequila glass. "I don't need to relearn my fucking craft, Sherry. I'm the best at what I do."

"Don't get your panties in a wad, hon. I'm just suggesting that maybe..."

"Maybe what?"

"Maybe this will be good for you."

"Maybe this will kill me."

"Nick. You know I love you."

"Right."

"And, as your friend, I have to tell you, I think you were on a dangerous path back here in L.A."

"What are you talking about? I was at the top of my game!"

"But it's not healthy. Drinking all night, smoking a pack a day. Having sex with a different girl every night."

"Not *every* night," he mumbled. "And I was always careful."

"I know. But despite all the fun you were having, you didn't seem happy. At least not to me."

"Well, you were wrong." She couldn't be more wrong. "And this is supposed to make me happy? Living in the middle of some forest, listening to crickets? Spending my time creating a hundred and one ways to make broccoli?"

"Maybe."

"You're full of shit."

"That's not true. I just had a colonic. See? I truly am an L.A. girl at heart."

He laughed at her change of subject. She really was a good friend to worry about him, even if her concern was misplaced.

"Listen, Nick. Just try to relax. Attempt to make the best of the experience. If you still hate it in a year, you can come back."

"Oh, don't worry. I'll be back."

"Good. Because I actually miss your sorry ass."

Nick smiled. "Back atcha, buttercup."

He hung up the phone, took a final drag from his cigarette, and leaned back in the swing. A breeze blew through the redwoods in a whooshing sound, and crickets chirped loudly all around the cabin. Consciously, he ceased the jarring motion of his leg moving, up and down, up and down.

Then there was nothing. No noise. No distraction. Just Nick Avalon, alone. Alone in his head.

His palms got sweaty, and he jumped up. He threw his cigarette butt on the ground and stamped it out. Slamming the porch door behind him, he went to the stereo and pushed buttons until the fast, electronic beat of a techno song exploded through the room. Finally he began to relax. He let the music invade his head, his chest, his soul. With the song blasting through the house, he undressed for bed.

But he couldn't wind down. It was too early. And somehow, even with the music pounding through him, it was too quiet. Standing in his room, he stared at his bed with disgust. The last thing he wanted to do was sleep. But what choice did he have?

There was really only one thing he knew that would calm his racing mind. So he went to the kitchen and started to cook.

Chapter Four

A rhythmic beat slowly drew Phoebe out of sleep. "What the...?" she muttered, opening her eyes. It was music. The unmistakable fast pulse of a drum coming through her open window. Or what should have been a drum. This sounded like some sort of electronic version of the instrument.

She glanced at the clock. "It's one o'clock in the effing morning," she said to herself.

Nick Avalon. Only one person would be blasting that annoying techno music in the early hours of the morning. "Inconsiderate jerk!" She threw off the vintage quilts that she slept under, then tiptoed out her bedroom door and down the old wooden stairs, being careful to skip the creaky one. If Jesse and Steve hadn't woken up yet, she didn't want to disturb them. Admittedly, Phoebe was a light sleeper, but anyone would agree that Nick Avalon was showing total disregard for his neighbors.

Still in her long nightgown and socks, she slid on the boots near the front door and stalked out into the night.

She tromped through the trees to the guesthouse, the music becoming louder as she made her way to the cabin.

How dare he? Does he think he's in an L.A. nightclub?
"Insensitive, conceited, stuck-up jerk!"

She didn't bother knocking on his door; he wouldn't hear her anyway, not over all that racket. Instead she barged inside, slamming the door behind her. The loud bang produced no response from Nick, so she called his name. Still, nothing. She went to the stereo and turned the music off. And even then, Nick didn't appear.

Then she paused as a waft of something sweet reached her nose. He must be in the kitchen. She followed the unmistakable scent of chocolate, her traitorous mouth already beginning to water.

She found him mixing what appeared to be batter. Dan and Sally had renovated the cabin not long ago, and the space was modern although it appeared rustic. Knotty-pine cabinetry lined one wall, and a faux-antique stove took up a large portion of the space. Despite the humble appearance, the kitchen was equipped for a chef.

And there happened to be one at the butcher-block island, mixing a bowl of something that looked creamy, chocolaty, and delicious.

Nick was staring into the bowl as he stirred. His expression was intent on what he was doing, and she realized he hadn't even noticed that the music had been shut off. She paused. She'd never seen this expression on his face. Normally he was so aloof, so standoffish. So intense he seemed wired to explode. But now, here alone in his own kitchen, his own element, she saw something different. He looked serene. Why didn't he ever look that way in the café?

Also, he never went without a shirt in the café, which, she had to admit, was a crying shame. Because just look at him.

She bit her lip. He was wearing nothing but pajama bottoms. His torso was lean but solid-looking, his arms defined. And then her gaze landed on the upper part of his chest. He had a large tattoo spanning the area just above his nipples. It was a word, decorating his skin in scrolling, dark script.

"Oh my God," she said.

Obviously startled, he dropped the spoon in his hand. "What the fuck? Phoebe?"

She stepped into the kitchen and crossed her arms under her breasts. "Do you have your last name tattooed on yourself? You really are the most narcissistic, conceited man I have ever met."

So why was there something about that particular facet of his personality that intrigued her? That shouldn't happen. But then, none of the things she'd been experiencing since she'd met Nick Avalon should be happening. For example, she was in her nightgown, staring at his naked chest as he mixed some sort of chocolate concoction. In the middle of the night. This entire scenario really shouldn't be happening.

But it was.

He picked up the spoon. "Yeah, well, no doubt I am the most narcissistic man you've ever met. So sue me." He looked her in the eye. "How many men do you know out here in hippie country anyway, Phoebe?"

She raised her chin. "Enough." But she had to admit, she didn't know a man who was anything like Nick. For better or worse, every time she watched his easy, proficient way around the kitchen her pulse raced with excitement, and it didn't seem to be a thing she could control.

He smirked. "I'm sure you know plenty of men. I bet

just last night you had a hot stud in your bedroom."

"How do you know that's not true?" Last night she'd spent the evening reading *The Honey Trail: In Pursuit of Liquid Gold and Vanishing Bees*. And even though she thought lessons on how to avoid the varroa mite fascinating, she couldn't focus. Her thoughts kept drifting to Nick.

"Anyway," she said, "I know plenty of men." They were all her brother-in-law's friends or men she'd known since she was in kindergarten, but he didn't need to know that.

"Been with a lot of guys, have you, love?" he asked, and his accent seemed stronger than ever.

She shoved her hands on her hips, arms akimbo. "It doesn't matter how many men I've known. The fact is, I don't need a man, and I don't have time for a relationship." She waved the spoon at him. "Why am I defending my love life to you?"

"I have no idea. But it's truly fascinating. Please, continue."

His sarcasm made her fingers curl to keep from punching his shoulder. For some reason he made her feel competitive, as if they were going for the same prize. Which was ridiculous. She was the boss. The only prize was continuing the success of the café. And they both wanted that. So why was he always taunting her?

Furthermore, why did she respond to his heckling?

"And," she added, "I'm glad to say none of them have ever been vain enough to get their own names permanently marked onto their skin. Or did you do it in case you forget who you are?"

"Actually, you're not far off."

She narrowed her gaze. "What do you mean?"

"I legally took my mother's name when I turned eighteen. This was my way of making it official."

"Making what official?"

She couldn't help it. *No, no. Don't go there; don't get personal.* But the night was already so strange, and whenever she was around Nick, her entire center seemed off-balance. And damn it, he was right. He really was totally unlike any of the men she knew.

Which was a good thing. The men she knew may seem boring by Nick's standards, but they were good, down-to-earth people. Trustworthy. Unlike Nick.

Spinning the bowl in a slow circle on the counter, he stared into the depths of what he'd been mixing. "I didn't want any ties to my father. The last time I spoke with him was twenty years ago. He was a bloody bastard, and I hated seeing his name every time I signed my name on something."

"Oh."

He shrugged. "Was getting this tattoo an immature thing to do? Probably. But it's done now, and I'm not having it removed."

Phoebe wondered what his father had done to make him so angry. Nick was confident, strong, and independent. It was difficult to imagine anyone making him feel bad.

At her farm, she often worked with abused kids. Every summer, a group would visit and learn about growing produce. She'd learned to distance herself somewhat from their situations so she could help them without becoming overly protective. But the thought of someone harming Nick...

It shouldn't make her feel a bit ill inside. But it did.

Shaking the thought aside, she stepped into the kitchen and peered into the bowl of chocolate. She'd found food was always a nice distraction from stress, and Nick's food was especially nice. "I came over because your annoying music woke me up. I mean, it's the middle of the night. Do you really need to be blasting what you claim to be music?"

"Oh, I'm so sorry. Did my loud tunes disrupt your beauty sleep?"

"It's rude. You had your stereo up loud enough to wake the entire neighborhood."

He purposely looked through the kitchen window and into the darkness of the forest. When he turned back to her and spoke, his sarcasm wasn't lost on her. "And the neighbors would be... who?"

"Me! And Jesse and Steve."

He shrugged. "I only see you, bumpkin."

She stepped forward. "Listen. You can't blast music all night long."

He threw up his hands. "Fine. Won't happen again. Promise. I'd hate to be the cause of anyone in the town being awake past midnight."

"Why do you have to be such a—such a...*prick*?" Immediately she put her hand over her mouth. Had she really just called her employee a prick?

Yes, Phoebe, you did. You're standing in your night-gown, in the middle of the night, calling your chef bad things.

He actually looked shocked. "Did you call me a prick?"

She moved her hand aside. "Um. I guess that was a bit... unprofessional." Had she actually hurt his feelings?

"I don't give a fuck if it's unprofessional. I'm just shocked to hear such a bad word come out of your mouth."

"I can say bad words."

"Obviously."

Okay, it was time to get some control over the situation here. She sucked in a deep, calming breath. But then her senses were filled with the sweet scent of chocolate. She glanced to the bowl on the table. "That looks good. What is it?"

"Melted chocolate, butter, and cream. Very bad for you."

"Looks yummy." She dipped her finger into the velvety mixture.

But then his hand was wrapped around her wrist, firm and unyielding. "What are you doing?" he demanded.

"Tasting." And wondering whether she was trying to irritate him or satisfy herself.

"Stop helping yourself to whatever I'm cooking."

She tried to yank her hand back, but he held her tightly. For such a lean man, he was incredibly strong. "Stop being so uptight," she said. God, it was *this*. This bickering that made something in her veins quicken. And it was bad. So, so very bad.

But she liked it. What was wrong with her?

"Phoebe. Stop trying to steal my food."

"No." Man, it was like an addiction. A dangerous addiction. She knew everything about this was wicked, that she should walk away and be an adult. The boss.

Sadly, she couldn't. Something in him called to her. He was like a big plate of pasta, and she was on a low-carb diet. He was bad for her; he was forbidden. And the more she tried to deny what she wanted, the more her mouth watered. The more she wanted to dig in and devour him.

This was going to end badly. She knew if she really wanted to do so, she could walk away. And yet there she was, holding his gaze. Her blood was rushing like a springwater brook.

Silently, the seconds stretched between them. Her heart went haywire. Then he said, "You really want a taste?" His gaze was direct and steadfast. Slowly, she nodded.

Oh yeah, she wanted a taste all right. A big fat forkful, smothered in sexy sauce.

Sexy sauce? Really?

And yet she nodded, because her mouth was actually watering.

For the pudding. Not for him.

For the food. Food only.

"Me first." His stare still holding hers, he raised her hand to his lips. Then he placed her finger, dripping chocolate, to his lips.

"What are you doing?" she asked. Her voice sounded high, shrill. Scared. But she wasn't scared. What could she possibly be scared of?

"This." He slid her finger into his mouth and licked, swirling his tongue around her skin, sucking off every last drop.

"S-stop." But her breathing was fast, and her nipples were pebbling beneath her nightgown.

Oh no, no, no . . .

He released her wrist, and she realized her hand was shaking. What was he doing to her? "I—I'm going to go now." She turned to move, but he reached out and grabbed her shoulder, stopping her.

"I thought you wanted a taste."

Looking away, she closed her eyes. Every nerve in her body was thrumming with desire. For her smug chef. For this man with his own name tattooed on his chest.

She was losing her mind.

Because she did want a taste. Of more than just chocolate.

Slowly, she opened her eyes and lifted her chin to meet his gaze. "I changed my mind."

He slanted her a wicked grin. "Is that so?"

"Yes." But even she could hear the uncertainty in her own voice.

He dipped his finger into the chocolate and brought it to her lips. "Are you sure?"

"Stop it."

He raised a single black eyebrow. "Stop what? I'm just giving you what you want."

"I don't want this."

"What?" His eyes twinkled with evil pleasure, and his voice lowered. "You don't want this?"

She shook her head, even as her entire body was screaming something totally different.

"I don't believe you." And then, as light as a whisper, he brought his chocolate-covered fingertip to her mouth.

Her breath hitched, and her entire body started to tremble. Her mind was telling her to walk away. But he was so close that she could feel the heat from his body. He looked as luscious as the dessert on his fingertips, and she wanted some. She licked her lips.

"That's it, baby. You can't resist, can you?"

She grabbed his hand. If he could tease, so could she. Maybe she couldn't resist this bizarre midnight tryst, but that didn't mean she couldn't take some control of the situation. So she held his hand steady as her tongue darted out to taste the sweet tip of his finger. She saw his eyes darken, and a surge of power washed over her. So she worked it. Holding his hand, she licked him, drawing his finger into her mouth. She captured his stare with her own and sucked him deep, using her tongue to glean every last drop of chocolate off his skin.

Only when she was done did she release him.

"Oh, is that how it is, Phoebe?"

Shit. Why did she feel as if she'd just unleashed a beast? And like a stunned animal, she didn't—*couldn't*—move.

Grabbing both her shoulders, he pulled her toward him. And then he kissed her.

She expected harsh, but he was shockingly gentle. He held his lips quietly against hers, not moving until she breathed. Then his mouth covered hers, his chocolate-flavored tongue softly licking her. He kissed her until her eyes drifted shut, until she felt as gooey inside as the pudding on the table.

Then he yanked the neck of her nightgown, tearing the flannel so he could pull the material down her shoulders, exposing her breasts.

She tried to pull the nightgown back up, but he stopped her. "Nick? What are you doing?"

"This."

Using his hand, he scooped up a handful of chocolate and spread it over her chest. "Oh my God. Nick—"

"Hush."

Damn it. She didn't want to be hushed. But as his warm fingers spread the creamy mixture over her skin, lust pooled deep inside her. And when he beaded her nipple between his moist fingertips, she moaned.

"You like that?"

"No," she said, squeezing her legs together.

"Then I guess you're going to hate this." He drew a nipple into his mouth, sucking and tugging until she was squirming beneath him, until she thought her legs wouldn't hold her up one second longer.

He backed her against the kitchen island and stepped between her legs. Then he moved his mouth to her other nipple, torturing her. Her pussy began to throb with want, and she felt herself getting wet.

He looked up, a wicked gleam in his eye. "You still don't like that?"

"Shut up."

As long as she was sassy, as long as she kept a distance, she could justify what she was doing. For now. Now, she was opening her legs wider, pressing herself against his crotch, feeling his erection through his cotton pajama bottoms. He was so hard, so hot. She'd never been so turned on, never yearned to feel the touch of any man like she did Nick's at that moment. She let her head fall back and exposed herself even more to him.

He grabbed her hips and lifted her onto the island. She squirmed, but his hands firmly held her still. "I know how much you loathe this, Phoebe. So I'm going to keep doing it. Just to torture you."

"I hate you," she said. But she was smiling. Smiling? How had he gotten her to this point?

Didn't matter. What mattered was that he was pulling up her nightgown and reaching between her legs.

"Open for me, Phoebe."

She did. She spread her quivering legs and exposed herself to him.

"Beautiful," he murmured. Then he knelt before her, and she felt his hands on the insides of her thighs, tracing her skin lightly. Touching her everywhere except that little spot where she needed to feel him most.

"Touch me," she whispered.

"Didn't I tell you to hush?"

She nearly cried out then. His words came out in a warm breath, caressing her damp flesh. Then she felt his fingers on her pussy, and that wasn't all she felt—he was spreading the chocolate all over the folds of her sex.

Her eyes drifted shut, and she gave in. She sank back onto the top of the island and let her fingers graze the still-moist skin of her breasts. She found a drop of chocolate he'd missed, and she brought the sweet mixture to her lips, sucking her own fingertip.

And then she felt his mouth on her pussy, warm and wonderful. He licked her as if he were savoring a luscious dessert. So slow it was a beautiful agony, he touched his tongue to every moist inch of her sex. Licking, sucking, even biting gently.

"Oh, God...," she gasped, bucking against his mouth. "That feels so...yes..." She could barely think. Lust raged through her blood, and everything centered around what Nick was doing between her legs.

He took her clit in his mouth, focusing his attention on that bud of nerves. With a cry, she arched her back as he flicked at her swollen flesh.

"Yes. Right there."

But he wasn't done. She felt his fingers—long and strong and driving into her—again and again.

"Nick, don't stop... Uh... Yes!" She'd never been so vocal before.

She'd never been so... yeah...

The orgasm screamed through her. Every muscle in her thighs clenched as she shouted his name, and her hands fisted at her sides. She couldn't tell if her climax went on forever or if he was simply sucking more of them out of her. She didn't care. All she knew was the pleasure was so intense that she couldn't contain her reaction.

She had no idea how long it took before her body settled down and the tremors that shook her started to fade. Panting, she lay on the kitchen island, unable to think or breathe or speak.

Eventually he got to his feet, and through heavy eyes, she watched him. He gave her a self-satisfied grin. Then he leaned over her and gave her another of those lovely, soft kisses. She sighed against his mouth. Maybe Nick Avalon wasn't so bad after all.

When she opened her eyes, he was watching her. "You okay, baby?"

Smiling, she nodded. "That was... amazing."

"You still think I'm the most conceited man you've ever met?"

"Maybe."

He winked. "Well, baby. I guess now you know why."

Chapter Five

All he'd wanted was chocolate pudding.

Standing in the shower, Nick let the hot water pound onto his skin. He must be really losing it to have gotten to the point where that crazy, frazzled hippie boss of his seemed irresistible. Not that she was. Irresistible. No female was. And he could have stopped at any minute. At any second of that encounter, he could have walked away.

Ah, but you didn't, did you?

No, he didn't. And he could still taste her. Not chocolate or sugar or butter. Her. Her skin, her essence. Her own sugary taste on his tongue.

It was killing him.

Well, his dick thought it was. Based on the painful way it was throbbing, he'd have thought someone had just slammed him between the legs with a sledgehammer. He turned under the showerhead, feeling the spray of water on his back.

It wasn't doing any good. He couldn't wash away the memory of her laid out before him like some sort of delicious, erotic buffet.

Out of all the women in all the world, he had to go and slather chocolate on this one. Certainly there were better options, even in this town in the middle of nowhere. Obviously, he needed to get laid. Hell, back in L.A., he'd had a buffet of lovely ladies to choose from every night. He never had to settle for anything less than top-of-the-line. So why was he here, standing under now-tepid water, waiting for his raging hard-on to subside?

More important, why did his cock jump at the thought of Phoebe Mayle? Why did his blood run hot when he licked his lips to savor her, still. Impossible. He shouldn't be able to still taste her.

But he did.

And he saw her. When he closed his eyes, he could clearly picture the way her pupils had gone dark and wide with desire for him. He could see the battle within herself, fighting her need to touch him. She hated him. Sometimes he could feel the emotion radiating off her like some invisible force that seeped into him. He barked a laugh, the sound echoing off the tiled shower walls.

She hated *him*. Well, she could join the fucking club. She could become an official member of the Nick Avalon Is a Bloody Prick Society.

And the thing was, he didn't even mind. In fact, he got off on it. Life was better when you knew exactly where you stood. And if you didn't give a shit what people thought, you didn't have to put up with any stupid pretenses like politeness.

Fuck that. Politeness was the most acceptable hypocrisy. Yeah, he liked that. Because Nick may be an asshole, a prick, and a son of a bitch. But he certainly wasn't a hypocrite.

And if people didn't like it, they could sod off.

It wasn't his fault that Phoebe couldn't deny her desire

for him. And it wasn't his fault she hated him. He was who he was. What people decided to do with it was their problem.

Right now, Nick had his own issues. He had to get the fuck back to Los Angeles. And he had to deal with this raging erection pounding like the beat of an electronic dance song.

He wasn't about to jack off. Nick hadn't needed to take care of himself in years, and he wasn't about to start now. He'd find some woman to take care of him. He always did.

And it wouldn't be his boss. There had to be some hick bar where he could find a willing partner. A woman who wanted nothing more from him than a wall-banger and a good-bye. Because that was about all Nick Avalon was good for.

But...damn it. Just the thought of touching another woman was more effective than that sledgehammer. The thought of another woman, some person who didn't have Phoebe's quirky smile, her honey smell, the taste of her skin...

Apparently, his dick didn't like that idea. The pounding arousal had begun to ebb. At the thought of another woman.

"That can't be good," he muttered to himself, the sound echoing off the moist shower walls. And of course, then he started thinking about her again and his desire started building up again.

Under the water, he turned again. Then he twisted the faucet until cold water shot him in the groin. A shiver ran through him and he gritted his teeth. But it did the trick. Not quite a sledgehammer, but his erection finally wilted.

Problem solved.

He turned off the water and grabbed a towel. Rubbing his hair dry, he stepped out of the shower and dried off the rest of his shivering body. Shivering was good. He tended to run hot in every sense of the word, and sometimes a blast of arctic chill was exactly what he needed.

And now his hard-on was good and killed. He didn't need Phoebe to take care of him. He didn't need anyone. For anything. He had himself, his skill, and he had tequila. What else could a man possibly require?

Phoebe grabbed a ceramic coffee mug off the shelf and slammed the cupboard door closed. When she'd come home from her little jaunt to Nick's last night, she hadn't been able to sleep. She'd taken a shower to scrub her body, sticky from chocolate pudding and Nick's mouth. Maybe it was the organic soap, but she didn't feel as if she'd washed everything off. She could still feel his hands on her skin; her body tingled everywhere he'd spread chocolate on her: her neck, her breasts, her mouth. Her pussy...

Not thinking about that. Even just the thought of his face between her legs sent a little pulse of lust right to the place his tongue had licked so adeptly.

"Morning!"

Phoebe jumped, practically dropping the mug, but catching it before it hit the hard wood. Taking a deep breath, she turned and tried to look normal as her brother-in-law came into the kitchen. She smiled. There. That had to appear somewhat natural, right?

He glanced at her. "What's wrong with your face?"

Her free hand flew to her mouth. Had she missed some

chocolate somewhere? In what she hoped was a subtle gesture, she licked her lips. No chocolate came back on her tongue.

Instead, she tasted *him*.

Oh, God, that couldn't be good.

Steve gave her one more *look* before opening the refrigerator door. "You seem a bit out of it this morning."

She supposed that was one way of putting it. *Frustrated, confused, horny, irritated.* Any of those adjectives would work, really. But sure, she could go with "out of it."

She grabbed the soy creamer out of Steve's hand and poured some into her still-empty mug and filled it with coffee. "I'm just thinking of all the things I have to do later. I think I'm going to teach the kids how to harvest honey today." She chugged a few gulps of coffee. "And I think the herb garden needs to be trimmed." Gulp, gulp, gulp. "Oh, and I got a fax last night from Edible Earth in Marin for ten pounds of carrots, so we'll have to pull and ship." She poured more coffee into her cup. "And I need to see how the eggplants are doing." Right. Eggplants.

She went to take a sip from her mug, but realized she'd drained the cup.

She turned and poured more organic, shade-grown, fair-trade coffee into her mug. It was the only type of caffeine allowed in the house. So it was a damn good thing that the coffee was delicious because Phoebe seemed to be drinking a hefty amount of the stuff that morning.

Steve asked, "You're not going to the café today?"

She nearly spit out her coffee but managed to swallow before answering. "What?"

He spoke slowly, as if she were incapable of understanding his words. "Don't you need to run by the café? You know, that restaurant in town you own. The one with the 'totally incorrigible chef'?"

You mean the one with the taut abs and shockingly hot tattoo across his lean, hard chest? She shook her head. "Um, no. I don't want to do him today."

Steve shook his head. "Uh, pardon me?"

"Huh?"

"You don't want to *do him* today?"

Crap. "I mean, I don't need to *see* him today. That's what I meant."

He continued staring at her.

"What?" She shifted on her feet as her neck heated. Damn pale skin always gave her away.

"Why are you blushing?"

"I'm not."

"You are."

"Shut up." She opened the refrigerator door and stuck her head into the cold air, pretending to look for something. But her brain wasn't inside the fridge so she pulled out a yogurt instead.

"Really?" she said, staring at the container. "Organic chocolate yogurt?" The label read '*Tastes like pudding!*'

"You have a problem with chocolate?"

"Definitely."

"Since when?" Steve asked.

She jerked her head up. "I mean, no. I don't have any issues with chocolate." *Especially when it's being spread all over your body by a hot chef with a big spoon.*

Crap. She really *was* out of it.

Steve leaned back against the counter and crossed his arms across his wide chest. Barely six feet, he wasn't a tall man. But he had a quiet presence that drew attention. His hair was long, his beard always shaggy. He was like a big teddy bear.

But he'd never quite gotten over the death of his wife, Phoebe's sister. Judy's death from cancer had occurred over five years ago, but as far as Phoebe knew, Steve hadn't so much as looked at another woman. He devoted his life to his hardware shop and his daughter, Jesse.

Steve took a few steps and placed a hand on her shoulder. "What is going on with you? Do you need a day off? I'm sure one of the kids can oversee the farm for a day."

She stared at the carton of yogurt. "No, I'm fine." She needed the distraction of the farm. Needed to dig in the earth and get her hands dirty. Needed to stay away from Nick Avalon.

Which, of course, would be difficult considering she owned the café where he worked, and he was her employee. But she could never, ever let him touch her again.

Why did that thought leave her feeling a little empty inside?

She smiled at Steve, hoping her expression seemed confident and sincere. "I'm fine. I promise."

He squeezed her shoulder. "You sure?"

"Definitely. I just have a lot on my plate."

"That's the understatement of the year. You always take on so much, Pheebs."

She shrugged. "I can handle it."

He kept staring at her.

"What?" she asked.

"Honestly?"

"When are you not honest with me? Spill it."

He released her shoulder and crossed the kitchen.

Turning, he crossed his arms before leaning back against the counter. "I don't like Nick. I don't trust him."

She laughed, but it was nervous and high-pitched. "That makes two of us."

"I see the way you look at him."

"Huh?" She tried to sound casual. "I don't *look* at him. And what do you mean, *look* at him?"

"Like you used to look at Bear back when we were in high school."

"Th-that's ridiculous! I never look at Nick that way." She shook her head. "And I never looked at Bear any way. I don't know what you're talking about."

"Come on, Phoebe. You're an open book."

She tore the lid off the yogurt carton and tossed the piece of foil into the garbage. She was too irritated to wash and recycle the foil.

"Steve. I'm not an open book. And even if I was, so what? I have nothing to hide."

Steve lifted a brow. "Is that so? Then where were you around three this morning?"

She whipped her head up to stare at her all-too-aware brother-in-law. "W-what?"

"I'm a heavy sleeper, but did you think I wouldn't notice someone coming and going in the middle of the night, in and out of the house where my daughter and sister-in-law live?"

She should have known. Steve might be laid-back, but he was also very protective of his family. And she knew if anyone ever threatened anyone he loved, he wouldn't back down. Phoebe knew her kindhearted brother would resort to violence if need be.

Phoebe should have thought about that.

She shrugged and pulled a spoon from a drawer. "You caught me. I went for a walk."

"A walk."

"Yup." She spooned some yogurt into her mouth.

Smooth, creamy, and chocolaty. She couldn't help but savor the flavor. And savor the memories of last night with Nick.

The *prick*.

"I know. But that doesn't mean you shouldn't take some time for yourself. Take a break once in a while."

She broke away from Steve's knowing gaze and crossed the kitchen. She placed her mug in the big white cast-iron sink. "No time. Even if I could, I wouldn't know what to do with myself."

"Why don't we take Jesse and go to the coast? We haven't been over to the beach in ages."

She glanced over her shoulder. Steve rarely suggested going to the coast. When his wife, Judy, was alive, they'd spent a lot of time at the beach. Since she died, it was difficult to persuade Steve to go. Too many memories. It was hard even for Phoebe. They'd spent so much time there, it seemed Judy's presence was washed into the air with each wave that crashed onto the sand.

"Really?" she asked.

Steve nodded. "Yeah. I think it would do us all some good."

"Okay. We'll plan it over the next week or two. If the weather's nice, we can camp." She turned back to the sink to wash her cup. Yes, a break would be a good thing. She *had* been working her tush off. Maybe that was why she was having this strange reaction to Nick. She was stressed and wasn't thinking straight.

Right. That had to be it. *Organic pudding is turning you on. Obviously, something is wrong with you!*

Because there was no way—no way at all—that she'd be attracted to him otherwise. Nick Avalon was trouble, and that was certainly the last thing she needed. She had enough going on in her life, and she simply couldn't afford to make things more difficult by allowing Nick to touch her—either physically or emotionally.

She straightened. *You're in charge. You're the boss. He's only doing this as a way to get some power over you.*

Well, he was going to learn a lesson about real women. There was no way on earth she'd let that man think he held any power over her, because he didn't.

None whatsoever.

Now she just needed to make sure he knew that.

She looked up and through the window over the sink. A soft wind blew through the redwood trees, and she heard the calming whoosh of leaves in the breeze.

What was she going to do now? Sex with Nick was totally inappropriate behavior on so many levels. She was his boss, for heaven's sake. She needed to be in control, and this certainly wasn't going to help a situation in which she barely held the reins as it was.

It couldn't happen again. Never. Ever. It was totally inappropriate. She needed to be able to assert her authority, and succumbing to Nick each time he tempted her with his delicious taste sensations simply would not do.

First, she needed some space. She'd go to the farm and work. Working on the farm always helped clear her mind, energized her, and gave her strength.

And she was going to need a lot of strength to stay away from Nick Avalon.

* * *

Sipping coffee on the front porch, Nick stared into the woods. They hadn't changed in the past week; really, nothing had.

The day stretched out before him—he didn't need to be at the café until that afternoon, so he had several hours to kill. It was 9:00 a.m., and normally he'd still be sleeping. But here in Redbolt there were no after-work parties to attend, so out of boredom he'd been going to bed earlier and earlier.

And he'd been waking up early, too. Back in L.A., he'd sleep the day away until it was time to get up and go to work. Eat, sleep, drink, fuck. That pretty much summed up his life. Oh, and driving of course. In L.A., a person needed a car like he needed oxygen. And if that person wanted to be seen as able to swim with the big fish, that person also needed a vehicle that announced that. Nick figured nothing announced who he was—and he *was* someone—like the huge Hummer he'd chosen as his method of transportation. Funny, no one out here seemed to care what they drove. Phoebe's Land Cruiser had to be about twenty years old and looked like it. Everyone drove beat-up old cars. He grunted a laugh. Judging by the selection of cars and trucks on the local roads, a person would have no idea what decade it actually was. Based on how people looked at his Hummer, one would think Nick drove an airplane around town.

Bumpkins. All of them.

He lit a cigarette and took a drag. But as he inhaled, the smoke tasted different. The smoke didn't really do anything for him; he didn't enjoy it and the cigarette tasted bad. After only a few minutes he put it out.

Staring into the trees, he stood. Nothing sounded good. He didn't want to smoke. He didn't have anywhere to go. He didn't have any girls he felt like calling for a quick shag.

Besides Phoebe, but going there was nothing but a train wreck.

He shook his head. Since when did he avoid train wrecks? It was as if he were living in an obscure alien universe, and nothing was how it was supposed to be.

He hopped down the porch steps and walked. And walked. He went into the woods, taking breaths of the crisp fresh air. It smelled like trees. The sun created shadows on the ground, and he dodged in and out of the sunlight.

He heard nothing besides the sounds of his sneakers' soles hitting the ground, which was covered in fallen needles. No cars, no people, no music. Nothing except the chirp of a bird or a breeze going through some high tree branches.

When was the last time he'd been so secluded from civilization?

He couldn't remember. Pausing, he thought back into his past. Way back. And he couldn't remember when he'd last taken a walk or a hike that didn't include going to a restaurant, or a kitchen, or a club—or to or from his car.

For some reason, that struck him as odd. He knew he was city-oriented, but still. Even a city bloke needed some fresh air once in a while.

Shaking his head at his thoughts—thoughts that would never have popped into his brain until he'd arrived here—he went on. He wound his way through the trees; there were no paths out here, and he navigated fern bushes and other shrubbery he couldn't identify.

After a while, looking through the thick branches he was pushing aside as he walked, he caught sight of something large that should have looked out of place but didn't. He continued toward what looked to be a rusted-out old farm tractor. When he was a boy, he would have loved making such a find. He would have enjoyed wandering around the tractor, looking at how it was made, wondering who'd driven it and how it had come to be abandoned.

Now, he stopped in front of the old thing and just stared. "Huh," he said aloud, and his own voice startled him. He was still unused to the silence of Redbolt.

Circling the corroded piece of metal, he felt the sun on his back.

Yeah, back when he was a boy, he would have enjoyed making a discovery like this.

Turns out, Nick still did.

Chapter Six

Phoebe came across him in the forest.

She'd been looking for wild mushrooms when she spotted Nick kneeling beside her uncle's old tractor, apparently inspecting something near the rear wheelbase.

So engrossed was he in the inspection of the tractor, he didn't notice her presence. She took the time to discreetly watch him. He wore dark jeans, those fancy sneakers that weren't nearly as shiny as when he'd first arrived, and a blue T-shirt with some sort of logo printed across the front. The short sleeves showed off his sinewy arms, and Phoebe took a moment to drink in the sight of him. His arms were long, lean, and tan as he brushed a bit of rust off the metal. He wasn't as pale as he'd been that first day he'd arrived.

Funny. One would think that, being from sunny Southern California, Nick would have arrived looking more like a sun god than a vampire. Well, Phoebe thought, it made sense. He probably worked late hours, partied after that, and slept his days away.

It had been a month since Nick's arrival in Redbolt. Watching him now, she realized there had been more subtle changes she hadn't noticed until that moment. Not only was his skin a healthy bronze, but his face looked a bit less gaunt. His hair was a bit shaggier, and he'd lost a little of that wolflike edge he'd arrived with. Not that she wasn't afraid he'd pounce on her any minute, but he was less... scary somehow.

In fact, he hadn't pounced on her at all since that night in his kitchen, two weeks back. That was good. It was a good thing. She'd pretended it had never happened and so had he. His point had been taken. He was a conceited bastard who could seduce any woman he wanted to, even her.

It was a big mistake. Clenching the bucket in her hand, she approached him. She almost wished he'd make a move on her again, just so she could prove him wrong.

Because she could resist Nick. She *could*.

Keep telling yourself that, sweetheart. Ugh. Now she was talking to herself in his voice. Irritation made her bite the inside of her cheek.

"Nick. What are you doing?"

With a jerk of his head, he glanced up. "Oh," he said, clearly surprised to see her. Wiping his hands on his jeans, he stood. "I was out for a walk and I stumbled on this. Just taking a look."

She couldn't keep the surprise out of her voice. "You went on a walk? Why?"

"Why not?"

"I don't know. It just seems out of character."

"Yeah, well, maybe you don't know my *character* as well as you think you do."

Huh. She really didn't want to think there was a chance of that being true. She didn't want to see any cracks in the character description she had in her mind. Because right now, she didn't like Nick, and she really wanted to keep it that way.

He shuffled his weight from one foot to the other, and she wondered why he seemed nervous. She'd never seen Nick Avalon as anything less than what he claimed himself to be, which was arrogant and conceited.

Which he was. Is. She knew it; everyone knew it.

So why was she having little nibblings of doubt? Because, no matter how much she wanted to deny it, she'd seen something. A smile here and there. A joke. A genuine compliment. And the way he worked with Jesse was impressive. He had shown such patience with Phoebe's niece it was surprising.

Or maybe she was just losing her grip on reality due to the fact that she couldn't stop thinking about Nick. About Nick's hands on her body, his tongue on her—

She derailed that train of thought and narrowed her gaze at him. "I've never seen you out walking before. What are you doing outside your cabin? Be careful. Mother Nature might get you!"

"I'm not worried about Mother Nature, and there's not much else to do in this Podunk town."

His attempt to insult her community had less venom than it normally did; it was almost as if he responded more out of habit or obligation than spite.

Now he was focusing on her, glancing up through dark lashes. His eyes were sparkling blue, reflecting the bright blue sky. His facial expression was soft, and for the first time, she noticed his features were actually much less harsh than she'd always thought.

What had changed?

"What do you have there?" he asked, glancing at her bucket.

"Oh, I was just out looking for mushrooms."

"Find any?"

Holding out the bucket in front of her, she said, "Just these."

He stepped forward and sized up her collection. With his long fingers, he plucked out a coral and brushed the dirt off the stem. "Nice. A *Ramaria rubinosa*?"

She hitched a breath and tried to ignore the way her heart fluttered a bit at his knowledge of mycology. "H-how did you know the proper name for it?"

He shrugged and wiped off some more dirt. The mushroom was large and beautiful, and she'd discovered enough to feature them on that evening's menu.

He said, "Believe it or not, I read about produce. And I like mushrooms." He had to admit he'd never had the opportunity to cook fresh mushrooms like these during any of his stints at restaurants in big cities.

"I suppose that makes sense," Phoebe said. "It's just that not even the locals know the proper names for any of the mushrooms around here."

"Well, I would hazard a guess that the locals are looking for a different variety entirely."

"What do you mean?"

Making a swirling motion with his hands, he said, "You know. The magic kind."

She jerked the bucket back. "That's ridiculous."

He stopped waving his hands. "Sorry. I didn't mean to offend you."

Now he was apologizing? Nick never apologized. For anything, and what he'd said was relatively low on the offensive scale.

She shook her head. "I'm not offended. It's just that those varieties don't actually grow out here in the wild."

Now he was the one who looked surprised. "And you know this...how?"

"Well, you can't just go feeding people random mushrooms. The majority of them will make you sick. I wouldn't be picking them if I didn't know what I was doing."

He took a step back. "Okay. Calm down."

"I am calm."

"Only you could make an issue out of a mushroom."

"I'm not making an issue out of it."

"You got all pissy at me just then."

"That's because you insinuated everyone out here is a bunch of hippies on hallucinogens."

"And they aren't?"

"Only a few. And not me."

"Of course not you. I'm sure you've never so much as taken a drag of a cigarette."

"Cigarettes are disgusting."

"Never touched a joint either?"

Biting her lip, she looked to the side.

Lowering his head, he took a step toward her. "Phoebe Mayle. Are you telling me you inhaled?"

"Maybe. Just once, though."

He laughed. "Did you like it?"

"Not really. It was a long time ago, and I remember I ate a bag of chips and fell asleep."

He smiled. "Yeah. I pretty much had the same experience."

She couldn't take her gaze off his smile. Silence stretched between them, but her brain had turned to mush, and she couldn't find one word to say.

She wanted to jump on him. Just like that. Standing

there in the sun, in the forest, talking about the most random things—she couldn't help it. She remembered the way his lips had felt on hers, the way his breath had felt soft on her skin, the way he smelled—like spices she couldn't quite identify, no matter how hard she tried.

She clenched the handle of the bucket in her hands. There was something about him, something that drew her. Raw. Physical. Hard. Heart-pounding. Lust.

As if some kind of magnetic force surrounded them, she could feel the draw between them. Tearing her gaze away, she moved toward the tractor and pretended to find it interesting. But then she felt him beside her. Her heart raced. Her skin flushed. He was so close, so close that goose bumps pebbled up her arms and her body tingled.

Oh, God, how she wanted to touch him. Just touch him . . .

And then she felt his hand on hers. Just the barest whisper as his fingertips went up the back of her hand, but that simple contact sent an electric shock through her, right to her core.

She glanced over, and he was staring at her. She felt her hands start to shake. But the pull was so strong, so exciting, she went with it. Allowed herself to enjoy the thrill of the moment.

All that talk about not doing this—not allowing herself to feel the pleasure of Nick's touch. It went out the window at a single touch.

He took the bucket out of her hand and placed it on the ground. Then he turned her toward him, using his hand on her neck to move her. She gazed up at him. His stare was so intense it was almost unnerving.

Okay, it was totally unnerving.

Hell, everything about him was unsettling. But the gentle grip with which he held her calmed her at the same time.

She'd never felt anything like it. She'd never felt a shiver go up her back like she did when he pushed the hair off her neck to slide his palm up her skin. He cupped her jaw and tilted her face up. She could have been chained to the spot, she was so unable to move.

"I know what you're going to say," he said.

"W-what?"

"You're going to tell me no, to not kiss you."

"It's a bad idea."

"You didn't think it was a bad idea that night in my kitchen."

"I-I was tired. And it *was* a bad idea."

Shrugging, he continued holding her face and, with his other hand, wrapped his fingers around her wrist. He had lengthy fingers, and they were strong. The simple way he held her froze her, even as she felt her insides begin to melt into butter.

Smiling, he nodded down at her. "Right. Very bad idea." But he was leaning down and his lips were closing in on hers. She thought he was going to kiss her, but he passed her mouth to nuzzle his nose at the base of her neck. She could feel his hot breath on her skin, and she started to tremble. Her eyes drifted shut as he inhaled and breathed out.

"You smell good, Phoebe."

So do you... The words were on the tip of her tongue, but she couldn't say them. She couldn't do anything except *feel*.

"You smell...fresh. Like the forest." And then he

kissed her neck. Gently at first and then with more intention. So good...it felt so good she nearly lost her balance. But he held her steady.

His mouth made its way up her neck, intoxicating. His mouth, his tongue, his warm breath, she'd never experienced anything quite like it. She wanted him to stop.

Oh, that wasn't true, was it? She wanted him to keep going and never stop. She wanted that mouth of his on hers. And she knew it was coming. But all she could do was wait. Again, she'd given up her power over her own reaction, over reason, over everything. Handed it all over to Nick like a chocolate Sunday with a cherry on top.

And though it was dangerous, her heart raced with anticipation and excitement. She couldn't deny herself this, no matter how much she knew she ought to.

Finally, his lips touched hers. She opened her mouth and let him lick her, kiss her, hold her. Her tongue mingled with his. Slow, hot, melting.

The kiss shot straight through her and landed directly between her legs. Pulsing right at her sex, she craved his touch right there. But she also wanted to feel *him*. Feel his body, his flesh. With her free hand, she grasped his firm biceps, pulling him closer.

Yes. He pressed against her, and every inch of her body that he touched turned to fire. And when she felt his erection push against her, separated by their clothes, her pussy dampened.

So simple. Just a kiss. But it had her entire sex dripping with desire.

Perfection. The sun, the trees, the soft breeze. A bucket of mushrooms she'd just picked. Nick kissing her. A satisfaction like she'd never experienced before settled over her, and suddenly images flashed through her mind.

This was what it could be like. A life of simple pleasures, of sharing her body with a man she desired. Who, despite his attitude, was starting to show tiny glimpses of something else. Something better than the bad-boy image he wanted so hard to maintain.

And that was scarier than any of the other reasons she had for staying away from him.

Her heart. Her heart seemed to be growing as he continued to kiss her and she kissed him back. Inside, her chest wanted to explode with something much different than pure desire...this was more. More than simple lust.

She jerked away. "I-I have to go."

He looked a bit stunned. "Phoebe?"

Grabbing the bucket, she tried to get a grip. These feelings were too much. If she continued down this road, it would lead to no good. Was she actually having thoughts of how perfect things could be with Nick?

Don't be fooled by his apparent attitude change. It's just a ruse, and even if it wasn't, it's a bad idea.

Nick Avalon, in general, was a bad idea.

"I'm sorry...it's just that I'm late, and I need to be at the café. Things to do, you know."

"Right." He was composing himself quickly. Part of her was disappointed. Part of her wanted him to stop her from leaving, to grab her by the shoulders and kiss her with the force of a man who wanted her. Like a scene from a movie.

Still shaking, she forced herself to look at him. "Stop doing that."

"What?" He looked sincerely shocked, but she knew it was all an act.

"Trying to gain power over me."

"What the fuck are you talking about?"

"You know damn well." Anger was overtaking the lust that had been rushing through her veins only moments before. "Do you think I forgot what happened the last time we—" She lowered her voice. "*You know.*"

"Know what?" he asked as he cocked a brow.

"The last time when you tried to have sex with me!" she said in an angry whisper.

"Why are you whispering? Are you afraid of offending the delicate ears of the trees? And anyway, who would they tell?"

"Shut up. I'm trying to make a point here."

"At least you raised your voice so I could hear you." He paused and tried to look thoughtful. "I'm not so sure that's a good thing."

"Can you ever just stay on topic?"

"Fine. What happened, the last time we, *you know*, poppet?"

"You..." She waved a hand at him. "And the chocolate...and you..."

"I didn't hear any complaints at the time."

"Well, I'm complaining now!"

He gave her a satisfied smirk.

"There! See? All you want to do is prove that you can have whatever you want."

"Can't I?"

Her face burned as she remembered how he'd ended their last encounter with the chocolate pudding. He'd wanted to show her a lesson, to prove he was better than her.

And he had.

She stared at him. Gorgeous. Even when she hated him, she thought he was gorgeous. He made her blood rush with desire. He made her nipples ache to be touched. He made her pussy wet with need.

Keeping her gaze fixed on his, she inched just a bit closer. Her pulse hit the accelerator, her heartbeat speeding up as she got closer to her target. She lowered her eyes to look at his lips.

She looked up. "Please stop."

"You really want me to?"

She searched his eyes, and when she spoke, her voice was soft. "I don't know."

He crooked his finger and nudged her chin up.

"Yes you do," he said. His eyes were now a dark shade of navy blue. Dark with desire. "You know exactly what you want."

After a second she nodded slowly, lightly. "You're right, Nick. I do want..."

"Say it, Phoebe. Say what you want."

"I want...I want..."

"Yes, love?"

She smacked his fingers off her face and shoved the bucket of mushrooms into his hands. "I want you to take these to the café, clean them, and make me a mushroom cream sauce for the buckwheat crepes on tonight's menu."

She couldn't help it. As soon as she crossed the first set of branches to obscure his view of her, she broke out in a huge smile.

Chapter Seven

People thought that because Jesse was eighteen, she knew nothing about love. That wasn't true. She'd seen the way her parents had looked at each other. She could still visualize the exact way her father had watched her mother when she was going about the simplest things. Like washing the dishes or talking on the phone or sipping her tea. He'd always seemed to be watching her. Not in a creepy, stalker kind of way, but because he'd just liked looking at her. His eyes would go all soft and mushy and full of what Jesse knew to be total contentment.

He never had that look anymore.

Jesse heaved a pot of boiling water off the Viking range and drained the organic wheat corkscrew pasta into a colander. Steam rose up, clouding around her face like vapor from a hot spring. She let it. It hid the tears that sprang up sometimes when she thought of her mom. She missed her. It was unfair. Mom had been a good person, and Jesse didn't need to be some sort of expert on the human race to know that the world was severely lacking in the good people department. So why her mom? Why did her mom have to get effing breast cancer?

It wasn't fair.

And she didn't even care about herself. It was her dad she worried about. It had been five years since Mom died. She knew her dad missed her mother just as much today as he had the days following that last, horrible stay in the hospital.

The steam evaporated, and she wiped her face on a dishtowel before throwing it into the laundry pile. She didn't know why she was thinking of her mom today. It was just like that sometimes. Maybe it was because she worried about her dad, and he'd been on her mind lately. She bit her lip. Yeah, he'd been on her mind because she'd been doing the one thing she knew would make him even more sad. She'd been learning how to cook meat, compliments of Nick Avalon.

And damn it, she liked it.

"Jesse!"

She whipped her head to the side to see Nick eyeing her. He was leaning against the counter holding a package wrapped in white butcher paper. Her heart gave a little jump. She knew that paper. It had become all too familiar since Nick had started working here.

"Oh, no," she said. "What is it?"

"Pork chops." His lips quirked, and he grinned evilly.

She couldn't help but smile. He really was charming sometimes. For an old guy.

But still, she must have looked worried because Nick said, "Don't fret, dumpling. I'm sure just yesterday these chops were on some pigs wallowing around in a free-range pen, chowing organic slop, happy as clams." He shook his head at his own nonsense. "Anyway, I assure you they were fat and happy little piggies before they got the ax."

Jesse put a hand to her mouth. "Nick! Don't talk like that!"

"My point is, we have an hour before we open for lunch. It's the perfect opportunity to give you a little lesson on how a simple technique can turn a humble pork chop into a delicious bit of piggy-meat heaven."

She really shouldn't. If her dad found out, he'd get that sad, puppy-dog look. And it would be her fault.

On the other hand, cooking was something that was becoming kind of an addiction. She loved learning techniques, especially the ones Nick had recently been teaching her, and she loved the end result. Out of all the hobbies she'd tried in school—painting, sculpture, poetry—nothing compared to the satisfaction she received from the art of creating the perfect béchamel sauce.

"Fine," she said. "But we have to hurry. We only have an hour."

Nick grinned. "That's more than enough time, cookie."

"Here's tonight's menu." Phoebe threw a piece of paper on the counter, where it landed in front of Nick.

He raised a brow and leisurely picked up the paper. He knew Phoebe created all the menus herself, usually based on what she was producing from her farm. She also typed up the specials menu daily, and he had to admit she did a decent job of it. No cheesy graphics. Just simple type with simple descriptions.

"It's Saturday."

He glanced up. "Yeah. I know."

"Fixed-price night."

He took a swig from his glass of tequila. "I'm aware of the concept."

"Good. Then read that over and make sure you can get it done."

She raised her little chin and added, "I know we serve a fairly humble menu during the week, but our Saturday prix fixe carte du jour is a bit more upscale. Think you can handle it?"

"Gee, ma'am. I'll try my darnedest." He gave her a mock salute.

With one last scowl she turned, her skirt swirling around her as she stalked back outside, her sandals hitting the ground like hammers. He laughed. For someone who came off as such a hippie, she sure was wound up like the worst kind of executive yuppie.

Nick took another sip from his glass and read over the menu. He hated to admit it, but he was impressed. Starting with an Andante dairy minuet with fennel and watermelon radish salad and Acme *pain epi* with Straus butter. Appetizers included risotto burrata croquettes with salsa verde, grilled artichokes, squash and Treviso radicchio with warm butter and aged balsamic...

The entrées included butternut squash ravioli with Lacinato and Nagoya kale, spring onions, and caramel almonds...rosemary crepes with rainbow chard, savoy spinach, leeks, and goat cheese...wild-mushroom shepherd's pie with caramelized onions, and a pinot noir mushroom sauce...

Damn. Even her wine suggestions were perfect, and he should know. He was good at a lot of things, but he had a special knack for pairing liquor with food. And not just wine. Sometimes wine just didn't cut it. Nick thought tequila was often preferable.

He took another sip of the said liquid that happened

to be right near his hand. Then he watched as Phoebe attempted to open the door to the café with a crate of artichokes in her arms.

She glared at him. "Can I get a hand here?"

"But it's so fun to watch you struggle."

"You're an ass." She finally made it through and the paned-glass door slammed shut behind her.

"So I've been told." He almost felt bad for not helping her. He might be a prick, but he still had the knowledge of basic manners. But something inside him enjoyed annoying her. It seemed every day she got more and more bossy, and it was now like a challenge. How irritated could he make her?

Because she was going to break sometime. And he wanted to be there to see it. He wanted to see her utterly give up control. And he wanted to be the one who enjoyed every second when that happened.

And she was changing. When he'd first met her, he could almost smell her nervousness when he was around her. But those nerves were slowly morphing into an almost comfortable irritation, and he liked that she was, apparently, beginning to feel less and less intimidated by him.

Dropping the crate on the counter next to the sink, she glared at him. "Did you look at the menu?"

"I did."

She made a gesture with her hand as if to say, *And...?*

Finally, she prompted, "And?"

"Are you sure about the caramel almonds?" Nick had no problem with caramel almonds, but he couldn't stop himself. He could stop taunting her, but he didn't feel like it. Why? Was he really that bored?

Could be.

And there was the fact that if he wasn't taunting her, he was thinking about her lush breasts, the taste of her skin, the way she smelled...

Better to taunt. "Because I think walnuts would be a better choice." He didn't even like walnuts.

"I made the menu. You just cook it."

"I'm just offering my opinion. You know, since I trained at—"

She rolled her eyes. "The Cordon Bleu. I know! We all know! Jeez, how many times do you have to tell us?"

Slightly taken aback, he drained his glass. The tequila burned its way down his throat and landed in his gut. "I'm sorry." He was apologizing? He never apologized. He said, "I think you people forget that I'm used to cooking—"

"Delicacies for patrons of the highest caliber! Trust me, we get it. *We know.*" Hands on her hips, she came at him.

He tried not to focus on the twisty little curl of hair that had sprung out of her braid. He focused on her pink little mouth, which was still moving. He couldn't help but think that she'd be a lot less able to rail at him with his dick in her mouth.

Damn it. The thought made him shift as his balls went tight. Better to listen, even if her voice was rising by the second.

"We all know you're way better than us, that you're used to cooking things bumpkins like us could never *begin* to appreciate. We know what you think. The thing is? *We don't care!*"

She was yelling at him. And flailing her arms. And

her hair was coming undone in frizzy, curly waves. He just stared at her. It had been a long time since someone shouted at him in a kitchen. Generally, it was Nick who was doing the bellowing.

This place really was backward.

He spoke calmly. "I was just trying to help."

Her chest rose and fell with her rapid breathing. She'd really worked herself up. It shouldn't be cute. But it was. So much so, he had to look away.

Then he looked back. "What got into your knickers? Oh, right. That was me."

He thought she might explode. She resembled one of those cartoons where the animated animal becomes so mad that its head turns bright red and turns into a steam-blowing contraption.

Quite the contrast from the sassy woman who'd walked away from him in the woods. No, he hadn't liked that very much. He'd been irked, yet he'd also been amused and somewhat surprised at her spunk. Not many people could stand up to him in the context of the two things he excelled at: cooking and wooing women.

Well, she may have been annoyed at him in the woods. Now she looked ready to kill him. He took a step back in retreat. She took a step toward him.

He put his hand out, palm facing her. "Hang on now, Phoebe. I was just giving you a hard time."

She continued to encroach on his space. He felt his ass hit the counter. With her index finger, she poked him in the chest.

"Ow!" he said.

"You ... you ... you *jerk*!"

"Wow. You really have a potty mouth, don't you,

love?" He was trying to sound casual, but his heart was starting to hammer. Why did it do that around her? He couldn't control his reaction to her, either physically or emotionally.

She made him feel. He wasn't sure what he was feeling, but it was there, and he wasn't at all cool with it.

He took her hand, the one that had been poking him, and clenched it in his fist. He could feel her bones. Long and delicate. But despite her fragile appearance, it was obvious she was anything but. She was a strong woman who wasn't intimidated by him one whit.

He needed to work on that.

Chapter Eight

Phoebe tried to jerk away from Nick's grip, but he held her firm. He was lean but freakishly strong, and he had no problem keeping her hand clenched tightly in his. A shiver went up her arm at the contact.

She glared up at him. "What do you want?"

Despite his casual appearance, she could swear she saw something in his eyes—something that belied his callous words and obvious attitude problem. His blue eyes bored into hers, and in those depths, she detected something strange.

"Oh, stop it," she said.

"You don't want me to stop anything."

She lifted her chin. "Don't give me that look."

He seemed genuinely surprised. "What look?"

"That one, the one that says you're trying to be all nice."

"Nice?"

In a flash he reversed their positions, so she was now backed up against the counter. "I'll show you nice."

He released her hand and grabbed the counter on each side, enclosing her. She sucked in a breath. She could feel him, feel his legs pressed against hers. And then he pressed his crotch against her, and she felt it.

He was hard. Like, really hard. Harder even than in the forest, and that had been quite impressive.

How could she—a woman who must seem so plain in comparison to all those L.A. girls—get a man like Nick Avalon so frisky? She wasn't insecure about her appearance. She knew she wasn't a total knockout, but she wasn't dog meat either. Still, why would a man like Nick Avalon be attracted to a girl like plain old Phoebe? Not that she was old. Thirty-two wasn't old. Well, maybe in L.A. But not here.

Was it?

He took her chin in his hand. "Stop it."

"What?"

"Thinking."

She tried to swat his hand away from her face, but he held her steady. "You'd like that, wouldn't you?" she asked.

"I would."

"Oh, I'm sure. Then you better go find yourself some bimbo with no brain."

"I fully plan on it."

"So why are you here—"

His lips stopped her words. His mouth pushed against hers, assaulting her as he pressed his jeans-clad erection against the flimsy folds of her skirt.

Damn. Much to her dismay, her body had already responded to him. She was wet, and her breasts were aching for his touch. His lips were warm, and his tongue was licking at her, trying to get her to open.

She opened. His kiss...it melted her. His mouth invited her in, teased her. Everything faded as her eyes closed, and she met him. His body was hard, imprisoning her to him. But his kiss was soft. Mind-numbing.

When her head was good and spinning, he pulled away. He had that little smirk on his face. If she weren't floating from the kiss, she would have smacked it off his face.

Instead she yanked his T-shirt and pulled him down to her, bringing his mouth to hers once more. But the dynamics changed. He pushed into her mouth. She pushed back. She grabbed his head. He held her shoulders. Push, pull. Attack and retreat. Phoebe felt like she was, for some reason she didn't understand, fighting for power. And so was he.

And it was all good.

She sucked his tongue into her mouth. Deep. Satisfaction went through her when he stilled. His eyes were closed, and he remained motionless. She was in control. *She* was the one kissing *him*.

But then he pushed her back. Panting, she looked at him. His eyes were dark, nearly black. His spiky hair was messy, messy from her hands.

He grabbed her arm and turned. "Come here."

"What?" She stumbled behind him. "What are you doing?"

"Teaching you a lesson."

"I don't want a lesson!" So why was her heart hammering with anticipation? *Yes!* her body was screaming at her. *Give me a lesson!*

Why was she allowing any of this to happen? Because no matter how much she told herself she didn't want him, no matter how much she denied it, the fact was that she was allowing it. Wanting it.

She wasn't walking out.

Nick dragged her through the kitchen, plucking a whisk off the utensil wall without slowing his pace whatsoever.

A whisk? What was he going to do with that? Turn her into a meringue pie?

He pushed through into the stockroom, pulled her inside, and slammed the door shut. Then he flipped her around so she was facing the door and pushed her up against it. Her chest beat against the wood, so heavy was her breathing.

"Nick?"

"Shhh...," he whispered in her ear. He pressed up against her back, and she felt the hardness of his body everywhere. Then he pushed aside the mass of hair that had come loose from her braid. His warm lips on her skin. His damp breath as he kissed her earlobe.

Just that. Just that had her leaning into the door, had her eyes drifting closed. And she could smell him, which was only making it worse. Or better. She couldn't decide.

He had one hand on her shoulder, gripping her. Stilling her. And his mouth...

So simple. Softly, slowly, he was licking behind her ear. She thought he'd never stop. Her body trembled as he continued to kiss her there. Shivers shot through her as her mind emptied. She couldn't stop the soft moan from escaping her lips.

"That's right, gorgeous. Let me have you."

His British accent was heavier than she'd ever heard it. And she hated that calling her gorgeous went straight to her head. And even more, she hated herself for nodding. *Let me have you.* She didn't want to give herself away. Not to Nick or anyone.

But, as she felt his hand caressing her back, felt his palm skim her rib cage, her hips and her ass...she couldn't help but let herself go. Just a little.

And then a little more.

And it felt so good to let go...He took her chin and turned her so the side of her face was resting against the door.

"Such a good girl," he whispered, and the words affected her. They satisfied her.

So when she felt him tug her skirt down over her hips, she didn't care. She wanted to be a good girl. Nick's good girl. When he caressed her butt, she sank deeper into the door because her legs were trembling, and she needed the support. He lifted her arms over her head to pull off her T-shirt. He tossed it aside, and then she was standing in her bra and panties. Still facing away from Nick. Somehow that was fine. She couldn't see him, but she could feel him. Feel his hands feathering down her back. Feel his breath on her neck. Feel his fingers as he reached around to press against her moist pussy.

"Wet, aren't you, babe?"

She was. Her panties were damp. Her sex was giving away her arousal. He reached inside the waistband to slide two fingers into her throbbing flesh. She gasped.

"That's my girl. So wet for me."

"Yes...Nick..."

With his fingertips, he rubbed her clit. Little circles with just enough pressure to make her cry out. Such a simple act, what he was doing. Touching such a small part of her body with his hands...but *oh my God*...the pleasure was shooting through her. She'd never responded to a man this way before, never felt such excitement, such total abandon.

Except for the last time they'd been together. What was it about Nick that made her so excited?

It wasn't just his hand between her legs. It was the unique fragrance of his body that was intoxicating her. It was the tequila-scented breath on her skin that was sending shivers through her system. It was the tone of his voice, commanding her.

It was him. She wanted to release herself. To *him*. When they'd been kissing earlier in the kitchen, she'd been fighting for power. But now he'd won. She'd given in to him. She had no idea why, but she wanted him to win.

Just this once.

And the lust pounding through her was taking over everything. Still working her pulsing clit, he increased pressure.

"Nick, yes. Right there!"

"I know, sweetheart. I know." But then he stopped. She hitched a breath when he slid his fingers out of her panties.

"Nick..."

"Don't move." He placed his fingers, the ones that had been touching her sex just seconds before, against her lips. "Taste."

He didn't give her a choice. He slid his moist fingers against her lips and then into her mouth. She tasted herself on his skin. She sucked on his fingers as he kissed her neck. Her pussy yearned to have him fill her with the erection pressing against her back.

"Such a good girl." He pulled his fingers out of her mouth.

"Nick. Please." How had he reduced her to begging?

But she was. No choice. All she knew was that she wanted this man fucking her. Hard. Rough.

She wanted him to *take* her.

But she froze when she felt the hard metal spokes of the whisk that he'd snatched from the kitchen.

Glancing over her shoulder, she was about to ask what he was doing.

But, once again, he turned her away from him. "Shhh," he repeated. "Be a good girl."

Did she have a choice? Her entire body was thrumming with lust and desire. Not just sexual, but so much deeper. She needed something more than a fuck. She needed Nick. She needed him to own her. Now that he'd won the battle, she wanted nothing more than to surrender completely.

She was on a precipice. And she wanted to jump. Somehow, somewhere deep inside her core, she knew Nick—the egocentric, irresponsible bad boy—would catch her. The thought was thrilling.

He was running the whisk over her body, gently over her shoulder blades, skimming her side, then across her ass.

"Lovely skin," he said. "So pale."

When he flicked her ass with the whisk, she jumped. But the sting was shockingly erotic. It amped up her already buzzing nerves.

"It's okay, babe. Just feel."

What he was doing seemed so naughty, so taboo. And she couldn't help but be a little bit exhilarated by it.

There had always been a part of her, a part she'd restrained, that craved dangerous things. But she'd never allowed herself to go there. She had a family to look out for, two businesses to run, impoverished kids to help. She simply didn't have the option to indulge her secret fantasies of bungee-diving from a bridge or jumping out of an airplane with nothing but a parachute to keep her body from shattering to a million pieces when she hit the ground.

This felt like that. As if she were indulging herself. She was exposed, under the influence of Nick Avalon, the most dangerous man she'd ever met. And she was allowing him to...

"Damn!" she cried out as he flicked the whisk at her ass once again.

"You okay, sweetheart?" His palm was flat on her back, holding her still.

She nodded. "Yes..."

He kissed her between her shoulder blades. "I know you are, sweetheart."

Of course he did. He could tap right into this place in her, a place she hadn't even been aware of. And now, like a chemical, something seemed to be releasing from her brain. Even as her nerves buzzed, something in her was calm. It was a heady combination, and she wanted more of it.

"Again," she said.

"That's my girl."

His words made her legs quiver.

The way he spanked her, just below the line of her bikini underwear, was quick and efficient. Each time she felt the sting—and the sting of the thin metal was sharp—she gasped. But also, each swat intensified everything she was feeling: lust, desire, exhilaration.

Harder and harder. Holding her still, he whipped her

ass until she felt as if she were floating. The sounds of her cries, of the metal hitting her flesh, of Nick's breathing, faded. Her body was going numb all over as the sensations spread through her. She knew he was hitting her more intensely, that she should be screaming from pain. But the pain felt good. Right. She'd never been so relaxed, so out of her head.

Sticking her ass out, she pressed her palms against the door. "Yes, Nick. Harder." She barely heard her own voice.

"Who knew you were such a naughty little thing, Pheebs?"

"Shut up and keep going."

She wasn't sure how many more times he smacked her ass. But he continued, and her mind kept disappearing. Then he whipped her hard, and this time it was much sharper, almost too much. But he knew exactly what she could take. And he paused a moment to allow her to catch her breath.

Her ass burned, but it was a good burn. Everything was good. Too good. She couldn't think. She couldn't speak anymore. She slumped against the wall.

"That's my girl."

Chapter Nine

The next thing she knew she was in his arms. He crossed the room to sit on a crate of canned organic garbanzo beans. He still held her. His arms were strong and reassuring around her. She didn't know what was going on, what had happened. Her entire body seemed to be connected to this man. Her heart seemed to be beating just for him. Her brain could only focus on him, and the sudden attachment to him that was threatening to blossom like an apple tree in spring.

Somewhere, she knew it was wrong. She didn't like him. She knew she didn't. So why did she want to sink into him? Why did she want to kiss his forehead and run her hands through his spiky hair? Why did she want to climb up, straddle him, and feel his cock inside her? She wanted him buried so deep inside her it hurt to even think about.

He kissed her forehead. "You okay?"

After a minute, she said, "I think so." Reality was starting to set in. The fog in her brain was beginning to clear. "What just happened?" And why did she feel downright giddy?

She'd never been giddy a moment in her life.

When she looked into his eyes, she saw he actually appeared a bit confused. Interesting. "I whisked you," he finally said.

She had to grin. "Yeah...you did."

He shifted beneath her, and she could feel his erection—long and hard and...*long*.

Okay, there was that lust again.

But it was more. The experience of what he'd just done to her had left her feeling open and vulnerable, and that should have been enough to make her jump off his lap and run away screaming. Allowing herself to feel those things was dangerous.

And it was clear she'd crossed a dangerous line. Nick Avalon was even more perilous than she'd ever imagined. What he'd done to her had been thrilling. Exhilarating. And easily addicting.

And this thing inside her—the way her chest ached from this connection he'd created—was the most dangerous part of all. It gave him power over her. It made her have feelings for him that didn't include irritation or hatred. Those feelings were things she could deal with, but that other stuff?

No way.

She went to push herself off him, but he stopped her. "Where do you think you're going?"

It was then she realized she was sitting on his lap in her bra and panties. Panic began to set in. "I need to go! It's nearly three. The night crew will be arriving any minute!"

Holy crap. What was she thinking? What if they got caught? Again, she tried to stand.

Again, he stopped her, holding her tight in his arms.

"So you think you can just go now because you want to?" He looked genuinely amazed that she would consider such a thing.

She pretended to think about it and then, "Yeah. I do."

"Not so fast."

"Nick. Let me go."

He reached around and grabbed her ass, the place where he'd used the whisk on her. "You liked it."

She felt her neck start to burn. "Maybe. So?"

"You gave yourself over to me, Miss Mayle."

"I did no such thing."

"Yeah? You were begging me for it. Begging me to hit that cute little ass of yours."

He thought her ass was cute? She shook her head. "I was curious, is all."

"Kinky is more like it."

She sucked in a breath. "Kinky! I am not!"

He laughed. "Is that so? Then why did you let me spread chocolate sauce all over your body and lick it off your pussy?"

Her cheeks were burning now. "I was...tired!"

But he was obviously enjoying himself. "And why did you let me take off all your clothes and beat your ass with a kitchen utensil?"

"Stop it." She started rebraiding her hair. "Just stop it."

He reached up to cup one of her breasts. She jumped. Her breasts were overly sensitive, and she yearned for him to do more than fondle her. She wanted him to rip off her bra, take her nipple in his teeth and bite—

Bite?

She punched his arm. "Let me go, you brute!"

"Brute? I'm sorry, love." He mockingly glanced

around the storage room. "Did we just travel back in time to Victorian England, and I somehow missed the journey?"

She gritted her teeth. "Just. Let. Me. Go."

Releasing her, he threw his arms out wide. "Of course, sweetheart. All you had to do was ask."

She jumped up, crossed the room, and started yanking on her skirt and top. Her ass was starting to sting, and not necessarily in a bad way. She glared at him. "You're a jerk."

He clasped his hands behind his head and leaned back against the wall. She wanted to punch him. Perched on a crate of beans in a storage room, his hair sticking up in spiky chunks, he still managed to look laid-back and suave. She, on the other hand, knew she was a damn mess. Her kinky hair was half-braided, her skirt was all wrinkly, and damn! She'd just put on her T-shirt, and the tag was poking her in the front of the neck. She pulled her arms inside the shirt to jerk it around. At least she'd noticed before she went into the kitchen with her shirt on backward.

Glaring at him, she placed her hands on her hips. "Damn you."

"You're welcome."

"I didn't thank you, Nick."

"Then clear it up, will you. What exactly did I do wrong?"

She pointed a finger at him. "You—you—you know exactly what you did!"

He gave her a smug smirk. "Took advantage of your helpless female self?"

Her mouth opened wide as she sucked in air. "What?

Are you even more of an imbecile than I originally thought?" She barked a loud laugh. "That's just ridiculous. Wait. You're right. It's me!"

"You?" He was looking at her as if he were observing a patient from an insane asylum.

"No." Blowing a curl away from her face, she started pacing back and forth. "You are right. I did let myself become helpless to your..." *Charm* seemed like the right word, but it really wasn't. She glanced at him. "Helpless to your *whisk*." More pacing. "But that's because of me, not you, you ass."

"You?"

"Of course. I've always tried to curb my draw to dangerous things."

"Is that so?"

"Yes! And don't give me that condescending tone either."

"I'll try not to, love."

"And don't call me love."

"Um, okay. Phoebe."

"Don't call me that either." She hated it when he said her name; it did funny things to her insides. "Obviously, I was weak today, after..." She threw a wave of her hand in his general direction. "After the other night. And it...it...has clouded my judgment. Ha, ha! Because there is no way I would ever, ever let you *do*...do those things you *did* to me if I was in my right mind."

He seemed confused. "So, is this my fault...or yours? You've utterly lost me, sweetheart."

"It's my fault." Was he stupid? "Because I, for some reason, behave totally irrationally when I'm around you!"

"Is that so?" He lifted his ass and pulled a pack of

Marlboros out of his back pocket. "Interesting." He extracted a cigarette out of the pack and stuck it in his mouth. Then he flipped open a silver lighter.

She gasped in exasperation. "What are you doing?"

He ignited the lighter and put a flame to the nicotine stick perched on the right side of his lips. "What does it look like, love? Surely out here in hippie central you've seen someone light up."

She stalked over and smacked the lighter out of his hand. "You can't smoke in here!"

"But you just keep talking. It's tiresome. I need a little pick-me-up."

She yanked the cigarette from his lips and threw it over his shoulder. "It's illegal! If the health inspector came in and saw you, we could get written up!"

He just looked at her. "That's easily taken care of, babe."

"Oh yeah? Do share your ultimate wisdom with this inexperienced minion."

"You give him a hundred bucks."

"What? No! We've proudly been scored 99 since the day this establishment opened. Fair and square."

He quirked an annoying dark brow. "What was the one percent you missed?"

She sniffed and looked down at him. "A patron snuck a dog into the restaurant inside her purse."

He laughed. Loudly. "You're kidding."

"Of course not. Why?"

Retrieving his lighter off the floor, he said, "That's just so...L.A. of you all."

"It was a special-needs dog."

"Is that so?" He stuck another cigarette in his mouth.

"Yes! It is. Was."

"So why'd you get written up? If it was, indeed, a special-needs dog?"

She smoothed a stray strand of hair behind her ear. "The patron didn't have the appropriate papers."

"And this special-needs dog was what? A golden retriever? A Labrador?" Once again, he flicked his lighter open.

Phoebe ignored it when he put the flame to the Marlboro stuck in his mouth. Trying to disregard the smell of burning nicotine that immediately swirled into the storage room, she said, "It was a hairless dog."

He coughed on some smoke. "A what?"

"A hairless dog. You know, it didn't have any hair. What harm could there possibly have been?"

"You mean like that cat from *Austin Powers*? Was the dog *shagadelic*?" He smirked at his own joke.

"Shut up." Stomping over, she plucked the cigarette out of his mouth. She then proceeded to put it to her own mouth and take a deep drag.

He was looking at her as if she'd just grown snakes out of her head. Well, if she looked in the mirror, she might think he was right. Surely, her hair looked a fright.

Closing her eyes, she let the smoke fill her lungs.

"What the fuck are you doing?" he asked incredulously.

Her eyes popped open, and she slowly exhaled, making sure to blow the smoke directly toward his face. "What?" she said, taking another drag.

He looked appalled. "You're smoking!"

"So?"

"You don't smoke!"

"How do you know?" No one knew she kept a pack of Camels hidden in her underwear drawer.

"Because you said it was disgusting!"

"Well..." She took a drag. "Well, it is."

"Then why are you doing it? I thought you were Miss Innocent Healthy Woman."

"I am!"

"Then?" He held out his hand as if expecting some sort of answer.

"You don't know everything."

"I know what you said."

"Phooey." Seriously? Did she really just say that?

"Did you really just say that?"

"Maybe!" she exclaimed. "Maybe it's time for you to get rid of all those ideas and concepts and ideas and stereotypes you have about everyone who lives here."

"Hey, love. I'm just stating the facts."

"Shut up."

"Don't smoke."

"Why?" she said, inhaling another drag that made her want to vomit. It was all too much. Now she was just proving a point. A point that might make her sick.

Nick looked alarmed. He went to swipe the cigarette out of her hand, and she jumped back.

"You think you know me?" she asked.

He stood, obviously thinking of making another attempt to get the Marlboro out of her fingers. She could do this. She was tough.

"Back off, Mr. Avalon." Resting her elbow in her hand, she took another drag. "You think you have it all figured out. You think you have us *all* pegged. A bunch of boring tree huggers living in the backwoods of nowhere."

He glanced around the stockroom for a second. "Well, yeah. Kinda."

"Ha!" She pointed the cigarette at him. "Ha, ha, ha!"

Looking genuinely concerned—or was it scared?—he said, "Phoebe, are you okay?"

"Don't say my name!"

"Okay. Love, are you okay?"

Was she okay? She had no idea. Her hands were shaking, and she felt shivers start to rack her body.

Nick took a step toward her. Slowly, as if approaching a wild, wounded animal, and he reached out his hand. "Babe. Come here."

"N-no." But her voice was shaky, and she didn't know what the hell was wrong with her. She tried to inhale more from the cigarette, but it just made her cough. She felt as if she were crashing off some high. All the things she'd been feeling throughout the day came at her in a rush, overwhelming her until her eyes began to fill. Anger, hurt, trust, exhilaration, lust, defense... It was too much. And it was all aimed at this one man. And even as she hated him, she wanted nothing more than for him to hold her and comfort her.

"Damn it!" she said, swiping at a tear.

When he took the cigarette from her, she couldn't—didn't—want to stop him. Her fingers were trembling too violently to hold it, and her throat was clenching. She saw him throw the cigarette on the floor and stomp on it with his expensive trainers. He took her in his arms.

"You'll have to clean that up," she said into his chest. And then she inhaled deeply, filling her lungs with the scent of him, and it was more calming and fulfilling than any cigarette could ever be.

Why was he doing that? Why was he holding her so tightly she felt like she could live here—*right here*? Why was he stroking the back of her head so soothingly she thought she could trust him? Why, why, why...

"Shhh," he whispered.

Oh, how she'd loved that earlier. Loved the sound of his voice in her ear. It had made her want to shush, made her want to give herself up, just for a minute. Because it was dangerous to do so. And he'd made her think that was okay. That it was perfectly safe to take that leap.

She pushed away so fast that he stumbled backward.

Nick Avalon was a mystery. The only details he shared about his personal life were shallow, usually having to do with parties or women. He never mentioned his family, or a history not related to cooking.

He was unpredictable, which was dangerous. And that was the very last thing she'd ever needed in her life.

"Leave me alone," she said, backing toward the door.

He looked genuinely confused. If she wasn't brainless, she'd think he even looked hurt.

And oh, how he could pull it off; as if he actually cared what she thought of him. But he was trying. His eyes appeared downright baffled. Sad even, when he said, "Phoebe, love. Fuck, what's wrong?"

"You. You're wrong. Stop doing this to me. *I'm* going to stop letting you do this to me." She yanked open the storage room door. "Don't look at me. Don't touch me. Don't...whisk me!"

"But—"

"No!" She put out her hand. "Shut up. You work for me. You're my"—she poked herself in the chest—"*my* employee. Now get out to the kitchen and start prepping.

We have an early crowd here. We're old and boring, remember?"

He was just staring at her. *It was an act.* He'd been a playboy since the second he'd gotten here, and she'd let him get to her. Why? Because he had *Danger* practically tattooed all over his arrogant face. She thought she'd tamped down that desire of hers long ago.

Now she wasn't sure. Not one bit.

Obviously, she'd been wrong. She should just jump out of an airplane and get it over with. Because free-falling ten thousand feet through the sky was certainly safer than letting Nick Avalon anywhere near her.

She glared at him. "Get to work." Turning, she spun on her heel and stalked away. It was then she realized she'd had her sandals on the entire time. He hadn't even bothered to take off her shoes.

Chapter Ten

Here you go, Dad." Jesse placed her father's order on the table. "Butternut squash ravioli. Nick made it. It's delicious. I tried some earlier."

Her dad looked up and smiled. It made Jesse's heart hurt. Every Saturday night, he came to the bistro at 6:00 on the dot. He always sat alone, at the table he'd so often shared with her mother when she was alive.

"Bon appétit." Jesse pasted on a reflection of his fake smile, turned, and went back to the kitchen.

"How is he?" Phoebe stuck two order tickets on the wheel hanging from the ceiling and spun it.

Jesse looked back at her dad, who was cutting a single ravioli with a knife and a fork. "The same." She faced Phoebe. "Do you think he'll ever meet someone?"

Her aunt's eyes went soft as she touched Jesse's shoulder gently. "When he's ready."

"What if he never is?"

"Oh, honey. Then that'll be his decision."

Jesse sighed. "I guess you're right." Anyway, she really wasn't sure how she'd feel if her father did, indeed, meet another woman. She wanted her dad to be happy, but no one could ever replace her mother.

With a sigh, Jesse glanced around the restaurant. The three other servers were busy, and Nick was sweating away at the big stove. The place was busier than it normally was on a Saturday night. But it was still unchanged. Same patrons, same decor, same...everything.

Jesse wanted out. She envied Nick and his background, and his stories about living in Los Angeles. And his awesome knowledge about food. She imagined his life in L.A. She pictured his chic apartment on the beach, the exciting parties, and the endless choices of things to do. It all sounded so cool.

It all sounded so unlike what she was used to. Redbolt wasn't exactly swimming with culture. She was sick of the same coffeehouse, the same grocery store, the same routine. The same people.

More than anything, Jesse craved more. That's all she knew. She wanted more.

"Jesse!"

Spinning, she saw Nick glaring at her beneath the warming lights. Yeah, he could be cool, but it was easy to see that he was a shark in the kitchen. She really didn't want to piss him off.

She plucked two plates off the hot counter. "Sorry."

"Yeah, well, sorry won't get this food to the tables, poppet."

Nodding, she headed toward the table and put the plates down. "Here you go, Rachel. And there you are, Rick."

The thirty-something couple smiled at her. Their San Francisco–based Internet start-up company had gone public a few years back, and they'd settled on a ranch about fifteen miles out of town. Jesse knew they were gazillionaires, but you'd never know it from their laid-back manner and casual dress. And every Saturday night, they came in for their standing 7:00 p.m. reservation.

"This looks delicious," Rick said, gazing at his vegan shepherd's pie.

Rachel picked up a fork and looked at her rosemary crepes. "What makes it all the more amazing is that our own Phoebe grew most of this right here on her local farm."

"Yup," Jesse said. "Phoebe is pretty amazing."

"That she is."

Jesse glanced over to the object of their praise, who was currently talking with the chef. Phoebe and Nick were head-to-head, trying to look casual but obviously fighting about something.

Well, that wasn't unusual. They were always fighting over something.

"Enjoy," Jesse said before heading back to the kitchen. She went straight over to Nick and Phoebe.

Nick had his hands on his hips and was leaning down to get right in Phoebe's face. "Who the fuck books ten reservations in the span of twenty minutes?"

Phoebe didn't back down. "What do you care? We have the space!"

"Yeah, but we don't have the fucking backup, *boss*. There's only one chef in this back room. Me!"

"I don't give a rat's ass who the chef is. There's only one *boss* in this place, and that is me!"

"The manager should know how to space reservations."

"Hey, buster!" She poked him in the chest. "For some reason, we're getting a lot more patrons since you've been here. I'm just trying to accommodate the demand."

Jesse couldn't help but be entertained by their disputes. She'd never seen her parents fight, not once. But watching Nick and Phoebe go back and forth like this, it was fascinating. Like watching professionals play tennis. Every night was Wimbledon.

Eventually, Phoebe tugged Nick into a corner where they continued their bickering, only now in furious whispers.

Why was she comparing Nick and Phoebe to her parents? That was strange. They were nothing like Jesse's parents, and they certainly weren't "together."

Nick had leaned right into Phoebe's face. Jesse could still hear them.

"Well," he said, "learn how to space out reservations before you piss off all your new money. Can't you see your waiters are getting buried, and the kitchen's in the weeds?"

Jesse bit her lip. All that was true. She and the three other servers had been rushing around all night trying to keep up. She'd personally handed Nick more tickets in an hour than she usually did all night.

But she'd never say anything to Phoebe.

Nick, obviously, had no qualms about standing up to the manager. He waved Phoebe away.

"Now, leave the kitchen to me and go help out your waitstaff."

Jesse sucked in an astonished breath. In all the time she'd known her aunt, she'd never seen anyone, not once, give Phoebe a command.

And Phoebe looked like she was going to explode. Her cheeks were red, and her deep-brown hair seemed to be unraveling from her braid in angry spirals. Her green eyes looked ready to throw sparks at Nick.

"Um, Nick?"

They turned their glares to Ethan, a shy seventeen-year-old with bright red hair.

"What?" Nick barked.

"A-a customer was wondering if he could get the butternut squash without the caramel almonds." Ethan's blue eyes were wide, and he looked scared.

"Hell, no!" Nick said. "The almonds are perfection. They make the dish." And then he turned his back on all of them and went back to the stove.

Phoebe was staring at him. After a minute, she turned to Jesse. "He likes the almonds?"

Jesse shrugged. "Um, I guess so."

"That's strange."

"Why?"

Phoebe shook her head. "Earlier he said he only liked walnuts." She shook her head. "Obviously, he was just trying to mess with me." And then she grabbed a plate and headed into the front room.

Astonished, Jesse gazed after her. Phoebe had done it. She'd taken an order from Nick Avalon.

"Excuse us. Mr. Avalon?"

Wiping his brow, Nick looked up as he set two plates under the lights. A man and a woman stood on the other side of the counter. Both looked to be in their mid-thirties, and both were beaming at him.

"Yes?" he said.

The man said, "We just wanted to compliment you on our outstanding dinner."

"Yes," the woman said. "I'm Rachel, and this is Rick. We've lived here about five years now."

"Pleasure," Nick said.

Rick leaned a bit closer. "I can't tell you how happy we are to have a chef such as yourself move to Redbolt."

"Yes." Rachel's smile got bigger, and it seemed genuine. "While we absolutely love living here, we have to admit the one thing we miss about living in Silicon Valley is the food."

"Right," Rick said. "And your shepherd's pie is absolutely the most delicious thing I've had in ages."

Rachel actually clapped her hands. "And my crepes. It was better than sex."

"Hey." Rick gave her a friendly nudge. "I take offense to that."

Rachel grinned at her husband. "Well, I suppose you can try to make sex better than those crepes. Maybe I'll let you attempt it later tonight."

Nick stared at the couple. Redbolt got stranger by the minute.

Rick cleared his throat. "Anyway, we just wanted to tell you how much we enjoyed our meals. Thank you."

Nick wiped his hands on the dishtowel tucked into his belt and held out his hand. "I appreciate it. Nice to meet you."

After Nick shook their hands, he watched them exit the front door. They seemed to be actually complimenting his cooking, and not in the ass-kissing way he was used to. For some reason, the interaction had brought him a small amount of satisfaction. Although he really didn't want to care what the townspeople thought of him, he couldn't help but appreciate the compliment.

In fact, as he glanced around the dining room and observed the crowd, he had to acknowledge there was a much different vibe here than at any restaurant he'd cooked for in L.A. People were laughing, talking, and sipping wine. No one was wearing designer clothes or obnoxious jewelry. No one was here to be "seen."

These were the locals, here for the wine and the food. And apparently, they liked what Nick was producing. Enough to sincerely thank him.

"You okay?" Jesse grabbed the two plates from under the lights.

He turned to her. "Yeah. Why?"

"I dunno. You're just standing there. You never just stand anywhere."

He took a sip from the small glass of tequila. Funny, he realized he'd been too busy to actually drink any of it; the glass was still nearly full. "I'm good," he said, and went back to the stoves.

The last customer left just after ten o'clock. Phoebe didn't want to admit it, but Nick had been right. She had overbooked the restaurant. They'd been running around like insane people trying to fill all the orders. Luckily there had been only one set of irate customers—a couple traveling to explore the great redwood parks of Northern California—who had gone bonkers when they were forced to wait thirty minutes for their table.

The clientele locals understood the place was abnormally busy and took it in stride. Also, giving complimentary glasses of a local wine helped relax most of the more surly customers.

The servers were doing the final cleanup. With a deep

breath, she glanced around the bistro. Despite her mistake, they'd come together. Nick had turned out every plate, and despite his grouchy demeanor, he'd done his job. And she had to confess he'd done it well. Very well.

She watched him as he cleaned the back kitchen. Every so often he sipped from his ever-present glass of tequila, but she hadn't seen him refill it in the last few hours. He'd kept his eyes on his work, looking up briefly to take a ticket or answer a server's question.

For once, he didn't seem to be bouncing off the walls. He was focused on what he was doing. His leg wasn't doing its jackhammer routine, and his fingers weren't tapping any available surface.

Now he was scrubbing a stainless-steel counter. He had tiny headphones stuck in his ears, and he appeared to be enjoying himself. He seemed lost in what he was doing, so Phoebe stole a moment to watch him.

Beyond the sleeves of his black T-shirt, his arms were sturdy. For such a lean man, he had well-defined biceps muscles. She couldn't help the flutter that landed in her belly when she remembered exactly how those arms had felt holding her. Strong and safe.

What the heck was she thinking? Nick Avalon was anything but safe.

"I haven't seen you look at anyone like that since Bear."

Phoebe whipped her head around to face Steve, who'd just finished sweeping. "What do you mean?" she asked. But she felt her face flush.

"You know. Bear? Your high school sweetheart? The one you were engaged to?"

"Steve. What's your point?"

"My point is, I think you have a crush."

"I do not." Maybe if she said it enough times, it would be true.

"I heard a rumor Bear's back in the country."

"Oh?"

"Yes. His mom stopped by the store and said he was in New York or something, and might be home for a visit."

"I hope he can make it by." And Phoebe meant it. She'd always considered Bear one of her best friends.

As a food research scientist and activist, her ex-fiancé often came and went. That was one of the main reasons they'd called off the engagement. Bear needed to see the world. Phoebe had ties to home. She didn't begrudge him his travels, not one bit. In fact, she respected his decision to help the world.

Phoebe wanted to do that, too. Just at home. With her farm and her bees and her summer students.

"Are you okay, Phoebe?"

Her gaze drifted back to Nick. He was still lost in cleaning and his music. "Yes, I'm fine, Steve. Why do you ask?"

"Just wondering. I worry about you."

Turning, she smiled at her brother-in-law. "I'm wonderful. Life is good." And it was true. She was a modern woman, in charge of her body. She didn't need Nick, Bear, or anyone else. She could take care of herself and not be needy. Sometimes she had sexual urges. (Nick was an urge. An urge, by definition, is temporary and goes away.)

She gave Steve a hug. "Really. I'm great. I couldn't be happier."

Steve wrapped his big arms around her, and she

enjoyed the comfort of her family in that one embrace.

Eventually they pulled apart. She noticed Nick and Jesse were the only other ones left in the place. It was time to lock up and go home. Phoebe was taking the keys from the pocket of her apron when the jingle of bells hanging on the front doorknob caught her attention.

She jerked her gaze up. Her breath hitched as the most beautiful woman Phoebe had ever seen in real life walked into her restaurant.

"Hello! Anyone here? I'm looking for Nick Avalon."

Blonde, petite, gorgeous, and perfectly made up, she reminded Phoebe of Goldie Hawn in her thirties.

Jealousy, pure and simple, coursed through Phoebe's veins. It was like a river. She couldn't stop it from rushing. The feeling was unfamiliar, and she didn't like it, but it was powerful.

Phoebe approached her. "I'm sorry. We're closed for the night. Can I perhaps make a reservation for you for tomorrow?"

The woman smiled brightly, and Phoebe thought her lips were just a bit too plump. Still, there was no denying her beauty.

She held out her hand. "I'm Sherry. I'm looking for—" Squealing, she ran to the bar and slapped her hands on the surface. "Nick!"

Obviously surprised, he looked up. Then his expression totally changed. A huge smile broke out across his face, such as Phoebe had never seen on him before. In awe, she stared at him as he slapped his white towel over his shoulder and jumped—literally jumped—over the bar. Who knew he was so limber?

Arms crossed across her chest, Phoebe watched as

Nick embraced the petite women in a big ol' bear hug. The hug seemed to last forever.

She didn't want to be jealous, really she didn't...

Why did Goldie have to look so damn good? Phoebe looked down at her own long skirt, dirty and wrinkly from a hard day's work. Her T-shirt was no better, and she wished she were wearing something a bit more feminine. Sexy. Revealing. Not that she had anything to reveal. Still. She couldn't help feeling nothing but dowdy next to the gorgeous blonde currently embraced in Nick's arms.

That jealous ball churned a bit more inside her tummy.

Goldie looked like she'd just stepped out of a catalog. Her jeans were obviously designer. And tight. Tight enough to show off an ass and legs that obviously spent many hours running on a treadmill to make them so firm and fabulous.

She wore boots. Spiky-heeled shiny black concoctions, into which were tucked the hems of those amazing jeans.

Phoebe shuffled in her sandals. Normally she didn't care about such things as clothing or being current with the latest fashions. She was who she was. She wore what went with whatever job she was doing. Most days, she went about her business in her beat-up overalls, which were usually dirty from farming. And at the restaurant, she just threw on a comfy skirt, a T-shirt, and her trusty sandals. It was fine. She fit in where she lived, and she was comfortable. It was important to be comfortable.

Right.

Finally, Nick pulled back to gaze at the blonde woman. "Sherry! What the *fuck* are you doing here?"

She gave him a little secretive smile that made Phoebe

want to hurl. Why she should be so affected by their secret little exchange was a total mystery.

And yet there it was. Jealousy that Nick shared something private with this woman, that they shared a past.
It was insane, but Phoebe couldn't totally repress a feeling of envy that this gorgeous woman had a history with
Nick.

The blonde said, "Pour me a glass of wine, and I'll tell
you."

"'Course, love."

And for some reason, hearing those words come out of
Nick's mouth, aimed at another woman, made something
deep inside Phoebe's gut feel sick.

And that feeling scared the daylights out of her.

"Excuse me. I have to...um..."

Everyone turned and looked at her. She felt her neck
begin to flush.

*Don't let them see you blush. Don't let them see any-
thing.*

"I have to check the stockroom. For cheese."

"Cheese?" Nick asked. "You keep cheese in the stockroom?"

Damn. "It's, yeah. Special aged cheese."

"And you need it now?" Jesse asked.

"I think it would be lovely with the wine. Okay, I'm
going to fetch the cheese now."

And as she marched toward the stockroom, she felt
them all staring at her. She slammed the door behind her.

Chapter Eleven

So nice to see you, love."

That was the first phrase she caught when she emerged from the stockroom. With a deep breath, she returned to the group so cozily gathered in front of the kitchen. "Well, I guess we're out of cheese."

Nick just looked at her but didn't call her on her obvious fabrication. He couldn't know, could he? That she'd spent five minutes breathing. Calming her nerves. Fighting this ugly feeling of envy geared toward a woman she didn't even know.

Love. He was calling this woman "love"? As if she needed reminding, Phoebe's ass immediately began to sting, and she remembered what he'd done to her in the stockroom. When he'd kissed her in the kitchen. When she'd kissed him back and later, he'd called *her* love.

Phoebe tamped down the reaction of hurt and, if she were being honest with herself, betrayal. Hating Nick, she watched as he jogged off toward the steps to the wine cellar.

Whatever vintage he chose was *so* coming out of his paycheck.

Familiar with the café, Steve had pitched in earlier, as

he did most Saturday nights. Now he was perched on a barstool, finishing off a nice cab they'd opened earlier. He was also staring at Sherry as if she were a movie star. Hell, maybe she was. Phoebe wouldn't be any the wiser. She wasn't exactly an expert on Hollywood stars.

Steve jumped up and pulled out a chair for Sherry. She perched her tight little ass on the stool and smiled brightly at him. Her brother-in-law turned bright red.

What the heck was going on? Phoebe thought she was the only one in the family cursed with the blushing gene. Furthermore, she hadn't seen Steve react to any woman since Judy had passed.

Walking toward them, Phoebe held out her hand. "Hi, I'm Phoebe."

Sherry turned on her stool and—if possible—her smile got even wider. Phoebe nearly flinched from the glare of her white teeth.

Still, Phoebe had to admit the woman seemed friendly. She considered herself a good judge of character, and there was definitely something sincere in Sherry's huge blue eyes.

"You must be the manager," Sherry said. "I've heard so much about you."

Phoebe narrowed her gaze. "You have?" She could only imagine what Nick had to say in regard to their working (or any other sort of) relationship.

"I certainly have." She lowered her voice and leaned closer. "And can I just say, I am impressed. I know what an asshole he can be, and based on how frustrated he is, I'm willing to bet you're holding your own. Good job!"

For a second, Phoebe was speechless. This woman, with her huge blue eyes, perfectly white skin, and perky lips, looked like a sweetheart. But she'd just called Nick, who was obviously a good friend of hers, an asshole.

Phoebe reached for two wineglasses and set them on the counter. Then she poured the remainder of cabernet out of the bottle on the counter.

She handed a glass to Sherry. "You obviously know Nick pretty well."

"He's one of my best friends. And I'm probably his only friend since I'm one of the few people who will actually put up with his bullshit."

Phoebe just stared at this doll-like person. "Who *are* you?"

"Sherry Hart." Closing her eyes, she took a small sip of the cab, swooshed it around her mouth, and eventually swallowed. Then her eyes popped open. "Lovely. *Ste. Michelle*?"

"Um, yes. How did you know?" Phoebe hadn't seen Sherry even glance toward the bottle.

"Oh, it's what I do. That's how Nick and I met. I'm a wine distributor."

"I see."

But Phoebe didn't see. She didn't understand Nick and Sherry's relationship, and she didn't understand why he'd been so happy to see her—certainly happier than Phoebe had ever seen him since he'd arrived.

If she did understand his reaction to her, she didn't want to admit it to herself.

She tamped down those feelings. That wasn't fair, not at all. But it was hard to ignore the feelings this Sherry person had brought on. None of these things were her business. None of these things she had control over. Yet...no matter how much she repeated the affirmation, it didn't sit right.

You can't control everything.

Nope. Not sinking in.

So no. Phoebe didn't see anything. Nothing made sense, not since Nick had arrived. Since the day he'd driven up in that yellow vehicular monster, she'd been covered in pudding, kissed senselessly by a man who thought waaaay too much of himself; she'd been whisked—

Sex in the stockroom. It sounded like a bad porn movie. She would have laughed at anyone who'd said she'd ever do such a thing. And yet she had several red, thin stripes on her bottom that told her she was perfectly capable of such behavior.

She glared down the hallway where Nick had just disappeared. It was him. He was making her do all kinds of things she wouldn't ordinarily do. And she was letting him.

She was giving him power over her. And that simply would not do.

"Here we are." Nick returned, holding a bottle of special reserve. He glanced up at her. "What?"

Phoebe tried to calm her heart, which was racing with irritation toward him. She narrowed her gaze. "What do you mean?"

"You're looking at me as if you want to tear my head off."

Nobody ever said she wasn't transparent. So she tried to laugh it off. A high-pitched sound emerged from her mouth. "I don't want to rip your head off. I would like a glass of wine, though. I see you picked my favorite vintage."

Ignoring her, he took a corkscrew from his pocket.

Yeah, that wine was definitely coming out of his paycheck.

"Thanks, Nick," Sherry said. "I'm just finishing up this lovely cab your boss poured for me."

"Well, there's always room for more good wine."

Sherry held up her glass. "Cheers to that."

"So," Nick began as he uncorked the bottle, "are you going to tell me what you're doing down here in Butt-Fuck, Nowhere, or not?"

Still not quite used to his tone, Phoebe flinched at Nick's description of their community, but she refrained from saying anything. Obviously, the minute he got around one of his hoity-toity friends, he reverted back to his true personality of überjerk.

"Well," Sherry said. "Guess who just landed the Northern California account?"

"Get out!" Nick poured himself a glass of Phoebe's finest.

"That's right," Sherry said. "I'm now overseeing this region for my company. I'll be coming up here all the time."

"That's great news," Phoebe managed, and gulped some wine.

"Wow." Nick held up his glass. "Congratulations!"

They clinked, and Nick glanced toward Phoebe. "I take it you met Sherry?"

Nodding, Phoebe swallowed. "Yup. Sure did."

He beamed at the blonde. "She's amazing. A true friend, this one."

"Uh-huh." Phoebe continued nodding. "That's... great!" And drinking. Before she knew it, her glass was empty. That was fast. Where had the wine gone? Silently, she held out her glass toward Nick, who filled it without so much as a glance in her direction.

Because his attention was fully focused on Sherry. Sherry, with the perfect hair and chic style and a truly amazing dentist.

She heard a cough and looked over at Steve, who was also focusing his attention on Sherry. "So. You'll be up here often?"

She nodded. "Indeed I will. And I have a feeling I'm going to truly enjoy my time here, Steve."

"Sherry," Steve said, his gaze fixed on hers, "you're a wine distributor?"

"I am. I've been handling Southern California, but we're expanding up here, and I'm going to oversee things until we hire a permanent manager. I'm going to start looking for new accounts first thing tomorrow."

"That's brilliant." Nick looked downright thrilled.

"Yeah. Brilliant," Phoebe muttered, and gulped more wine.

Why should she care? It made no difference to her—none whatsoever—if this Sherry person was suddenly going to be around all the time.

Obviously, Sherry and Nick had some type of relationship, and from the way they were looking at each other, Phoebe had to assume it was intimate.

She supposed that meant there would be no more trysts involving chocolate or whisks, but oh well. It was actually a good thing. Really, a very good thing.

Phoebe didn't care one iota. Not one little bit. No sirree.

"Slow down, killer." Nick nodded at her glass, which was nearly empty. Again. "This didn't come out of a box, you know."

Did he call her killer? From *love* to *killer*? Nice.

She glared at him. "I know. This came from my cellar, remember?"

"Yes, I do remember." He was speaking ridiculously slowly. "Because the cellar is where I retrieved it from. I'm just saying, you might want to go a little slow on the wine. It's your last bottle of this vintage." He gave her a wink and took a tiny sip from his glass.

"What?" Despite the way she was chugging, this was actually her favorite wine, and he knew that. "Then why didn't you bring out something different?"

"Because I wanted to pour something special for Sherry."

"We have many special wines. Why did you have to go and pick this one?" Phoebe knew she was freaking out over nothing. She knew it, but for some reason she couldn't stop herself.

"You did it just to annoy me. And by the way, where did all the other bottles go? We had ten as of last weekend."

He shrugged. "Let me see...Just a crazy thought, but perhaps someone...*bought them*?"

"All righty, then." Sherry slid off her stool.

Phoebe felt her neck burn. She couldn't believe she'd been bickering with Nick like a teenager. In front of Sherry, no less. Now Sherry would believe all the horrible things Nick surely said about her management abilities.

"It's been a long day. I think I'll get back to the hotel and call it a night."

"What hotel?" Nick said. "You can stay with me."

"No!" Phoebe slapped a hand over her mouth. Looking around, she saw all gazes land on her.

She gathered herself. "I mean, there's no guest room in the cabin."

"So?" Nick said.

So? So they were going to just sleep together? After what Nick had done to Phoebe just hours ago? She thought her insides might explode.

Nick shrugged. "I'll sleep on the sofa. Sherry can have my bed."

"Oh. Oh." Phoebe nodded. But they were still staring at her as if she were a crazy person. "I just...um, well, that won't be very comfortable."

Maybe she was a crazy person. Nick certainly made her feel that way. After all, why should Phoebe care where Nick or Sherry slept?

"Why don't you stay in our guest room?"

Phoebe turned her glare to Steve, who had just made the offer. The offer of Sherry staying in *their* house.

"Oh, no. Thank you, but I couldn't." Sherry slipped her big fancy purse over her shoulder.

"It's really not a problem," Steve said. "We have plenty of room. You'd have your own bathroom. And full use of the kitchen."

Phoebe could hardly believe Steve's pleading tone of voice. Had they entered the twilight zone?

Sherry shook her head. "Really, I couldn't impose like that."

"And she can stay with me," Nick said.

"No." Phoebe pasted on a smile. "Steve's right. I mean, that's what I was going to say earlier, Sherry." Phoebe gulped. "You should stay with us. We have room and a friend of Nick's is a friend of...well, you know."

Sherry looked from Phoebe to Nick, who shrugged. "They do have a huge place," he said.

She glanced back to Phoebe. "And you're sure it wouldn't be an imposition?"

"No. Of course not."

"If you're positive..."

"Yes, we're very positive." Steve pushed himself to his feet. "Do you have your things with you?"

Sherry nodded. "Yes. I haven't even checked into the hotel yet. I wanted to come straight here and see Nick."

"Then you can follow me. I'll show you the way."

And just like that, Sherry, Nick's best friend, was Phoebe's newest roommate.

"You." Her gaze landed on Nick.

He eyed her warily. "What?"

"Ever since you arrived it's been nothing but chaos and mayhem and...and...whisks!"

"Chaos and mayhem and whisks? Oh, my."

"Shut up."

"You started it."

"No, you did!" The restaurant was almost clean, the staff had gone, and they were the only ones left.

She poured herself more wine. "You don't listen. You can't take an order. You think you're the king of, of... *everything*."

He slanted her a smug smile. "I didn't hear you complaining earlier, love."

The word was like a punch in the gut. "Do you call everyone that?"

"What?"

"*Luuuv.*" She drew out the syllable with a fake uppity British accent.

"No. Why?"

"You just seem to toss the word around as if it means nothing."

"It's just a word."

She stalked around to the other side of the counter and started putting clean pots on the shelves.

"Phoebe?"

"What?"

He put a hand on her shoulder, stopping her. "What's wrong?"

She met his gaze. "Nothing. Absolutely nothing."

"Then why do you look as if you want to rip my head off? Again."

Because I do. "I have no idea what you're talking about." She tried to shake him off her, but he held her firmly in place.

"Stop doing that," she said.

"What?"

"Touching me. It's inappropriate."

He raised a brow. "Really? So how was it appropriate earlier when I had you naked in the storage room? Was it *appropriate* when I was spanking your ass?"

Her faced burned, but she lifted her chin. "No. That was very inappropriate."

He took the soup pot out of her hands and placed it on a shelf. Then he turned to her. "You're crazy."

"You make me crazy."

"I do what I can."

She clenched her fists to keep from punching him. "I swear...sometimes I could just kill you." And even as she said the words, her heart pounded with a need for him to touch her. To feel his breath on her skin. To hear his soft voice in her ear.

She really was crazy. How in God's name could she be this attracted to Nick Avalon? She didn't even like him.

He leaned his hip against the counter. "Aw, but you don't want to really kill me, do you?"

"You have no idea."

"I don't think you want to kill me. I think you want to fuck me."

Flinching, she stepped back. "Don't talk like that," she said in a low voice.

"Why? Are you telling me it's not true? Are you telling me you don't want to rip off my clothes, get on top of me, and fill yourself with my cock?"

"How could you even say those words? Your *girlfriend* was just here!"

"Sherry?" He laughed. "Oh, she would never have me."

Her stomach lurched. "So you want *me* since you can't have *her*?"

For a second, she wanted to vomit.

He simply stared at her. "No, Phoebe. It's not like that."

"Then what's it like?"

"Oh my God! You're the one making me crazy now."

"Good. Now you know how I feel. So go ahead. Tell me what it's like. Tell me what it is you want from me."

What was she doing? Her entire body was trembling. She really didn't know how much more of this she could take.

"You want to know what I want?" He was nearly yelling now.

"Yes." She probably didn't want to know the answer, but she had to ask anyway.

He came at her.

Somehow, she was ready.

When his mouth hit hers, she was already open. When he lifted her, she wrapped her legs around his waist. Tongues, lips, teeth. Legs, thighs, chests. All colliding, coming together in something so intense, it was nearly violent.

"This is what I want," he said. "You. Now."

"Yes." She was panting, breathing so hard she could barely talk. "Yes, Nick."

As he carried her, she clenched her thighs around his hips as he walked out of the kitchen. Kissing her, he continued down the hallway. He managed to get them into the large restroom at the end of the corridor and then he kicked the door shut behind them.

"Nick..."

His lips silenced her. He picked her up and used the weight of his body to hold her against the back of the door. Her shoes fell off. He tugged up her skirt, and she felt his jeans on the naked flesh of her inner thighs.

Somewhere in the back of her head, it occurred to her that she was pushed up against the door of the bathroom while her chef ravished her. That had to be bad. Had to.

She pulled away from his mouth. "Wait...what are we doing?"

"Oh, right. See, I'm about to fuck you." He pressed his erection against her damp sex, but stopped kissing her. She cried out in protest. She needed him to be kissing her. She needed his mouth, hot and intense, on her lips.

"First I'll rip off your panties." He gave said panties a

tug. "Then I'm going to take out my dick and drive it into your pussy." He pushed against her sex, and she gasped. Loudly.

Pulling away, he oh-so-innocently looked her in the eye. "You want me to stop?"

"Oh, God..." He felt so good *right there*, between her legs. She could feel his cock, so hard. It jerked against her, and she melted even more. Her sex was swollen, sore with want. Ever since that night in his kitchen, she'd wanted this. Wanted it so badly, she knew that she wouldn't say no.

She ground against him. "Hell, no. Don't stop."

"I didn't think so."

The sound of her panties being torn echoed off the walls. He tossed them aside, and she watched the white cotton fabric as it hit the ground. Yeah, Nick did to her self-restraint exactly what he'd just done to her underwear. He'd torn it off and thrown it away.

And so she looked him straight in the eye and said, "Nick. Take off your pants."

Chapter Twelve

Nick didn't need any further invitation. In fact, he was so lost in his desire for Phoebe that he barely needed any invitation at all. If Phoebe had actually wanted him to stop, it would have been incredibly difficult. His cock would have said it was impossible.

Thank God, she hadn't said no.

He yanked her T-shirt over her head, and his gaze fell on her luscious breasts. "Fuck, Phoebe."

She stilled.

He saw the vulnerability in her eyes, and he kissed her gently on the lips. "What's wrong, babe?" he asked.

"I know I'm probably not like the typical girls you see...not what you're used to."

Her words, and the look on her face, caused a tiny hurt in his chest. He kissed the top of her cleavage and felt a shudder go through her.

"You're right," he said. "You're not like most of the girls I've been with."

She started to struggle, but he held her tight.

"You're real."

She laughed bitterly. "Real what?"

"Beautiful."

That stopped her. So the bossy, confident Phoebe Mayle was just as susceptible to compliments as the rest of the female population.

The thing was, Nick realized he meant it when he whispered against her smooth, soft skin, "It's true." He lifted her breast from the cup of her bra. "So beautiful."

"Stop it."

Not this again. He looked up. "Stop?"

"Saying those things...things you don't mean. You don't understand. I don't care what you say."

"Is that so?"

"It is. Now come on." She wiggled against his groin, and he stifled a groan.

She brought his mouth to hers once again. He kissed her; he touched her. He crushed his pounding erection against her naked pussy.

"I need to be inside you, Phoebe."

"Yes." She continued to kiss him, and he felt desire in her complete abandon. And it was that abandon that fueled his lust.

If she was surprised he had a condom in his pocket, she didn't show it. But, hey. It was habit for him. Back in L.A., he'd never known when he'd need one. Now he held it in his teeth as he unzipped his jeans and pulled out his cock.

She took the condom from his mouth, ripped it open, and handed him the rubber.

"Thank God you have one," she said.

He smiled. "I can be a useful fellow when need be."

He held her against the door as he reached between them and slid the condom on.

She raised her brows. "Seems you've done this before."

"I like to be prepared. What can I say?"

"I don't want you to say anything, Nick."

"Really?" He pressed against her sex, and she gasped. "How about, do you want me to fuck you?"

She clenched his shoulders. "Do you really have to ask?"

"No." He thrust into her. She was so wet. He slid in so easily, so deeply...

"Uh!" She threw her head back. "Yes, Nick."

"Fuck." He withdrew and entered again. "You feel so fucking good. So tight."

"Yes..."

He could see it in her eyes; she was so turned on by him. Her green eyes had gone dark, emerald.

"So good..." He barely knew what he was saying. Everything centered around being in her. Fucking her. Feeling her.

Her legs, wrapped around him, were trembling. But she clung to him, positioning her body just right so he could fit inside her perfectly.

It felt too good. He could already feel his climax building. The intensity of fucking this woman overcame him.

When he looked into her eyes, he saw that she was staring at him. He couldn't look away; he could just withdraw and enter, again and again, gazing into her eyes. Listening to the little cries that escaped her lips each time he filled her.

He felt her come. Her pussy clenched around him, and she clung to him everywhere, so hard—as if she were holding on for dear life.

It undid him.

He drove into her one last time as his own climax tore

through him. He shouted—actually shouted—her name.

He was pretty damn sure he'd never done that before.

Finally, he came back down to earth. His heart was pounding. His T-shirt was damp from his own sweat. His head was...

Fucked.

He pulled out of her and placed Phoebe on her feet. Silence screamed through the small room as reality set in. He stared at the concrete floor as he zipped his pants, focusing on one crack that spread the span of a few feet. That's what his chest felt like. Cracked.

He racked his brain for a witty retort, something to save him. But his head was blank. He could still smell her, feel her stickiness on his cock. He could still hear her...her cries of pleasure.

"I gotta go." He spun on his heel and charged for the door.

Her eyes were wide and questioning. "What's wrong?"

"Nothing. I just..." He ran one hand through his hair. "I have to finish cleaning up the kitchen."

She bit her lip. Damn it. Just the sight of her little pink tongue on her mouth caused a new jolt of lust to shoot through him.

He yanked open the door. "I'll see you tomorrow."

Phoebe stared after him. What the hell had just happened? Other than the fact that she'd just had sex in her own restaurant. Yeah, that was something she'd never thought she'd do. But even more confusing? Nick Avalon running away from her after the deed was done.

Because that's exactly what he'd done. He'd run away. She went to the mirror. "Nice," she muttered. Of course, she was a total disaster. Her hair was sticking out in a brown, kinky mess. The only makeup she wore was some mascara, and that was pretty much a dark mess under her eyes. And her lips were dry and swollen from the intensity of kissing Nick.

Shrugging, she went about trying to put herself back together.

Why had he run? The look in his eyes had seemed downright scared. That made absolutely no sense. What would freak him out so much? He'd already seduced her with a bowl of pudding and spanked her with a whisk. What had freaked him out?

Who knew? One thing she'd learned about Nick was that he wasn't as predictable as she'd originally thought. That sarcastic nonchalance he wore around him like armor wasn't as thick as she'd first assessed. She'd seen some cracks. She'd seen something more than the smoking, tequila-drinking, conceited bad boy who'd shown up just weeks ago in his great big Hummer.

After he'd put her on her feet, she'd expected some mocking remark. She'd totally anticipated his giving her some flippant comment and walking out.

What she hadn't expected was to see those cracks in his armor. But she had. And they left her more confused than ever.

Chapter Thirteen

The scream caught in Phoebe's throat.

Her hand on her pounding heart, she sank back into the pine chair and tried to catch her breath.

"I'm sorry. I didn't mean to startle you."

"It's fine..." Phoebe looked across the kitchen to Sherry, who she'd totally forgotten was staying in her house.

In her flowing white-satin robe, Sherry had wafted into the kitchen like some kind of ghost. Phoebe had been staring into her mug of cold chamomile tea, pondering what to do about the situation with Nick, when the apparition—*Sherry*—had come in.

Sherry looked at the cup clutched in Phoebe's hand. "Do you mind if I join you?"

Of course she minded. The last thing Phoebe wanted to do was make chitchat at 2:00 a.m. with one of Nick's exes, who had her widowed brother-in-law giving her puppy-dog eyes. But Phoebe said, "Of course not. Would you like some tea?"

Sherry pulled out a chair and floated into it. "That would be lovely."

After a second, Phoebe stood. "Right. Let me get it for

you." What? Did the woman think she was running some sort of bed-and-breakfast here? The expectation loaded in Sherry's question made Phoebe's hands clench with irritation. She gave the other woman a once-over.

And why did she have to look so elegant? It was two in the morning, for God's sake. Like some thirties film-and-screen actress, Sherry sat there in her shiny white nightclothes. Her blonde hair was brushed into a chignon (a chignon! at 2:00 a.m.!), and Phoebe swore the woman was wearing eye makeup.

Maybe she thought Nick was going to ring her up for a late-night booty call.

Maybe Nick was already making pudding. Creamy, chocolate pudding, all mixed up and ready to spread on Sherry's flawless pale skin.

The woman lived in Southern California, for goodness' sake. Shouldn't she be all tanned and wrinkly? But *no-o-o-o*. This Sherry had skin as perfect as an untouchable white cloud.

Shaking her head, Phoebe pulled out another mug and turned on the gas stove to heat the kettle. She wore her same old flannel nightgown and old beat-up slippers. Her stomach turned. This woman—Sherry—was what Nick was used to. So why had he gone after Phoebe? It made no sense.

"He doesn't make sense."

Phoebe nearly dropped the box of chamomile tea she'd just lifted out of a basket on the counter.

Glancing at Sherry, Phoebe said, "What?"

Sherry gave her an impish smile. "Nick."

"W-what makes you say that?"

She smiled. "He's just a bit confusing at times."

Remembering the way Nick had split after their earlier romp in the restroom, Phoebe had to laugh. "Yeah. I'm getting that about him."

Sherry rested her chin on her hand. "He's afraid."

"Afraid? He seems so confident." But then she remembered the look on his face as he'd fled from her.

"It's just a front, a facade," Sherry said.

Phoebe placed the tea bag in a mug and filled the cup with hot water. "I imagine he needs to be strong for his job."

Sherry looked thoughtful. "There's definitely that aspect of it. But there's more."

Phoebe crossed the kitchen and set the steaming cup of tea on the table. "What do you mean?"

"I don't want to say too much. I mean, you are his boss and everything."

"Right," Phoebe said, slowly taking a seat opposite Sherry. There was that little fact of her employing the subject of their conversation. But she wanted to know more about him.

She wanted to know everything.

Shaking her head, Phoebe tried not to pry.

And didn't succeed. "You don't have to share anything you don't feel comfortable with." She rubbed her fingertip across a scratch in the table. "But. If there's something you think would help me do my job better...please, feel free." Right, Pheebs. *You want to know all about Nick so you can do your job better.* Would Sherry buy it?

And anyway, she didn't want to know! "Never mind."

"No, it's okay. Anything to help you handle Nick." Sherry paused and then said, "I'll just say he's not as tough as he puts on. He's had a..."

Phoebe looked up. "Yes?" she encouraged. "A what?"

"A hard life. He's been through a lot."

"A hard life? It seemed like he had it all in L.A. He makes it sound like he had the perfect life."

Sherry sipped her tea. "On the surface, he did. He had a high-profile job, a great income, and any girl he wanted. And I do mean *any* girl."

Phoebe coughed. "Right. Any girl. Great job. So what was the problem?" She really did not need to hear all about Nick's escapades and his perfect girls.

"It was superficial. He lives his life trying to get out of his own head. Alcohol, parties, sex...It's all a distraction so he doesn't have to deal with what's in here." Sherry touched one red fingertip to her temple.

Phoebe stared at Sherry. "What do you mean?" And was he having sex with Phoebe just because he needed the distraction?

Sherry shook her head. "I've already said too much. I guess what I was really getting at is, I think this move has been good for him."

Phoebe laughed. "All he does is complain. He's bored here. He hates the people. Heck, he hates everything about it. I have no idea why he took this job." She took a large gulp of cold tea. "Other than the fact that no one else would hire him, of course."

"You're right about that. No one wanted him. And I think that was the hardest thing for him to handle. Being dismissed so easily...It ripped him apart."

"But he's amazing at what he does!"

Sherry shrugged. "Doesn't matter. There are a lot of talented chefs in that town, always someone ready to take your place. Yes, Nick is good at what he does. But he doesn't know how to leash himself. And it all went to his head."

Phoebe continued tracing the line on the table. Finally, she looked up into Sherry's big blue eyes. "Why are you telling me all of this?"

Sherry smiled, a small spread of her perfect lips. "Because I don't want Nick to fuck this up." She waved around the kitchen. "This is good for him. It's forcing him to take a break from all that craziness. It's making him get some perspective. Get back on track."

Phoebe glanced up sharply. "What do you mean, get *back* on track?"

Sherry shrugged one satin-clad shoulder. "You know. Get his life back in order."

"And then what?" For some reason this conversation was making something in Phoebe go cold. "And then what happens?"

Sherry's blue eyes searched hers. "I . . . I don't know." Picking up her still-full mug, she stood. "I'm sorry. It's late. I've been driving all day." She laughed, but it sounded falsely light. "I never know when to shut up."

Phoebe watched the other woman take the damp tea bag out of the mug and toss it into the garbage. Why had this conversation left her feeling as if she were missing some piece of the puzzle?

"Sherry, I don't understand. What are you saying?"

Sherry dumped the amber liquid into the sink. "Nothing. I'm sorry." She glanced over her shoulder. "I was just trying to say I think this entire experience is good for Nick." She punctuated her statement with a smile that Phoebe was sure was meant to be reassuring.

It wasn't.

Phoebe stood. "This experience? Like does he think this is summer camp or something? Are his parents going to pick him up at the end of three months?"

She didn't miss the way Sherry's shoulders clenched at Phoebe's statement. But then, turning, Sherry's big blue eyes looked worried. "No, of course not. Please, don't read too much into what I said. I honestly don't know what I'm talking about."

Phoebe didn't understand why panic was rushing through her. She pushed the chair she'd been sitting in under the table. "I just want to know. Are you saying Nick is simply here on some sort of hiatus?" Phoebe knew their contract was a year at least. It took a lot of work to train someone; she didn't want to do this again in less than a year. She'd barely gotten to the point where she felt she could leave Nick in the café without any supervision.

And it was more. There was a part of her that had been opening up to him. Starting to trust him. Starting to like him. Not romantically, of course, but she was gaining glimpses into the good side of him, and she didn't want it to be false. If he really was planning on simply using her and the café—the thought made her heart hurt.

Phoebe said, "I just want to know if he has something else planned. I mean, I've been spending a lot of time training him. To, you know, run the kitchen. Be the chef at the restaurant. To learn the fixed-price menu on Saturday night…" She sounded pathetic. She sounded needy. She sounded like all the things she hated.

Sherry was backing out of the kitchen, her satin gown whispering against the hardwood floor as she glided away in retreat. "I know you have. Like I said, I don't know what I'm saying. Just forget everything. Nick is doing great here!"

She sounded so enthusiastic that Phoebe wanted to vomit.

"So, thanks, Phoebe. I'm just going back to bed now."

Phoebe put her hands on her hips and faked a smile. "You do that."

"Okay. Yeah, I will." Sherry nodded. "Oh, and thanks again. You know, for the tea."

"Anytime," Phoebe muttered. *Yeah, any time you're up in the wee hours of the morning, I'll be here! Just waiting to make you some organic chamomile!*

Still walking backward, Sherry said, "It was really good. The tea, that is."

"Thanks. It's, um, organic."

"I can tell! Okay, then. Night."

"Night."

And then Sherry was gone, disappearing into the darkness of the hallway like some sort of gorgeous blonde phantom.

Phoebe stared after her. In the quiet of the kitchen, she replayed their conversation. Her head swam with everything Sherry had said. Obviously, she knew Nick wouldn't be in Redbolt forever. But was he just here biding time? Was he simply putting up with them until something better came along?

Was he putting up with *her* until something better came along?

No. He wouldn't do that. Phoebe put the cups in the dishwasher and shuffled out of the kitchen, up the stairs, and back to her room.

Still, she couldn't stop the questions going through her head. Why had Sherry come here? Why had she appeared in the kitchen in the wee hours of the morning to put these ideas in her head?

Then another thought occurred to her. Phoebe did not like Steve's response to Sherry, not one bit. Sure, she'd hoped Steve would eventually find a partner, someone to replace Judy, Phoebe's sister. Phoebe'd always thought the phrase "God brings his angels home early" was definitely appropriate when it came to her sister. Judy had been kindhearted, generous—always welcoming people into their home for supper. She'd carried Jesse in a sling for two years and had loved her unconditionally. Her death had been a tragedy, a loss for the entire community. No one would ever replace her.

Especially not some starlet from Southern California.

Phoebe's stomach turned at the idea of someone like Sherry coming into the family.

He's only just met her tonight. You're being ridiculous.

Yeah, the idea of getting worried when they'd only met the woman once might seem a bit preposterous. However, since Judy had died five years ago, Steve had never, *not once*, responded to a woman like Phoebe had seen him do tonight.

With Sherry. Nick's girlfriend or ex-girlfriend or whatever she was.

It was amazing how one person could have such an effect on so many of Phoebe's emotions. A Buddhist quote she had printed out and pinned up in her office flashed across her mind:

A family is a place where minds come in contact with one another. If these minds love one another, the home will be as beautiful as a flower garden.

But if these minds get out of harmony with one another, it is like a storm that plays havoc with the garden.

Harmony. She needed to keep her family in harmony, and suddenly everything seemed anything but harmonious. And why? Because of Nick and Sherry? Phoebe laughed bitterly in the darkness. They weren't family—why was she allowing them to affect her? And why was Sherry sleeping under their roof, when she saw the effect she'd had on Steve?

Because Phoebe had acted on fear and jealousy. She knew these emotions were unproductive and damaging, and she had the power and wisdom to overcome them.

So far she'd failed at following Zen instead of flying off the handle. She'd allowed the negative thoughts and emotions to guide her decisions, and she had to let them go.

Nick had Jesse cooking meat. And despite how she'd defended Steve, she did know he wouldn't be happy about it. Even if Phoebe thought Jesse should have the choice of cooking whatever she wanted, she did know it would upset her brother-in-law, whether he admitted it or not. And Jesse probably hadn't noticed, but Phoebe had observed her niece watching Nick like he was some sort of hero. Her niece was blossoming, and a true love of cooking, of food, was surfacing in a way Phoebe couldn't deny. Jesse hadn't had quite that spark in her eye when she was in the café before Nick had arrived. However, every day Phoebe watched Jesse's skill improve, and her confidence grow.

A thought occurred to her. Maybe if Nick did leave, perhaps Jesse would want to take over the café. The thought resonated in Phoebe's mind, and the more she thought about it, the more it made sense. Jesse was going to be a responsible, smart woman, capable of being in charge of a business. She'd been working for Phoebe, at the farm and at the café, for years.

The more she pondered the thought, the happier Phoebe became. It was perfect, really. She'd allow Nick to train Jesse in the hopes Jesse would one day take over the café. Then if Nick left (and she knew one day he surely would), the Green Leaf would be successful and still kept within the family. Harmonious.

But, at the moment, nothing was harmonious. She'd been shoving questions and uncertainties to the back of her mind ever since Nick had arrived. She hadn't wanted to seriously consider them, but that damn blonde bombshell had thrown them in her face.

Phoebe crossed the room straight to her bed and fell onto the soft mattress. Through her open window, the moonlight illuminated the glow-in-the-dark stars she'd pasted to the ceiling when she'd been just a girl.

Just a girl. Had she ever been that? Just a girl. Maybe once...

Her parents had died when she was fourteen and her sister was seventeen. Their aunt and uncle had taken them in, but Phoebe had always felt as if she'd taken over the role of parent.

Her relatives were kind, generous, and supportive. But they hadn't been ready to take on the responsibility of two teenage girls. Ironically, they'd been so busy with the restaurant that there was never any food in the house for Phoebe or her sister. Her aunt and uncle would bring home delicious leftovers. Phoebe and her sister went many a night hungry, eagerly waiting for their guardians to arrive home with the food.

Organic quiches, quinoa salads, tempeh lasagna... The girls had truly obtained a palate for gourmet food, thanks to their aunt and uncle.

And then Phoebe had discovered the garden. One afternoon, after school, she'd wandered into the weeds and plopped down under the sun. It was the first day in weeks that the fog hadn't been looming over the area like the lid of a coffin, smothering everything. No one was home, and instead of going inside the house and doing homework or making dinner, she'd meandered into the fenced-in, overgrown garden and allowed herself a moment of peace.

Just one moment, she'd told herself.

But then, as she reclined back on her elbows, she'd glanced over and seen a leafy green plant that somehow differed from all the weeds and wildflowers surrounding her. She reached over and pulled the feathery plant out of the dirt. It was a carrot.

She wiped the dirt off and stared at the root vegetable. She'd pulled that plant out of the ground. She'd extracted something that had meaning. It wasn't just a useless weed; it was food. And as she stared at that carrot, she felt a sense of accomplishment as never before.

It made no sense. But the next thing she knew, she was on her knees, crawling through the overgrown mess of the garden, tugging out random plants.

It didn't take long. Soon she knew what leaves could be pulled to produce carrots, and there were more. She found celery and fennel. Basil and cilantro. And as she pulled out every plant, it brought a memory.

Her mother had gardened. She'd helped her mom when she was very little, and as she crept through the dirt, it was as if her mom were right there next to her. They'd sow and nurture, watching things grow. And every seed turned into something that ended up on the dinner table.

So many memories... Everything came back in a rush. It was too much. She started digging. She plowed into the earth with her bare hands, and before she knew it, she had an entire pile of vegetables and herbs.

Covered in dirt, she'd brought that pile of food into the very kitchen beneath which she currently slept.

Her straight-A report cards, her soccer trophies—none of those things compared to the sense of pride that filled her chest simply by looking at a pile of produce she'd discovered in the long-ignored garden.

That summer, she worked every day in that plot of earth. She spent hours at the local garden center, learning about what would grow the best. She came home with packets of seeds, mulch, and fertilizer. By the time fall came, she was harvesting enough produce for her aunt and uncle to start putting the food Phoebe grew on her aunt and uncle's menu.

Sadly, unlike her mother, Phoebe had little talent when it came to turning the food she'd created into anything edible. Still, her lack of culinary skills didn't detract from her newfound love of gardening. She just needed someone else to actually prepare the results of her labor.

Like Nick did. The things he could do with food. When she pictured him in the kitchen, deftly slicing onions and mincing garlic...

It sent a shiver through her.

Why? Why did she find his skills so attractive? Sometimes, when he threw a handful of herbs into a sauté pan, she became fixated on his arms. Just fixated. She loved watching his tight muscles flex. She loved looking at the veins that ran in stiff cords beneath his skin. She loved the little mole he had on his right biceps.

But most of all, she loved watching him turn simple food into something so delicious, the simple scent of his cooking made her mouth water.

And then there was the sex. She flopped over and pulled her pillow over her head. She could not believe that she'd succumbed to Nick's advances. She couldn't believe she'd had sex—against a door, and in a bathroom—with her employee.

It had to stop. She wouldn't do it again.

Nope.

Never.

She wouldn't even think about it.

But what had happened when he'd spanked her? It had hurt and yet it had exhilarated her. The pain had made her feel as if she were flying. Skydiving.

It was fun and naughty, and she loved every little minute of it.

Loved it too much. She couldn't believe she'd actually smoked part of Nick's cigarette. It scared her. The whole thing—the café, the forest, his kitchen. As much as she knew every part of it was wrong, she couldn't help the little smile that came over her when she thought about so many of their interactions.

He made her heart race with excitement. And with fear. Because she couldn't deny the fact that her feelings for Nick were a mixed bag. It wasn't just attraction. She kept getting these little glimpses of him that drew her to him as a person. She found herself wanting to get to know him better. Sometimes, she actually enjoyed her time with him. Sometimes, these flashes shot through her brain of what it could be like if she decided to actually have a relationship.

And those were all bad, bad things.

Nick was trouble. She didn't have time in her life for anything or anyone else. And now there was this Sherry person to worry about.

Grunting, Phoebe turned onto her side. Surprisingly, her bottom was still sore, but it only reminded her of what Nick had done to her. The red marks on her ass felt as if they were some sign of ownership. A branding.

And she shouldn't like it. Not one bit.

But she did. She liked it so much that when she thought about the experience, her center began to throb and she could feel her own juices coating the lips of her sex.

How could she be aroused when she'd had Nick's cock inside her only hours ago?

Nick's cock. Damn, she never should have thought about that. Because it only made her body thrum with lust. Her sex pulsed. Her breasts ached for his touch.

Throwing the pillow aside, she leaned over, opened the drawer to her nightstand, and pulled out her vibrator.

The irony didn't escape her. For quite some time, her vibrator had been her battery-operated boyfriend. Now she'd finally gotten laid, and she was still using her little toy just hours after the fact.

Not that her vibrator was very little.

She ran her hand over the phallic-shaped piece. It was simple, really. Just a lengthy pink piece of plastic. But there was a dial on the bottom, and now she twisted it so the thing began to softly vibrate in her hand.

Reaching under her nightgown, she pressed the pulsing tip to her clit. Already she was so sensitive, just from thinking about Nick. She gasped as the instrument beat at her sensitive bud. She spread her legs wide and closed her eyes.

"Nick." She barely heard the word escape her mouth. But in the dark, with the vibrator pressed against her wet sex, she couldn't help but think about him. Wished it were him between her legs. Wished it were his tongue licking that sensitive, aching part of her body.

"Yes." Through the fabric of her nightgown, she took her own nipple between her fingers and pinched. The sharp bite of pain caused her hips to buck against the vibrator, and she cried out again.

She needed more. She turned up the power of the vibrator and pressed it against her pussy. She held it there, letting it strike a consistent, constant beat against her clit.

Nick. She wanted to taste him. She wanted to feel him, his skin on hers. She wanted to suck his cock and feel him come in her mouth...

"God!" As she masturbated, the fantasy of sucking Nick's cock was so real. She licked her lips; her mouth was dry from her deep breathing. She wanted him so badly, so badly...

The climax hit her. With her eyes closed and her legs spread, she froze. Holding the vibrator hard against her pussy, she let the shivers rake over her. Her sex contracted in tiny pulses until finally she stilled.

After she'd come down, her skin was sensitive against the vibrator, and she turned it off. Without the soft buzz of the vibrator, the room was silent, and her thoughts returned to Nick.

Didn't they always?

Her orgasm had been acceptable, but compared to the reality of coming with Nick inside her, the climax was superficial. She needed him.

Damn it. She'd been walking a fine line ever since he'd pulled into town in his obnoxious car. She wanted him, but she knew it was wrong. Yet she couldn't stay away...

Turning onto her side, her thoughts returned once again to Sherry's words. Phoebe was impressed with how he was running the kitchen, even if he could be a total pain in the butt. She was beginning to depend on him.

Which was also dangerous. Phoebe could depend on her family. That was it. And her goal in life was to keep her family harmonious. Depending on Nick for anything was a direct threat to that, and she had to do whatever it took to keep everyone in her family happy.

She wasn't about to fuck it up just because she thought she might be developing feelings for Nick.

Flipping onto her back, she started to meditate. Breathing slowly, she focused on her breathing and repeated the word *harmony* every time she exhaled. She attempted to push away all thoughts and images from her head. But Nick kept appearing. So she did what her meditation teacher had advised whenever a worry or concern kept her from clearing her mind. She visualized.

She imagined him walking away from her and jumping into a pool of fresh springwater. And there he stayed, along with all her other problems, waiting to be dealt with another time.

Finally, Phoebe cleared her mind and focused on her breathing word. *Harmony.* She silently chanted it until she fell asleep.

Chapter Fourteen

What are you working on?"

Jesse quickly shut down the browser she'd had open on her computer. Turning toward the door, she smiled at her dad. "Just a paper for school. Science. A science paper."

It tore her up to lie to her dad, but she didn't have a choice. If he knew what she was really doing, he'd be hurt. And anyway, it was just a pipe dream. Nothing was going to come of it. He didn't need to know that she'd been looking at culinary schools all over the country. And farther. Paris looked amazing...

It was fun to look, to daydream. But she knew she could never leave her father. She was stuck in Redbolt.

And that was just fine with her. It was a nice place to live. Really, it was.

And that's what she'd keep telling herself.

Standing, she tucked a dreadlock into her scarf. "I'm just working on a paper on...global warming."

Her dad came into her room and sat on the bed. "I'm so proud of you, Jesse. So your classes at the community college are going well?"

She nodded. "Yes. Definitely."

And why wouldn't they be? The local JC was basically

just an extension of high school. The majority of her graduating class from Redbolt High were taking the same courses she was. There were a few older students who were going back to school, but Jesse knew most of them as well.

Nothing ever changed.

"And work at the restaurant is going well?" her dad asked.

She sat on the bed across from her dad and crossed her legs. "Of course. Nick's an amazing chef. I'm learning a lot." She tried not to sound too excited. Sure, her father would be happy she enjoyed working at the family business, but Jesse was concerned her zealous enthusiasm would give away her love of cooking nonvegetarian items. "Yup," she said. "Nick's a great teacher. I'm learning a lot…" She looked up. Damn it. That was *so* the wrong thing to say. "About vegetables."

"Oh? Like what?"

Damn. Picking a thread on her quilt, she said, "Oh, you know. Some new techniques." Like how to make a slow-roasted pork loin that melts on your tongue. But yeah, she wasn't about to say that to her vegetarian dad. "Like, we made broccoli millet croquettes the other night."

"Very nice." Her dad glanced out the window, and when he looked back at her, Jesse thought he was about to say something more.

But he was interrupted by the Hollywood bombshell, who breezed into the room. "Good morning! How are you two doing today?"

Jesse wasn't sure what to make of Sherry. She'd been staying with them for two days, and despite the fact that she never did her own dishes, the woman seemed nice enough. One thing was for sure: the woman dressed impeccably. In fact, Jesse didn't think she'd ever seen a woman who always appeared so put together and chic.

Chic. That was a word one didn't use every day in Redbolt.

Today, chic Sherry wore her blonde hair in a tight, high ponytail. She wore a flouncy blouse that would have looked frumpy on anyone else Jesse knew, but Sherry worked it. The blouse was tucked into a tight skirt that showed off legs that were the perfect amount of muscle and curve. And even though Jesse had never considered herself one of those "shoe girls," she had to admit that the high-heeled red patent pumps adorning Sherry's feet were luscious.

And really high. Jesse wondered how the woman kept from toppling over.

Something in her chest gave a little tug. She couldn't help but stare at this glamorous specimen. Sure, Jesse had seen beautiful, fashionable women before. In movies, on television, and once in a while, a tourist would catch her eye with some kind of stylish accessory Jesse had never seen before. She'd always looked away from those in-person encounters. She wasn't sure why, but whenever she'd see someone who obviously lived in a city, where fashionable stores were plentiful, Jesse would feel dowdy. Like a bumpkin, as Nick would say.

Even though she was from L.A., Sherry epitomized what she imagined every woman in Paris looked like. Her heart gave a little tug. She was envious.

She wrapped a dreadlock around her finger. She'd starting growing them so many years ago that it was part of her very identity now. She couldn't imagine having real-girl hair. She couldn't imagine styling and blow-drying and curling.

It just wasn't who Jesse would ever be. She knew who she was, what she was about. Where she lived. Like Phoebe always said, all they had was each other. Family.

That was her life, and it would always be the same. She unwrapped the dreadlock from her finger and tucked it behind her ear.

Still, Jesse's eyes were drawn to those amazing shoes and her toes twitched with a crazy urge to know what they felt like.

She stilled her toes. "Mornin', Sherry."

Running his hand through his hair, her dad stood. "Sherry. How are you today?"

Jesse looked at her father. If she didn't know better, she'd think her dad was blushing.

Impossible.

"I'm wonderful." Sherry smiled brightly. "Well, I just wanted to say hello before I head off to work."

"Oh? Do you have a plan for the day?" her dad asked.

Sherry reached into the fancy briefcase she held at her side. "I have a list of restaurants I plan on visiting."

Her dad's eyes sparked with interest. He loved planning. And it could be anything from a menu to a car trip to how to arrange the kitchen. Just say the word *plan*, and he got all excited. Secretly, Jesse called him Planny McGee.

"Mind if I have a look?" he said.

"Not at all." Sherry handed him the piece of paper.

Her dad's brow furrowed. "Hmm."

"What?" Sherry said, taking a step forward.

"It's just that it's Monday, so several of these places are closed today. Oh, and Christie's is closed for the month."

"Really?" Sherry looked shocked, as if anyplace being closed was totally incomprehensible. "The whole month?"

"Yes. The family always takes time off to go camping and get away before the summer season starts. They say it's refreshing for the body and soul and allows them to continue their business every year with new perceptions and ideas in regard to our society."

Jesse cringed a bit internally at the new age sound of her dad's words. Oh well. Welcome to Redbolt. It might be strange, but it was home.

However, Sherry smiled brightly at Jesse's dad. "That sounds like a wonderful idea."

"Anyway." Glancing at Sherry, her dad shifted on his feet. "I could help you. You know, drive you around. Since I know the area and all. I mean, if you like."

Sherry positively beamed. "You don't mind?"

"Well, my shop's closed today as well. You know. Since it's Monday."

Sherry put her hand on his shoulder. Jesse just stared as she watched her father's neck turn a definite shade of red.

What the heck was going on here? Was her dad—a man she'd only seen interested in one woman, who happened to be Jesse's deceased mother—actually interested in Sherry?

Wow. Jesse knew Sherry was a pretty woman and all, but she'd never known anyone who could turn her dad's head.

As she watched them leave her room, Jesse just stared. She wasn't sure how she felt about her dad's new interest.

Arms across her chest, Jesse shook her head. Watching

Sherry was like a lesson in how to make a man's brain disappear. For some reason, Jesse thought that might be a good technique to acquire.

Well, that and maybe a few pairs of those amazing shoes.

"It's low tide."

Phoebe looked up. Her gaze landed first on a pair of fancy trainers, then traveled up, up, up to skim jean-clad legs that could belong to only one man. She knew those legs. They'd held her up against a wall while the owner of said legs had ravished her.

Nick.

She was on her knees, trimming basil in the side garden of the farm. She'd been so engrossed in what she was doing that she hadn't noticed Nick approach. Now he loomed over her, his hands on his hips and a cocky smile on his face.

She blew a stray curl off her face and pushed back her wide-brimmed hat. She tried not to think about the fact that she was covered in dirt, her overalls were tattered, and she hadn't even bothered with mascara today.

Nick, of course, looked as handsome as ever. His black T-shirt hugged his lean chest. His long, muscular arms were crossed in front of him. She tried not to think about the obnoxious tattoo she knew was just a piece of fabric away on his chest.

It was an utterly narcissistic tattoo. It wasn't sexy *at all*.

She cleared her throat. There, on her knees, she was nearly at eye-level with his crotch. She swallowed, but her throat was dry.

"What does low tide have to do with anything?" she asked, raising her gaze to his face.

He was grinning and looked downright excited. "Oysters!"

"Oysters?" Slowly, she put down her shears and removed her gloves. "Nick. What are you talking about?"

He crouched down just as a cloud passed over them, casting a shadow across his face. His blue eyes darkened as he gazed at her.

Her pulse jumped. She hated being this close to him. She hated the fact that she had to clench her fists to keep from taking his head and pulling his mouth to hers.

"I'm talking about oysters. You know, those little things that live on a reef...kinda slimy. Very good when roasted over a fire pit."

She took off her hat and attempted to put her hair back into some semblance of a braid. "I know what oysters are. What I don't understand is why you keep repeating the word."

Standing, he took her hand and tugged her to her feet. "Leave your hair. I like it wild."

"But—"

She tried touching her hair again, but he slapped her fingers away. She gave him a dirty look. "Why are you going on about oysters?"

"Because. I heard from a vendor that right now the tide is low and you can walk right out onto the reef and harvest as many as you want."

"And?"

He sighed, looked away, and then back at her. "And, we should go get some."

"We?" She smirked. "Why don't you ask Sherry to go

with you?" She tried not to sound bitter, but she was fairly certain she didn't succeed.

He laughed. "Sherry?" he said incredulously. "Have you seen her?"

Phoebe ran a hand over her hair. "Yes. In fact, I have."

"Can you picture her getting her hands dirty looking for shellfish?"

Phoebe thought about it for a second and realized the answer was no. She couldn't.

Hands on her hips, she looked warily at the sexy Brit standing in front of her. "So. I'm second choice to Sherry when it comes to sex and oyster harvesting?"

He blew out a heavy breath. "Oh, for fuck's sake! Do you want to go with me or not?"

She did. And she didn't. Every second she spent with Nick was bad. Dangerous.

The beach? Oysters? Nick? That would take an entire day!

She shook her head. "I don't have time."

"What do you have to do that's so important?"

Besides stay away from you? "I have to finish here in the garden. I have to contact the youth group to arrange for this summer's volunteers. And"—she straightened her back—"I have to work on my brownie recipe for the cook-off." She'd been trying. Repeatedly. But she just couldn't get the damn thing down.

"Do you need some help with that?" he asked. "Because I'm sure with a little help we could—"

"There is no *we*," she said in a rather loud voice, which she calmed before she continued. "I can do it."

"Really? Because from what I've seen, I would say otherwise."

"I can," she ground out.

"Fine. You can make your family recipe for the world's best brownies, win the bumpkin cook-off, and die a happy woman."

She clenched her fists. "Why do you always have to make everything I do seem so stupid?"

He actually looked a little abashed. After a minute, he said, "I don't mean to. I'm just kidding."

"No, you're not."

"Well, your brownies are atrocious, but I don't mean to make you think I believe you to be stupid."

"I don't believe it. But you still come across like that's what you think. Like I'm some lowbrow twit."

"I'm sorry. Like I said, I'm just kidding. Mostly."

"Well, maybe your friends back in Hollywood think you're a real laugh riot, but I don't."

He held out his hands, palms facing front. "Fine. I apologize. I will make great effort in the future not to offend you."

She grunted a response.

"So...," he said. "Are you going with me?"

"I told you, I have things to do."

"Right. Brownies. Way to change things up on your day off."

"Stop it."

"Right, sorry. Forgot the rule: no jokes."

"That's not what I meant. I can take a joke."

"Okay, good. We're back on. So?"

"So what?"

"Are you coming or not?" He softly punched her shoulder. "Come on. It's Monday. Everything's closed."

Why did she suddenly feel like he was a kid wanting

some friend to play with after school? He looked sincere.

Oh, he was so bad. So dangerous. And he kept making her do things she knew she'd regret. And still, she straightened her back and said, "Fine. But I'm driving."

Chapter Fifteen

W hy in the hell would we take your car when we can take mine?"

Phoebe opened the trunk of her old Land Cruiser and tossed her bag into the back. "Because I refuse to go anywhere in that yellow monstrosity."

"It's not a monstrosity." Nick threw a couple of mesh containers into the Toyota. "It's a valuable piece of machinery. It's the most uncompromising off-road vehicle available." He threw a bucket and some gloves into the car.

She slammed the trunk closed and tilted her head. "And you need that in Los Angles...why?"

"Because..." He paused. "Because they're really cool."

She couldn't help but laugh. "Okay, then. Get your ass in my real off-road vehicle and we can get going."

"Real off-road vehicle?"

"Yeah. What?"

"A Hummer is definitely an off-road vehicle."

"Really? Do ya mean like you take it off the freeway sometimes?"

He scoffed. "Yeah. Well. Maybe."

"Just get in the car. Killer." She walked to the driver's door, opened it, and sank into the seat.

A few moments later Nick opened the passenger door.

Phoebe went to start the engine, but he put his hand on hers, stopping her from turning the key. A spark of electricity shot up her arm and landed in her chest.

She hated that.

"Did you just call me killer?" he asked.

She looked sideways and tried to appear innocent. "What?" She remembered when he'd called her that same name, and it had annoyed her so. Did it annoy him?

Didn't look like it. He seemed to be trying to bite back a smile. "You called me killer."

She tried to look nonchalant. "So?"

"Come here."

"What?"

"Aw, fuck it." He released her hand and grabbed her head. Then he was kissing her. His lips were warm and soft and gentle. When he touched her, every part of her mind and body seemed to liquefy and dissolve into glue, pouring into this one person.

She fought it. She fought it so hard he had to hold her head steady while he kissed her. So she kissed him back, tried to take control. When she felt him relax a little bit, a sigh of satisfaction escaped him. She wanted to sink into him; every part of her wanted to give in.

But she couldn't. She could not give in one inch. Then he'd be in control, and she couldn't have that. When he was in control, he did things like spank her. Feed her. Fuck her.

And she liked it way too much.

It was so enticing. She wondered if she could just have fun and not worry about her feelings. About falling for him.

Maybe, just maybe, she could.

Could she enjoy it? Could she separate herself enough to give in and be okay when he left?

The thought was somewhat enticing. She knew if she gave in again, it would open yet another door. She would be jumping down the rabbit hole. The question was, How would she feel when he was gone?

At least a year. He'd be there at least a year, and hopefully longer. And when she thought about it like that, the possibility opened just a bit. Could she do a temporary relationship with Nick?

If so, she didn't want him in control all the time. It was fun to fight him, so she did.

She grabbed his head and held him steady. She pushed her way into his mouth. There was nothing but this, this battle between them.

A subtle battle of control.

Just kissing. Just their hands and mouths and tongues. A battle she knew she was fighting, and yet it was smooth. Natural. This struggle between them. Fight, retreat. Back and forth. Lick, suck. Push, pull.

It was a fight as natural as the moon's battle against daylight.

It was he who released her.

She blinked a few times before she could focus, and when she could, she saw he was staring at her.

Her defenses were still up. She met his gaze. "What?"

He shook his head. "Nothing."

"No." She wasn't going to let him off the hook. Why did she always feel so challenged by him? And even more important, why did she enjoy the battle so much?

"Why are you looking at me that way?" she asked.

"What way?"

"Like you want to laugh at me."

"I'm not laughing at you. Trust me."

"Trust you? Why the heck would I do that?" The words just flew out of her mouth. She didn't know where they came from. But there they were. Her heart hurt with the need to trust him. He'd gotten her to do just that time after time . . .

But that had been a mistake. A fun mistake that had led her here, to now.

He just shook his head and leaned back into his seat. "I'm letting you drive, right?"

"Letting me?" She barked a laugh. "What do you mean, *letting* me? You think because I'm a woman I should just hand over the reins?"

Without turning his head, he slanted her a look. "Are you driving a horse?"

"Yes. This is my horse." She tapped the steering wheel. "And these are my reins."

"Giddyup, then."

Why did he make her laugh? *Why?* But turning to start the engine, she couldn't help but chuckle.

"You know," she said. "For such a prick, you can be kind of funny."

"Did you just call me a prick?"

She pulled out of the driveway and onto the narrow two-lane road that led away from the house. "Don't act all offended. I'd bet money on the fact that you've been called a prick dozens of times."

"And that makes it okay?"

"It proves my point. You can be a prick. Everyone thinks so." But she was still smiling when she said it.

"Ah, but a funny prick. Right, love?"

She maneuvered around a hairpin turn, and her hands clenched the steering wheel. Not because of the dodgy thin road that led to the coast, but because of his words. That word. *Love.*

"Nick, I thought I asked you to stop calling me that."

"No, you didn't."

If she hadn't been driving, she might have punched him. "I know I did." Because she'd hated it when he'd said the word to Sherry.

"No. You yelled something like, '*Don't call me that!*'" He mimicked her tone in a high-pitched yell that made her cringe. "You didn't ask. You demanded. In fact, you're a pretty demanding woman in general."

Watching the road, she straightened her back. "Fine. As long as you know I was right."

"You always have to be right, don't you? *Love.*"

She ignored the taunting word. "No." She paused a moment before continuing. "Well, I guess I do."

He patted her knee. "Admitting you have a problem is the first step to recovery."

"Oh, go jump off a cliff. I'm in charge of a lot of things. I have to be confident and sure of myself. The minute you back down, people start to run you over."

He glanced out the passenger window. "Yeah. You do have a point there."

"I'm sure it's that way for you, too."

Looking back at her, he said, "Yes, you have to be sure of yourself to run a kitchen. If any of the sharks sense blood, you'll be ripped to shreds."

The tone of his voice had changed. He sounded pensive, and even a little sad. Her heart went out to him.

"Is that what happened to you?" she asked softly.

He jerked his head back. "What? Hell no."

The road was getting windier, and Phoebe drove the SUV around another tight curve. The closer they got to the ocean, the foggier it became. It was going to be cold and damp at the beach.

"Right," she said. "Sorry I asked. Of course, you would never be anything but one hundred percent self-assured. Must be nice."

"Ah, that's where you're wrong, poppet. It's not about what you are; it's about what you let others perceive you to be."

"Ha! So you're saying your whole 'I'm Nick the Prick and I'm perfect' personality is just an act?"

"No. I really am a prick."

"I know."

"But I'm not perfect."

"What?" She feigned disbelief. "You are admitting that you're not Mr. Perfect?"

"Of course I'm not. If I was, do you think I'd be here?"

She clenched her jaw. She wasn't going to say anything. She really wasn't.

"Then why the heck *are* you? Here, that is?"

Too late. She could never keep her mouth shut.

"Honestly?"

"Please."

"Well, Phoebe, I came here because I couldn't get a job anywhere decent."

"Thanks."

"My visa only allows me to work in California, and let's face it. There's really only two decent cities in this state."

The fog was getting heavier, and she had to slow down to a crawl just to see the road. "And they would be?"

"Los Angeles and San Francisco."

"Why didn't you take a job in San Francisco?"

Out of the corner of her eye, she saw his shoulders tighten. "Every offer I got was a step down from where I was. I couldn't do it."

"But coming here wasn't exactly a big step up in the ladder of your career."

With one long fingertip, he rubbed the fabric of his jeans where it covered his knee. "That's true. But at least here, no one knows me. No one here knows or cares what I was before."

"You really care that much about what people think?"

"No. I care what I think about myself. And living in the city and working at some chain diner would make me want to—" He ran one hand over his head. "I'd rather stick a knife in my eye."

She continued to crawl through the fog. "You're right about one thing, Nick."

"What's that?"

"No one here cares."

He jerked back. "Okay."

"What I mean is, this isn't L.A. This isn't some back-stabbing city where everyone has an agenda."

"I suppose you're right about that."

"People here actually care about the community. And we have a pretty high tolerance for the mistakes people make."

"Are you saying you wouldn't fire an employee if he made a mistake?"

"It would depend on the mistake. If he'd lied, stolen,

or cheated, then yes. But if it was an honest mistake, then I'd give him a second chance."

He grunted.

"All I ask out of the people who work for me is one thing."

Sinking into the seat, he crossed his arms over his chest. "What's that, love?"

"All I ask is loyalty."

She glanced over and saw that he'd closed his eyes. His facial expression was relaxed, but she could see every muscle in his body was tense. Why was that?

"You can be really draining," she said.

"Now what are you going on about?" he asked.

"I never know with you. I never know what will flip a switch in you that changes your entire demeanor from utterly nonchalant to ultratense."

"For fuck's sake." He reached into his inner coat pocket and pulled out a flask. "Can we just be quiet for a minute?"

She swiped the flask out of his hand. "You can't drink that in the car. It's illegal!" She threw the flask into the far back of the Land Cruiser.

"Hey! It wasn't as if I was going to give the driver any."

"It doesn't matter. It's still totally illegal!"

"Well, what do you want me to do? Sometimes you just keep hammering on and on. Talk about draining."

"Fine. Let's just be quiet for the rest of the drive."

"Thank God."

And that was the last they spoke for the next thirty minutes.

Chapter Sixteen

Phoebe pulled the car into an empty gravel parking area and came to a stop. Glancing over, she saw Nick's eyes were still closed, but she doubted he was asleep.

She punched him in the arm. "Wake up."

He opened one eye. "Are we there yet?"

"Yes. Now get up and let's get going. It looks chilly out there."

Straightening, he gazed through the windshield to the sandy beach that ended just a few feet from where she'd parked. Beyond the sand were rocks that jutted out of the ocean, and the waves crashed against the boulders and tide pools in violent bursts.

"Wow," Nick said.

She glanced at him. "What?"

"Nothing. It's just...it's gorgeous. Reminds me a bit of home, actually."

"Really?"

"Yeah. They don't have beaches like this in Southern California."

"No, they don't." She stared at the turbulent water. "I've always loved it here. It's very peaceful to hear the waves crashing, to wander around the tide pools. I don't know why I don't come here more often."

"You have a lot going on, Phoebe. With the farm and the restaurant. Jesse and Steve."

"Yeah. But still, it's important to make time for yourself. To regroup." Still staring at the water, she said, "Right?"

"I suppose, yeah."

"And anyway, now I have you to run the kitchen. That's helped me tremendously. I really should make more time to do some things for myself."

She turned to him. "I really do think you're doing a fabulous job in the café, Nick. Thank you. You obviously know what you're doing—"

He rolled his eyes.

She ignored him. "So I'm going to step back. Let you do your job without me hovering around all the time."

"That's very...shocking to hear."

"Why? You're the one who's always telling me how great you are."

"And you're the one who's always telling me not to question your authority."

"Look, Nick. All I'm saying is, thanks to you, I can start focusing more on my farm. And maybe even myself." The simple thought scared her. But she was starting to see that she couldn't do everything. At some point she needed to delegate, and Nick was slowly proving he could handle the responsibility.

He shifted and reached for the door. "Shall we?"

She watched him exit her car. His body was stiff, and his movements were fast and jerky.

Now what? What had she done to piss him off this time?

Opening her own door, she sighed and let it go. She realized she was never going to figure out Nick Avalon. But that didn't help get rid of her overwhelming desire to know him. In fact, the more time she actually spent with him, the more she liked him. When they weren't arguing, of course. Because then she often just wanted to throw rotten fruit at him.

They retrieved their oyster-gathering tools from the trunk. As Nick grabbed some gloves and a basket, Phoebe pulled her North Face jacket tight around her neck. It had been so long since she'd been to the beach she'd forgotten how cold it could be, even at the start of summer.

There was a mountain that separated the ocean from the valley where Redbolt was located, and the weather could change drastically by simply driving "over the hill," as the locals called it.

A chilly breeze whispered the back of her neck. Luckily, she always came to the beach prepared for cold weather, and now she dug a knit hat out of her backpack and pulled it onto her head.

"What?"

Nick was staring at her. "Nothing. You just look so..."

"What?!"

"Cute."

"Oh, shut up." Apparently his hissy fit was over.

"Phoebe, why can't you just take a compliment for once?"

"Because I don't believe you." She picked up a basket and stomped off toward the reefs.

"You don't believe anyone except yourself?"

She glanced over her shoulder. "Sometimes."

He whistled long and low. "Wow."

Stopping, she spun around. "Now what are you talking about?"

"You. You just have so many defenses up. And I bet no one even knows it." He smiled smugly. "Except me."

Just then a cold burst of air hit her in the face, and she wiped at her nose, which had started to run. "You have no idea what the heck you're talking about."

He came closer. Her instinct was to back up, but she didn't. She lifted her chin and met his gaze.

"You're scared of me," he said.

"Are you totally insane? Why the hell would I be scared of you?"

"Aha!" he said, as if he'd just discovered something.

"What now?" she yelled, frustrated.

"You said a bad word."

"I did not!" Had she? He made her so mad. He had her totally out of her mind and she didn't even know what she was saying anymore.

"You said *hell*."

"That's not a bad word."

"It is when Phoebe Mayle says it."

She spun on her heel and made her way down to the oyster bed. Why was he doing this to her? One second he was flirtatious, the next he was pensive, the next he was a prick.

When she looked back, he was still at the car, changing into rain gear. She watched him.

He was making her crazy.

And he was making her incredibly turned on.

It had to be the boots. Pausing at the edge of the water, she watched as he waded into the sea toward a reef of oysters. He wore knee-high rubber boots like those fishermen wore. His khaki pants were tucked into the boots, and he wore a heavy white cable sweater that looked straight from Ireland.

He wore a black cap on his head. He looked like he could have just stepped off a fishing boat. This was a far cry from the hip version of Nick Avalon that had shown up at her door. The boots were a far cry from the hip trainers he normally sported.

And she found them kinda hot.

He obviously knew what he was doing. Phoebe had come out and collected oysters before, but Nick did so with an intensity and purpose that sort of shocked her.

He wore heavy rubber gloves and carried a big wire basket in one hand. In his other hand he wielded a small black rake, and with this tool he began scraping oysters from the reef and dropping them into the basket.

She watched. She didn't know why it was so fascinating to observe Nick like this, but it was. He seemed so comfortable out here in the wildness of the sea that it surprised her. She would never have expected Nick Avalon, the snooty chef from Los Angeles, to wander out in the cold waters of the northern Pacific Ocean to gather oysters.

He looked up at her and smiled.

Right then, her heart melted a little bit. He looked so happy, like a kid. She smiled back, and it came from deep inside her. He made a motion as if he wanted her to join him, but she was nailed to her spot.

The wind whipped at her, and she pulled her hat farther down on her head. She didn't care how cold it was. Watching Nick out there, stepping carefully through the rocky reef, was simply fascinating.

He was fascinating to her.

And, for some reason, she was starting to trust him.

And there was no denying her body's response to his touch. Just the thought of his fingers on her skin sent a shiver through her, a shiver that had nothing to do with the chilly fog surrounding her.

She loved being touched by him. Loved it so much it scared her.

She'd had casual sex; she'd had sex when she was in a serious relationship. Until she'd met Nick, she'd thought sex with Bear was as good as she was ever going to get. And the casual sex filled a need.

But, there was nothing casual about the way she felt when Nick touched her. When they had sex, it touched her somewhere, everywhere. From her toes to her chest to her head. She'd experienced a connection with him unlike anything she'd ever encountered before.

She hugged herself tightly as another breeze hit her. Yeah, she was starting to recognize how she felt about Nick. The question was, How did he feel about her?

When he was young, the one place Nick could go to get away from everything, the one place he felt safe, was the beach. Now, as he raked up another shell, he retreated to that place. He lost himself in the salty air, the sounds of the waves. He forgot about his father, his job, where he was...He forgot how easy it was to lose himself from everything.

Well, everything except *her*.

Nick thought he'd never seen anything as cute in his life as Phoebe at that very moment. Standing there on the beach, in her puffy jacket and faded jeans and colorful knit hat; he waved at her, and she waved back. It made his chest clench.

She was starting to trust him. Just a little bit, but it was there. And despite the fact that he'd always considered himself a heartless bastard, he couldn't help the tug of guilt that was getting stronger every day.

He was going to leave. He was going to leave this place and leave Phoebe. Even now, as he raked up another oyster and dropped it into the basket, he was resolved to go.

He couldn't—wouldn't—give up all he'd worked for to live the rest of his life working in a tiny café in the middle of nowhere.

Oh, his dad would love that. His dad, who'd told him cooking was for "sissies" and thought he could beat the idea out of him. As if smacking Nick across the face would make him a "real man."

Nick had proved his father very wrong. He'd become a chef and had earned a reputation as one of the baddest boys in the industry.

He laughed to himself. Maybe all those beatings his father gave him had been a good thing. By the time he finally moved out at seventeen, he'd developed a thick skin. And to succeed, Nick had certainly needed to be tough. If his father had taught him anything, it was the ability to be strong. To overcome anything.

So why was he having such a hard time with the idea of leaving? He glanced back at Phoebe, who was still watching him. A vision flashed through his mind. Here, cooking what she produced and collecting food from the sea. It could be a good, simple life.

And the thought made his heart pound with anxiety.

He wasn't meant for anything good or simple. He was meant to prove himself, every day. Prove he was a man.

Prove his father wrong.

And cooking vegan brunches in the middle of nowhere was not any part of that plan.

Phoebe smiled at him. He smiled back. And he ignored the way his heart hurt because he knew he'd be leaving her.

She'd be pissed, but she'd get over it. She was a strong woman. And if she didn't get over it, well, he'd live with that. He was used to living with people hating him. She'd just be one more individual in the world who thought he was a prick.

Well, according to what she said, she already did. He was just going to prove her right.

Chapter Seventeen

Her dad still hadn't come home from his day out with Sherry. Nick and Phoebe had gone to the beach. Which meant Jesse was alone.

Lying on her bed, reading a biography of Julia Child, she tried not to even look at her computer. But it seemed to be calling to her.

Jesse! it was saying. *We have lots of culinary schools for you to research! New York, Madrid, Paris...Come check us out!*

"No," she said aloud. Then she slammed the book shut and flopped onto her stomach. She was going crazy. Was she really talking out loud to her computer?

Yeah, Jesse. You are.

It was like torture. Why would she do that to herself? Going to culinary school was totally out of the question. For one thing, they were all off-the-hook expensive. And for another thing, she could not leave her father.

Come to San Francisco; it's not that far away!

But that wasn't where she wanted to go. She wanted out. She wanted totally different. Sure, San Francisco had a decent culinary school. But she wanted to go someplace totally unlike what she knew. Somewhere out of California, out of the entire country.

She thought about Bear. He was living his dream, traveling the world. Every time he came back to town, she loved hearing his stories, especially since so many of them involved the local cuisine made from food he'd helped cultivate.

But even while she envied Bear, she couldn't quite forgive him for breaking his engagement to Phoebe. Her aunt had taken the news gracefully, but Jesse wasn't so dense that she didn't know it had affected her aunt more than Phoebe would ever admit, even to herself.

Breaking the engagement had been hard on Phoebe, but they all understood that Bear would never be happy living a stationary existence here in Redbolt. And part of Jesse envied that he had the guts to pursue his dreams, living his life on his own terms. Even if it meant hurting those around him.

Jesse wished she had the guts to do the same.

So she pushed herself off the bed and headed toward her computer. Why was she opening her browser and typing in the web address to the school in Paris? She knew the address by heart now, and she reread the pages that she'd already read dozens of times before.

The courses included stocks, sauces, forcemeats, and dough...mastery of "haute cuisine"...and what she really wanted to learn was the French language for gastronomy.

She sighed. Julia Child went to France and came back one of the most renowned chefs in the world. Not that Jesse thought she was anything like Julia, but still. What an adventure it would be!

She heard a car pull into the gravel driveway, and she immediately shut down her computer. Then she went to her bedroom window to see who had pulled up.

It was her father and Sherry. Her dad bounded out the driver's side of the car and jogged around to open Sherry's door.

Jesse put her hand to her mouth. Was that really her dad? He laughed at something Sherry said. And as she got out of the car, he held out his hand to take hers, helping her to her feet.

She touched his shoulder. Sherry. Was touching. Her dad's shoulder.

And he didn't seem to mind.

Jesse's first reaction was shock. She'd never seen a woman who wasn't related to her father show affection. And she'd certainly never seen her dad smile quite the way he was currently, not at any other woman.

Her dad looked downright happy.

Through the window, Jesse watched them come into the house. Her father shuffled along, his hands in his pockets. But there was no denying the fact that his expression was joyful. Content.

Jesse hadn't seen her father look truly content since before her mom died.

Was it actually possible that her father was developing a crush on a woman who wasn't Jesse's mom?

She went back to her bed and sat down. It was interesting, and normally nothing would have made Jesse happier than seeing her dad cheerful. But she couldn't deny the fact that Sherry was here for only a little while. What happened when she left?

If her dad really did develop feelings for this woman,

what would happen then? When she went home?

Her dad would be sad once again. And alone.

Jesse pulled a dread out of her scarf and twisted it around her finger. It would be just one more reason that she could never leave this town.

Chapter Eighteen

When Nick came back to shore, his basket was nearly overflowing with oysters. He was grinning, and his joy was infectious. Phoebe had to smile back at him. Her heart skipped when she saw the pure joy on his face. So rarely did she see him like this—she absorbed it like a sponge cake soaks in a cream sauce. And the feeling was just as delicious.

She glanced at her own basket. She'd harvested a few oysters, but mainly she'd just ambled around the rocks. Instead of oysters, she'd found some gorgeous shells to add to her collection.

"Wow." She glanced at his basket. "You hit the jackpot."

"I know. Let's fire up a few of these babies."

"What? Here?"

"Of course, here." He glanced around. "I'll just find some driftwood that's dry enough to burn."

"O-ok-kay."

It was as if he'd just noticed she was there. His gaze assessed her in one big sweep. "You're freezing."

"N-no." But she was. It was getting late, and even

though it was foggy, the sun had provided a bit of warmth. Now, as it became darker, the cold was seeping into her bones.

Dropping the basket, he came to her and wrapped her in a big hug. She couldn't help it; she sank into his warmth. He rubbed her back with his big, strong hands. She buried her nose in his sweater, inhaling the scent of the sea and him. Nick. The ocean with all its pungent smells couldn't take away from how she felt when she buried her nose into Nick's body and smelled his own unique, spicy scent that turned her insides into a puddle of mush.

"Let's go home and get you warmed up."

"I thought you wanted to build a fire."

"I do, but not if you're going to die of hypothermia."

"I'll be fine once we get a fire going." For some reason, she wasn't ready to leave, even if she was shivering from the chilly air.

Holding her shoulders, he pulled back and looked her in the eye. "You're sure?"

She nodded.

"Right. Okay, hang on." He jogged off toward the Land Cruiser. After a while he came running back. His arms were full, and he nodded to his right. "Come on."

She was surprised when he led her to a grouping of rocks that circled a patch of sand. In the center of the rocks were the remains of many previous bonfires. She knew he'd never been to this beach before. He must have scoped the spot out when they'd first arrived.

He sat her down and wrapped a wool blanket around her shoulders. "Just wait, I'll have you warmed up in a few moments."

She could simply nod. Who knew Nick Avalon was such a Boy Scout? Determinedly, he went about gathering dry wood, and then returned with an armful and dropped the pile onto the sand.

It didn't take him long to get a nice fire going. Obviously, he'd done this before. One swift strike from a match and he had a burning ember going, which soon had the entire pile of wood blazing with heat.

Phoebe held her hands out in front of the fire. "How did you become such an outdoorsman?"

He shrugged. "I used to spend a lot of time outside when I was a kid."

"In England?"

"Yeah. We lived near Portsmouth."

"Is that where you learned so much about the ocean? And building fires?"

"I suppose." He dumped the contents of her basket into a tan canvas bag and placed the now-empty wire container over the fire. Staring into the orange flames, he went on. "I'd do anything to get out of my house."

"Really? Why was that?"

But he'd shut down—she could see it in his blue eyes. And by now, she knew better than to push him.

"I just liked being outside." He poured the majority of the oysters that he'd harvested into the canvas bag, but left a few in the basket. He then stacked the basket with the remaining oysters onto the one already placed in the fire.

He stared down at her, and she could see the orange blaze reflected in his blue eyes. His demeanor had changed. Gone was the Boy Scout. Nick Avalon, sexy bad boy, was back. She saw it in the gleam in his eye, and the way he slanted her that wicked grin.

"Now. Are you ready for something delicious?"

She nodded. "Yes, Nick. I am."

He pulled a pair of tongs from his back pocket. "Then be a good girl for me. I want to feed you."

Chapter Nineteen

I want to feed you.

Such a simple statement, but it made her stomach quiver. When he spoke to her like that—those simple commands of his—it did funny things to her brain.

She wanted to obey. She wanted to give in.

She wanted to trust him. She wanted to so badly it hurt. But every ounce of what was left of her self-preservation was telling her not to.

Still, she found herself walking to the edge. Ready to jump. Ready to let him catch her.

"Here." He extracted his flask from his pants pocket, untwisted the cap, and held the bottle out to her.

She wasn't much for tequila, but she took the flask anyway and brought it to her lips. The liquid burned its way down her throat and landed in her stomach. She shuddered.

"That good, eh?" Nick said with a smile.

She nodded. "I'm just not used to drinking anything but wine."

"Sometimes it's good to mix things up."

Eyeing him, she said, "That is very true." And she took another sip. A gulp, actually.

"Slow down, killer. I don't want you passing out on me."

She scoffed. "Right."

"Oh, you're such a big drinker, are you?"

"No. But that doesn't mean a few sips of tequila are going to knock me out." To prove her point, she took another. And shuddered once again as it flowed through her body.

But she could already feel the effects of the alcohol.

She licked her lips. "I like tequila."

"So do I," he said, taking back his flask.

He sipped from the bottle, and they both stared into the fire. She was warming up, and she wasn't sure if it was the fire, the tequila, or the sexual energy pulsing between them.

Eventually he took the tongs and poked around the pile of oysters cooking inside the basket. He glanced up at her. "Clasp your hands behind your back."

For about half a second, she thought about arguing with him. But really, what was the point? She knew damn well she wasn't going to deny him anything.

More to the point, she wasn't going to deny herself anything.

She moved to hold her hands at the base of her spine.

The opened oyster in his hand, Nick brought it to her mouth and tilted the shell. She opened her lips and let the smooth oyster flesh slide into her mouth.

"That's a good girl. Swallow it down for me."

Swallow... She wanted to swallow more than an oyster. She wanted to feel his cock in her mouth and suck it until she could swallow his very essence.

But for now, she obeyed and settled for an oyster.

Of course, he'd cooked the oyster flesh perfectly. It

was barely seared, and the taste of the fresh salty tissue needed no seasonings other than what the sea naturally had provided. It slid down her throat.

Of course, she'd heard that oysters were an aphrodisiac. She happened to know that the idea was total folklore. However, she couldn't disagree with the fact that there was something very sexy about the way Nick fed her. No, the lust coursing through her veins had nothing to do with the chemical effects of the seafood.

Adrenaline raced in her blood, causing her heart to pound, and she felt little tremors rack her body. Because, as she'd been telling herself since the second she'd seen Nick Avalon walk into her café, he was dangerous. She'd been telling herself to stay away. To be the boss. To not succumb.

So why was she sitting on a rock on the beach with her hands behind her back? Why was she letting him feed her scrumptious, fresh oysters?

The answer was easy. She wanted to.

She realized she not only wanted to give him more power in the café, but also more power over her. She liked it. It was fun. She liked him. She figured if she could take a chance and let the café be vulnerable to Nick, why couldn't she do the same thing for herself?

His gaze was fixated on her mouth, and she thought she should try to make this whole situation as normal as possible. Despite the fact that her hands were still clasped behind her, they were just eating, right? He was just feeding her?

And yet it was so much more than that. Due to her position, her breasts jutted out. And they were warm and tingly. They were wanting, aching.

She was getting used to his touch, and her body squirmed with the need to feel his hands on her.

Looking up at him, she licked her lips, wanting him to know she was ready to be fed. Pressing her legs together in an attempt to tamper down her throbbing pussy, she watched Nick's mouth as he ate.

And as he ate, he watched her mouth. His blue eyes were dark in the dim light and sparkled as his gaze moved up to fix on hers. Her heart skipped. What was it about this man that could turn her to mush in a simple glance?

She watched him as he swallowed. She fixated on the corded muscles of his neck, the way they moved. The ocean crashed against the shore. The fire shot up a blast of a spark. Nothing distracted her from him. From watching him. From simply being near him.

Watching Nick eat was the sexiest thing she'd ever seen. She wondered if she'd ever be able to have their pre-dinner-rush meals together in the café without jumping his bones.

Probably not. She was more at ease with the idea than she might like to be.

She was totally unsure what normal actually consisted of anymore. This—this moment—felt nothing but normal. The sea, the fire, the food. Being with Nick. This feeling of excitement coursing through her. This was what felt good. Right.

She let him feed her. Her eyes drifted shut, and she tasted the slick oyster as it slid into her mouth.

"That's my good girl," he said. His voice was deep and husky. Her trembling moved from her limbs to her center. God, how she wanted him. She thought about the incident in the storage room, when he'd pushed her against the wall, pulled off her skirt, and spanked her.

That feeling. He'd had total control over her. And yet she'd felt free for the first time since she could remember. That feeling was here. Right *here*. Right now.

She could feel it. She was hovering over it. She craved it. She wanted to jump into it as if it were a pool of warm water.

She unclasped her hands and put them to the zipper of her jacket. Meeting his gaze, she started to unzip her coat.

"You want a good girl?" she asked.

He quirked a brow, but his stare remained fixed on hers. Nailed to hers.

"You like being my good girl, don't you, Phoebe?" he asked.

She pulled the zipper down and shrugged it off her shoulder. "I'm not yours." *Yet.* She couldn't help it; the word just popped into her brain, and she tried to poke it away. But it was like a bubble floating around, and no matter how hard she tried, she couldn't pop it.

Yet.

Her senses seemed to be amplified. The ocean sounds seemed like thunder, and the fire sparked like miniature bomb blasts. She thought her eardrums might explode. A crisp wind whispered against her warm cheeks and seemed to burn her skin. Her heart hammered in her chest, louder than any churning ocean waves.

The moon burned through the fog, shadowing Nick's face in chiaroscuro shadows that hollowed out his cheekbones and highlighted the angle of his long, thin nose.

Do you want to be a good girl?

Above the blare of noise around them, the question resonated. Deafening.

Of course she did. She wanted to be Nick's good girl. When she was playing that role, there was nothing else. No family, no restaurant, no farm. Just them.

She tossed her jacket onto the sand and smiled. Crossing her arms near the hems of her sweater and T-shirt, she tugged the clothing up. The glow from the fire illuminated the newly exposed skin of her belly. She smiled at him.

She lifted her sweater and shirt over her head and threw them on top of her jacket. Then she sat across from him. She smiled when she saw his gaze fall on her breasts, covered only in a cotton bra. She reached behind her back as she nibbled her lip.

She unclasped her bra and tossed it aside, where it joined the pile of clothes on the sand. "Of course I want to be a good girl, Nick. But you have to make me."

As soon as the words left her mouth, her heart pounded a fraction faster. She'd just issued Nick Avalon a challenge. And she knew he wouldn't back down.

Holy shit.

Nick's mouth was dry. He couldn't keep his gaze off Phoebe's glowing skin. Looking at her taut breasts, he had to clench his hands to keep from feeling her up like a teenage boy at his first dance. Her nipples were rosy and tight in the open air, and he wanted to suck on them. Bite. He wanted to throw her down onto the sand and lick every inch of her exposed skin. He wanted to bury his hands in her hair as he ravished her mouth.

He wanted to taste the flavor of oysters and tequila on her tongue.

He wanted...What he wanted was to fuck her bloody brains out.

But no. She'd thrown down a gauntlet, and Nick had never been the sort of man who shied away from a battle. And that's what Phoebe was offering him. A battle. But it was just an act. He could see it in her eyes; she wanted to be taken over. By him.

The thought gave him pause. Because he did feel a sense of possession over her, unlike what he'd felt for any of the women he'd been with before. In fact, the thought of anyone else touching her like he did made his stomach turn with the unfamiliar feeling of jealousy.

But he wasn't going to focus on that now. Not when he had something so beautiful right in front of him. Waiting for him.

Shifting to give his aching cock some space, he slowly pulled the basket out of the fire and set it on a rock beside him. He glanced up to find her watching him. She was trying to look relaxed, but he could see the rapid rise and fall of her chest.

He pushed himself off the rock and knelt before her.

"What are you doing?" she asked.

He lifted one of her feet and placed it on his knee. "You didn't think you were just going to take off your shirt and leave the rest of your clothes on, did you?"

The saucy thing leaned back on her hands, basically pushing her breasts out at him.

Taking it slow was going to be a real problem.

"Can you ever answer a simple question?" she asked.

He began unlacing her boot. "Can you ever stop asking questions?"

"Yes. I just often choose not to."

He threw her boot aside. "Now would be a really good time for you to practice the whole silence thing."

"Make me."

"Woman, you are driving me nuts."

"I think you're already nuts."

He made quick work of her other boot and tugged it off her foot. "You definitely bring it out in me."

"Ditto."

Looking up at her face, he couldn't help but smile. "You must have a death wish."

Her expression changed, and he saw a flicker of panic flash in her eyes.

"Why do you say that?" she asked.

He climbed onto his knees to pull off his sweater. Leaning into her, he watched her breath catch as he brought his face close to hers.

He pushed himself against her body, and through the fabric of his T-shirt, he felt her hard nipples and the soft flesh of her breasts.

"Nick. Why did you say I have a death wish?"

He gently rubbed his lips against hers. Her breath was hot and sweet against his mouth.

"Are you asking questions again?" he asked.

She nodded. "So answer me."

"Sweetheart, you have a death wish because you fuck with me. No one else does that. And if they do, they heartily regret it."

"Is that so?"

He pulled back an inch. "Are you laughing at me?"

"No." But she was biting her lip.

"You are. You're laughing at me."

"I swear, I'm not." A bubble of laughter escaped her mouth.

"You cheeky little bitch," he said.

"It's just that, I mean, I can see why some people would think you're all big and scary." She said the words *big* and *scary* in a sarcastic tone that should have annoyed the heck out of him.

"But I'm starting to think Nick Avalon isn't very scary at all."

It was cute. She was trying to convince herself that he wasn't scary. However, despite her steady voice, he could see her hands were shaking. It was all an act.

"You keep telling yourself that, sweetheart." He placed his hand on her breast and beaded a nipple between his fingers. She gasped.

"Come on, love. You know damn well you're frightened of me. That's what you like about me." He whispered the words against her lips and gave her nipple a twist.

"Not. True." But her words came out as breathy gasps.

He ran his tongue across her bottom lip. "You need to be scared of me, love. Trust me on that one."

"I'm not...I don't."

He took her other breast in his free hand. Slowly he circled her nipple until he saw her breathing go more shallow. "Are you sure?"

"Yes," she whispered. "Yes..."

Just when he could feel her entire body go soft, he released her breasts and grabbed her shoulders. Jerking her against him, he kissed her.

Tongues collided. Teeth hit. Lips crushed. This kiss was churning, churning and as violent as the sea in the distance. And each second that passed, each second he held her to him and kissed her, he could feel the resistance draining out of her.

She tried to act so tough. But it was so easy.

He released her. Her eyelids drifted open, and she gazed up at him. Yeah. He could see it in her eyes. The spacey gleam that told him she was his.

His. The very idea scared the shit out of him. Because the idea of Phoebe being his made something in his chest tighten with want. This woman. He did want her. He did want to own her.

And, in return, he wanted her to own him back.

Bad thoughts. He shook them away. *Don't think about that. Think about now. Sex. Fucking. Because in a few months this woman will hate you.*

His stomach turned at the thought. He ignored it.

He grabbed the blanket that he'd tossed near their stuff, whipped it out, and threw it on the ground where it landed in a large square in the sand.

In one fluid motion, he yanked Phoebe to her feet and pushed her down onto the blanket. He followed her down, covering her body with his.

Instinctively, she placed her palms on his chest as if to push him off. He didn't budge. Instead, he took her wrists in his hand and pulled her arms over her head.

"I thought you wanted to be a good girl for me, love."

She squirmed, but he restrained her by shoving his need between her legs and holding her hands tight.

She met his gaze. "I said I would if you could make me."

"Oh, I can make you, all right. You're mine."

She just stared at him.

As soon as he spoke the words, he wanted to kick himself. "You're mine tonight, babe. Tonight."

She nodded. "Right. I knew what you meant."

Yeah, he could walk out on her business. But he had to make sure that he didn't walk out on her. Or her heart. He had to keep being a dick so she didn't develop feelings for him. At least she was a nice distraction. Even if she was too smart for her own good.

Nick knew that Phoebe understood the score. That was good. Sure, she felt guilty about having sexual relations with Nick—an employee—but Nick thought that was an advantage. It was his safety net.

Nick knew Phoebe would never want a guy like Nick, not in the long run. She needed someone reliable, someone who didn't abhor small towns. And even if he was enjoying Redbolt and the sea more than he'd like to admit, he still knew he was never going to be local enough for her.

She needed someone like Bear.

The thought sent his blood rushing through him like boiling water, and he tried to turn off the heat. Instead, he focused on now. The present. Phoebe. At least for now, she was his.

He reached into his pocket and pulled out a length of corded twine.

When she saw what was in his hand, she gave him one of those looks he was getting to know.

"Whatcha got there, Nick?"

He dangled the edge of the rope, letting the soft edge caress the skin under her arm. "You've never been bound before?"

She narrowed her gaze. "I try to reserve kitchen twine for Thanksgiving. You know, to truss a turkey."

Grinning, he placed a soft kiss on her lips. "Don't worry, baby. I won't eat you up. Unless, of course, you beg me to."

She struggled in his grasp, but he held tight. "You didn't answer the question." He kissed her again, and this time her arms relaxed in his grip. "Have. You. Ever. Been. Bound." He punctuated each word with a kiss.

Her hips moved beneath him, and he sank farther. His dick was hard, so hard it hurt to press against her. It hurt to feel the clothes separating them. It hurt to want her so fucking badly it made his chest constrict. It hurt to feel...

Anything.

And so he pulled her arms long and tight over her head. He kissed her. He ground his hard, hurting cock between her legs. He compartmentalized his brain so all he felt was the physical sensation of arousal. Nothing else.

That was something he could do. That was something he knew how to do. Fuck. And that was what he was doing. Fucking.

It was Phoebe. She was just a woman. A woman he wanted to fuck. It—*she*—was no different at all.

His hand still held her arms over her head as he placed his free hand on the button of her jeans. He popped open the first button.

"So, baby?" He undid another couple of buttons and pulled aside the waistband of her jeans. He skimmed his hands down from her waist, feeling the sharpness of her hip bones beneath soft skin.

"Nick?" she said, her voice breathy. "Do whatever you want to me. Take me." Her gaze was steady on his. "Fuck me."

"Yeah?" he said, his adrenaline pumping at her words.

"Yes. Take me. I'm yours."

And for the rest of the night, she was.

Chapter Twenty

Jesse entered the house and shut the door behind her. "Hello?" she said. But she could tell no one was home. Everything was quiet and dark. She turned on the hallway light and kicked off her worn sandals.

Looking down, she hitched a breath.

There they were.

Shiny, cherry-red, and so pretty . . .

Glancing over her shoulder, she leaned down and then gingerly picked up one of Sherry's red shoes.

With her index finger, Jesse caressed the red patent leather across the toe. It made her heartbeat speed up. A lot.

So pretty. So sophisticated. So shiny.

Something about just holding the beautiful pumps in her hand gave her a sense of satisfaction. And want. She wanted to wear these shoes.

Jesse knew the house was empty, but she glanced around anyway. Her pulse beat a nervous rhythm as she bent over and slipped the shoe onto her foot. Like Cinderella, it slid on perfectly. She put her foot on the floor and lifted the other foot to place her weight on the high-heeled foot. Wow. It was really uncomfortable.

The skirt she was wearing that day was floral printed and fell just below her knee. When she looked down at her leg, she could see the way the shoe made her calf look long and streamlined. She could see the allure of such a sexy piece of footwear.

It was obvious she really needed to try on the other pump. No one would ever know, and Jesse would always have the memory of knowing she'd actually worn a pair of shoes that probably cost more than she made in a week at the café.

And so, before she knew it, she was standing there in both of the red shoes. Wobbling to the front door, she peered through the window to make sure no one had pulled in. She knew they hadn't because she hadn't heard anything, but she was being paranoid.

Although she doubted Sherry would freak out if she caught her trying on her shoes, Jesse still thought it best to keep it a secret. After all, she didn't need her family thinking she was developing some sort of creepy shoe-stealing fetish.

But she really, really wanted to see what they looked like in a full-length mirror, and the only one was upstairs, in her room.

She looked up the staircase. She'd never noticed how steep and long it was before. But before she knew it, she was walking toward the first step, the bottom of the shoes making sharp clicking noises on the hardwood floor. Her ankle twisted, and she caught the banister before she fell.

Jesse's opinion of Sherry multiplied ten times. Any woman who could manage to maneuver daily in high heels like these had to possess some sort of special skill Jesse obviously didn't own. And if it was all about practice, Jesse had even more respect for any woman who'd spend that much time learning how to walk in torture for the sole purpose of looking sexy.

No, feeling sexy.

As Jesse made her way up the stairs, there was no denying, even in her clumsiness, that she felt a little bit sexy. She didn't think she'd ever experienced such a thing before. But it was pretty much impossible not to feel a little bit seductive when she walked with these beautiful, shiny, sophisticated pumps on her feet.

Jesse made it to her room. Slowly she entered and approached the mirror nailed to the wall near the closet.

Looking at her reflection, she couldn't help the little jolt of excitement she got from seeing how amazing the shoes looked on her. Jesse spun around, looking over her shoulder to gaze at the back image of her reflection.

Wow. Just wow. They may not be the most comfortable footwear in the world, but they were soooo worth it. Because the shoes were luscious, and the way they made her feel was so... feminine. Sexy. Confident.

All from a pair of shoes? Who knew?

She couldn't stop staring at them.

"Gorgeous, aren't they?"

Jesse whipped around and stumbled. She stopped herself from falling by catching herself on the post of her bed.

The words had come from Sherry, who was watching her. Leaning against the doorway, her arms were crossed over her chest.

Jesse felt her face burn from embarrassment. "Oh my God," she said, reaching down to take off the shoes. "I'm so sorry."

Sherry pushed herself off the doorframe and entered the room. She waved a hand dismissively at Jesse and smiled. "No worries. Do they fit?"

"Oh, I was just…" Jesse's face burned like a roasted tomato. "But I shouldn't have tried them, I know. But they were in the hallway, and I've never worn anything like them before, and I was going to put them right back. I swear."

"Honey, don't worry about it! At home I share shoes with my girlfriends all the time. You never answered me. Do they fit?"

"Um, yes."

"That's great! We're the same size! I let all my girlfriends borrow my shoes, so help yourself."

Jesse wasn't sure what she thought about Sherry referring to her as a girlfriend, but at least the woman didn't appear angry.

"Don't take them off unless you want to. They actually look cute with your outfit."

Slowly, Jesse straightened and checked out her reflection in the mirror again. Her skirt had red flowers, and she was wearing a gauzy white blouse. The shoes definitely were a lot more stylish than her outfit, but they certainly added a look of sophistication.

And she liked it.

"I actually got those in Paris. I was there meeting with some sommeliers, and I popped into this little shop in the Sixteenth District." Sherry closed her eyes as if remembering the taste of a magnificent crème brûlée. "You should have seen it. The shoes in that shop were so amazing. Orgasmic."

Jesse blushed at the phrase. She'd never had sex, but she knew what Sherry meant.

Jesse crossed the room and sat on the bed beside Sherry. "You've been to Paris?"

Sherry nodded. "Several times. It's such a wonderful city . . . so romantic and beautiful. It charms you."

Jesse wanted to hear more. She wanted to hear all about Paris. But she didn't want to ask. She didn't want to seem silly.

Sherry smiled. "Every girl should go to Paris, at least once."

"Yeah." Jesse slipped off the beautiful shoes. Immediately, she felt frumpy. "I bet it's amazing. I'm sure I'll never be able to go, though."

"Why not?"

"Why would I?"

"Don't you want to see the world?"

"Well, yeah, but . . ." The conversation was hitting a bit close to home. "My dad needs me here."

"Oh, I'm sure your dad would be just fine on his own if you wanted to see the world. And remember, you only live once. You're young! The world is your oyster. Take my advice. Travel while you still can."

"But you still travel and you're . . ." She was going to say "old" but realized that sounded offensive, so she ended with "not eighteen."

"I know. But things change as you get older. You get more responsibilities and less freedom."

"And you get stuck in places like Redbolt instead of Paris?" Jesse couldn't help the little bite of defensiveness in her voice.

But Sherry just tilted her head and gave her a soft look. "I'll tell you a secret."

"What?"

"A long time ago, I was married."

"Really? What happened?"

Sherry shrugged. "I was young. I married my high school sweetheart, and before I knew it, I was thirty-two. And very, very unhappy."

"Why?" Jesse didn't want to pry, but she found everything about Sherry fascinating.

"Well, it turned out my high school sweetheart was a cheating bastard, but that really wasn't the problem."

"Then what was it?"

"He wanted a housewife. And I was happy doing that, and I love my son more than anything. When my son got older I wanted to travel, to see the world. I wanted to be able to buy shoes like those." She pointed to the pumps now resting on the floor. "I wanted to know I made the money myself to do so. I just wanted more." She took a deep breath and exhaled. "So, when I discovered he'd been screwing around behind my back, I took it as an opportunity to start my life over."

"What did you do?"

"Well, I've always loved wine. So I went to school, learned all there was to know, got a job in the wine industry, and now I'm loving every minute of my life."

"Wow. That's a great story."

"Yes. I wouldn't change a thing about my life."

Must be nice, Jesse thought, then quickly pushed the pessimistic notion out of her brain. Jesse did have a great life. She had nothing to complain about.

"But," Sherry continued, "it took a lot of work to get where I am today. Do you believe in destiny, Jesse?"

"Um, sure. I think so. Do you?"

"A little. But I also believe you control your own destiny. And at the end of the day, you need to make yourself happy. And you're the only one who can do that."

"What makes you think I'm not happy?" Jesse said.

"I'm not saying you're unhappy, honey. I just think it's a good idea for us all to ask ourselves that question every now and then."

"Well, I am happy. I like living here, and I'm sure Paris is lovely, but I'm needed here. With my family. And that makes me happy."

"I'm glad. Because Nick says you're a very talented chef-in-training, and you never know. One day the Green Leaf may just need someone like yourself."

Jesse jerked back. "W-what? What do you mean?"

Sherry stood. "I'm just saying if you like it here, and if you end up being as good a chef as Nick says you have the potential to be, and if family is what makes you happy—well, then, maybe one day heading the kitchen of your family restaurant would be a dream come true for you."

Jesse wasn't really sure what she was going to do when she grew up, but being head chef of thc Green Leaf had never entered her mind.

In fact, the very idea made her cringe a little inside.

Which was ironic, because based on everything Jesse wanted to believe, Sherry's words should have brought her great joy.

Instead, Jesse felt like her throat was closing in and she was being suffocated.

"Um, thanks for letting me try on your shoes, Sherry."

"Help yourself, Jesse. You know where my room is."

Wringing her hands, Jesse nodded. Suddenly she felt as if her entire life had just flashed before her eyes.

Chapter Twenty-One

How are those delicious lumps of death coming along?"

Phoebe didn't look up from the batch of brownies she'd just taken out of the oven. The cook-off was coming up fast—one week away to be exact, and Phoebe thought she was finally making some progress. The brownies were actually starting to resemble those that her aunt and uncle used to make. A small resemblance, but there none-theless.

With a bit more practice, she just might have a chance.

"My offer for help is still on, you know."

"Thanks, but no." She wanted—needed—to do this on her own. If she could do this, it would mean she was a suc-cess, that she could effectively carry on the legacy her family had left her. And she needed to prove it all by herself.

"So," Nick said, slicing an onion with quick, sharp slices of his big knife, "tell me more about this cook-off thing."

"It's a tradition," she said. "The county has been hold-ing it for over twenty years. For ten of those years, my aunt and uncle have won the dessert category with their delicious brownies. Every year. They've become some-what legendary."

"And you're trying to carry on the tradition."

"Not trying. Succeeding." She cut a slice through the brownies in the pan. The knife slid through nice and smoothly. She smiled. Yes, she was definitely making progress.

Nick sauntered over and picked up the old, tattered piece of paper on which the recipe had been handwritten by her aunt. Studying it, he said, "Huh."

Phoebe looked up. "What?"

"These measurements are...interesting."

"Well, that's what makes them special."

"Yeah, but—"

She held up the knife. "I don't want to hear any 'buts' out of you. I don't want your opinion, and I don't need your help."

He was still staring at the piece of paper. "You sure?"

"Absolutely."

He dropped the paper onto the counter. "As you wish." He walked behind her, and she felt his hand on the base of her spine. The result of which was an electric thrill that went straight up her back.

"What are you doing?"

"Nothing." But he was moving her hair away to kiss that place on the back of her neck...the place that, when he put his lips there, made her brain go a little bit fuzzy.

"Stop," she said. But her protest sounded weak.

"No. I like the way you smell." And then she felt his tongue on her skin, licking just under her ear. "You have a little chocolate on you. Just thought I'd get it off."

"Thank you."

His lips lingered a little too long on her skin before he whispered, "Welcome, love," and walked away.

It wasn't until he left the kitchen that she allowed herself to smile with pleasure.

"How are things going with Phoebe?"

Nick picked a pack of cigarettes off the arm of the porch chair and glanced toward Sherry. Funny, it was the same pack he'd purchased several days ago. He used to buy one about every day. Why had this box of smokes lasted so long?

It was exactly one week since that night at the beach with the oysters and sex that churned like the crashing waves of the ocean.

Every time he thought about that brilliant night, he got hard and broke out in a cold sweat. And so he tried not to think about it. But every time he saw Phoebe, he'd barely been able to control himself. And sometimes he hadn't been able to at all. The storage room was becoming quite familiar.

Today the restaurant was closed, and it was Nick's day off. He hadn't seen Phoebe all day, and she hadn't called him. He hadn't called her. There was no reason to.

So why did he feel as if there was something missing that day?

Sherry snapped her fingers in front of his face. "Earth to Nick. I asked you a question. How are things with Phoebe?"

"Things with Phoebe?" he said. "Fine. Why do you ask?"

Sherry took a sip from the glass of red wine she held in her hand. "I was just wondering."

"There's nothing to wonder about. She's my boss. I do my job."

Sherry laughed. "I don't think that's all you're doing."

"What are you talking about?"

"Oh, come on, Nick. I know you."

"Yeah?"

"Of course I do. Are you really going to try to tell me you aren't fucking Phoebe Mayle?"

"What makes you think that?"

"The fact that every time she's in the room, you look like a dog in heat."

"How can I be a dog in heat? I have a penis, not a vagina." He took a drink of tequila. "I'd have to be a woman to look like a dog in heat."

"Okay, you got me there. Fine. Whenever you see her, you look like a man with a big hard-on for his boss. Furthermore, you get this puppy-dog look in your eyes."

"What's with all the dog analogies?"

"I can't help it if you look like a lovesick puppy whenever she's in the room."

He nearly choked on his tequila. "What the hell are you talking about?"

She crossed her legs. As usual, the woman was dressed impeccably. She'd worked that day and was still in her dress clothes. He didn't know how she managed it, but Sherry could pull off a miniskirt and high heels and still look classy.

"If you think I'm horny," he said, taking a drag from his cigarette, "maybe I should just fuck you." He exhaled a breath of smoke.

A loud guffaw escaped her mouth. "You already tried that."

"Obviously not hard enough. Hey, speaking of which, what's up with you and Steve?"

"Don't try to avoid the question."

"I'm not. I'm just wondering. What's he got that I don't have?"

She pretended to think about it. "Let's see. Manners, a nice personality, respect toward women, a connoisseur's taste in wine."

"Hey, I have that, too."

Her eyes actually turned a bit dreamy. "Not like him." Then her voice rose a pitch. "I don't think I've met anyone outside France who has a palate like his. He can tell you the exact acre where any of these local wines come from. I haven't seen anything like it outside the Loire Valley."

"Impressive."

"Yes, and he's very sweet."

"Good. I'm glad you like him. But, aside from his amazing ability to decipher geographic tannins, what do you like about him? Is he special or is this just a tryst?"

She paused, and Nick was surprised. She seemed to be actually considering the question. In all the years he'd known Sherry, she'd been like him. She'd wanted to have fun, to be herself, to live without the restraints of having a partner. He realized he kind of thought of her as a soul mate that way. Two of a kind. And a kind of panic washed over him at the thought that maybe he'd been wrong. If Sherry could actually fall for a guy, and be serious about it...where did that leave Nick?

"So?" he prompted. "You actually like this guy?"

Slowly she nodded and then finally said, "Yeah. I really do."

"But why?" And this time he heard the wonderment in his own voice.

"What can I say? He likes me."

He laughed, and it sounded a lot more bitter than he would have liked. "He likes you? Sherry, a lot of guys like you. A whole hell of a lot. And you're getting all mushy over some hick from Nowhere, California?"

"Don't call him that. Did you know he went to Stanford?"

"So?"

"So he's not a hick."

"He owns a hardware store."

"And what's wrong with that, Nick?" She turned to face him. "What's wrong with not living in Los Angeles? What's wrong with not worrying about where the next big party is? Or enjoying life in all its simplicity?"

"Is that what you want, Sherry? To leave L.A. and live in Hicksville?" He took a deep drag from his forgotten cigarette. "You've only been here a little while. How can you think like that?"

"Oh, hang on there! I'm not saying I'm up and going to move. I love Southern California."

"Then I don't get it. Why are you going on about Steve if you're just going to leave here?"

"Love is strange that way. Love makes things work."

"Love?" he asked incredulously. "You're telling me you're in love."

She gave a small shrug; he knew she'd picked up that habit in France. "I don't know. All I know is that when I'm with Steve, I feel..."

"Bored?"

"Safe. He's a lot more worldly than you might think."

"Is that so?"

"He was in the Peace Corps. Lived in Bolivia for many

years. Lived on a boat. Rode a motorcycle around Colombia."

Nick had to admit he was surprised. He never would have thought Steve had left Humboldt County, and those other things were actually impressive. In fact, the more time he spent in this seemingly backwoods place, the more Nick discovered the people weren't as backwoods as they seemed. Truth be told, he'd encountered some of the most cultured and educated people here he'd met in a long time.

Like Andrew, who owned the movie theater. It was ten years ago that Irish Andrew had come through Redbolt on a backpacking trip. Andrew had been an actor back in Dublin, and now he was here, running the film projector for whatever movies he thought the community ought to see. And Nick was actually impressed at what he brought into town. Most were Sundance winners or arthouse flicks Nick would have thought were never viewed outside Hollywood or New York.

So when Sherry was talking about Steve's worldly experience and his Stanford education, Nick really wasn't as surprised as he would have been when he'd first arrived. Actually, nothing about this place surprised him anymore. Funny, that.

"You never answered my question, Sherry. Lots of guys like you. So why Steve?"

"Because he likes *me*." She pointed to her chest. "He doesn't care that I used to be married to John McDavid, owner of the L.A. Spartans baseball team. We talk about wine and art and France and the vineyards in Chile. We talk. He likes me, and I like him, too."

Nick grunted. "I'm smart, and I liked you."

"You know we would never work, Nick."

"I don't want things to work. I just want to get laid."

"Stop acting like a prick."

"That's me. Nick the Prick."

"Shut up. You're not a prick. You just played one on TV."

He studied her face for a few moments. She was probably one of the most attractive women he'd ever seen. And that was saying a lot considering the array of beautiful ladies he'd had access to in L.A.

Had access to. Past tense. But now he couldn't think of a single woman who was more beautiful to him than Phoebe.

You bloody moron. Get those thoughts out of your head.

He was silent for a moment. Then, "Seriously, Sherry. Why don't you think things would ever work between us?"

Their being together should work, he thought. In theory, they should make a great couple. Sherry got his sense of humor. She was gorgeous. She put up with his shit. They both liked food and wine. On the surface, they would be perfect together.

With a blank expression, she stared at him. "What the fuck are you talking about?"

"I'm serious. We have a lot in common. You're gorgeous. We get along. Why don't we ever give things a go?"

"Oh, holy shit." She leaned back in her chair and sipped more wine. "Holy effing shit."

"What?"

"You stupid fucking moron."

"Hey," he said, somewhat affronted. "No need to get nasty."

"You realize what you're doing, right?"

"Oh, God. You're going to go off on one of your psychoanalyzing rants, aren't you?" He stubbed out what remained of the cigarette and pushed himself to his feet. "I'm gonna need more tequila for this."

"Bring back the bottle of wine, too."

"Yes, mistress." He took his time getting the drinks. He hated it when Sherry gave him one of her lectures. She was always so...right.

He could drag out the minor task only so long before he finally went back to the porch. After refilling Sherry's wineglass, he took his seat and swallowed a gulp of tequila.

"Proceed with the sermon, ma'am."

"I shall."

"Fine."

"What's with all this talk about you and me?"

"I thought this was a lecture. Not question-and-answer time."

"It's both, Mr. Avalon."

"What was the question again? You talk so much you lost me."

She sighed and looked at him as if he were an annoying student. "Why did you ask why we"—she waved her hand between the two of them—"never got together?"

He shrugged. "I don't know. It just popped into my head that we would work well together."

"Right. Now I remember why I called you a fucking idiot."

"I believe you said 'moron.'"

"Either label is appropriate. First of all, since when does Nick Avalon want a relationship with anyone?"

"Are you saying I'm incapable of having a relationship?"

"No. I'm saying you run away from commitment as if the very idea were an exploding grease fire."

He shrugged. "Maybe I've changed."

"I see that."

He lit another cigarette. "You're driving me crazy."

"You're driving yourself crazy."

Exhaling, he said, "No. I'm pretty sure it's you that's making me want to stab sharp objects into my ears."

She uncrossed her legs and repositioned herself to face him. "The only reason you brought up such an insane subject is because you're scared."

"Scared of what? I can't wait to hear this one."

"Scared because I think you like—like, *really* like—Phoebe."

He jerked back as if she'd tried to coldcock him. "What are you talking about?"

"It's simple. You like her. You like her more than any woman you've known in a long time. You can't control how much you like her. So that scares you. And what's an easy way to cut off the possibility of liking a woman—maybe even *loving* her? To run the very opposite direction and ask *someone else* if they would like to attempt a relationship together."

He just stared at her. Crickets chirped. A truck rumbling down the road echoed in the night air. More crickets chirped.

Finally he shook his head. "You're crazy."

"So are you."

"That's utterly ridiculous."

She raised her glass as if making a toast. "So are you."

"I'll admit I like Phoebe. She's smart, funny, and attractive. I admire her."

"Admire? That's a big word coming from Nick Avalon. I thought the only person you admired was yourself."

"Shut up and listen, you cheeky bitch."

"Listening."

"Stop reading so much into it. I fuck her sometimes. She likes it. I like it. That's it."

"Right."

"And besides, even if I did like her, I'm still getting the fuck out of here sometime in the near future."

"Yeah. About that."

"What?"

"Have you given Phoebe any indication that you don't plan on staying here for at least the agreed-upon time?"

He took another drag from his cigarette and finished off what was left of his tequila. "No."

"I thought not."

"Are you still planning on leaving?"

"If I get a better offer, hell, yes."

She shrugged.

"What?"

"Nothing."

"Spill it, woman."

"Fine. It's just that maybe you should reconsider your big plan to get back to L.A."

"Why would I do that?"

She pretended to think for a second. "Um. Maybe because you're happy here?"

"I am not." But even he had to admit the words sounded hollow and not very convincing. "I hate it here. I never needed to know how to cook ovo-lacto-pesco anything." He looked into the trees. "The air is so clean it makes me crazy. And furthermore, there's absolutely no nightlife whatsoever."

"That's not true. Have you been to Joe's?"

"Who's Joe?"

"It's not a person. It's a bar. Everyone goes there."

"You've been here less than a week. How do you know where everyone goes?"

"Because I make an effort to actually get to know the people I'm working with. I've been there twice already. It's fun."

"Whatever. I don't really consider some Podunk bar nightlife."

Sherry put down her glass and stood. "We're going."

"What?"

She took the glass of tequila out of his hand and placed it on the table between the chairs. "Come on. We're going to Joe's."

"I'd rather be poked in the eye with a sharp stick."

She grabbed his hand and tugged. "If you go in with your usual attitude, that might be in your future."

Chapter Twenty-Two

Hello, beautiful."

Phoebe looked up from her pint of beer. "Bear?" She jumped off her barstool and fell into the arms of her childhood friend and former fiancé. His hug was tight, and his flannel shirt was warm against her face.

He smelled like...mud. Not spices or Nick.

Good Lord. She pulled back. "Oh my God!" She scanned his face. His blond hair was shaggy, and he had light stubble on his face just like always. "What are you doing here?"

He ordered a beer and turned back to her. "I just returned from South America. My latest Food for the World stint was in Africa. What an amazing place."

Staring at him, she shook her head. "Wow. Were you working on local agricultural development again?"

Nodding, he brought the pint to his mouth. "Yup. It was amazing, but I always love coming home."

She stared at him, and for the first time since she'd known him, she realized she felt no romantic feelings for him whatsoever. He was a friend. Her first love, but now he was just...Bear.

He'd acquired that nickname back in high school when, over one summer, he'd shot up two feet and grown the facial hair he still sported. He'd grown his hair long, and to this day, he wore it in a shaggy cut hanging just under his strong jaw.

But it wasn't just his looks that had attracted Phoebe to the man. He'd always had an adventurous streak she envied. He was the boy who'd jump off the highest cliffs into the ocean. The first boy who'd jump into the crashing waves with his surfboard. He was the guy who joined Green Peace the minute he turned eighteen and headed for some country none of the rest of their community had ever heard of.

Bear still had a house in Redbolt, though. And every so often, he'd pop back into town between his missions.

He placed a hand on her shoulder. "It's good to see you, Phoebe."

Smiling, she touched his hand. "You, too. We miss you around here."

"You know this will always be my home." He leaned a denim-clad hip against the bar. "So. How's your life? How's the café?"

She rolled her eyes. "Hectic as usual. But I hired a chef who is actually turning out great."

"Yeah?"

She nodded. "It was a bit touch-and-go at first, but he really seems to be working out." She felt her face starting to heat. Why was it she couldn't think about stupid Nick Avalon without blushing?

"I'm glad you found some good help, Phoebe. You always try to do everything on your own. You always have been that way."

"Are you saying I'm a control freak?" She laughed. Bear had always said that.

"You know it," he said with a smile. "But an adorable control freak."

She lightly punched his arm. He was such a flirt. But it was just in good fun, even if they had been engaged.

So why now, when she looked up and saw him staring at her, did it feel different?

"You look good, Pheebs," he said.

Out of the blue, a flash of nerves settled in her belly. She'd never been nervous around Bear before. Why now?

She was being silly. Bear would never actually be flirting with her. They were done. He'd never be happy here, with her.

Right?

Hoping it would calm her nerves, she took a gulp of her cold beer.

She looked up. "Thanks. You look good, too."

It was then she realized he was standing close to her. Just a little too close. Just enough to wonder if he was, indeed, actually flirting with her.

"Bear, are you flirting with me?"

He chuckled. "Um, yeah. In case you haven't noticed, I always flirt with you."

"Well, that's just . . . that's just messing around."

His expression became more serious. "Maybe for you it is."

"Are you high?" she asked.

There was that deep chuckle of his again. "No. Phoebe, I've always told you. You're the perfect woman."

"As a joke." Even if it wasn't a joke, she hadn't been perfect enough to make him want to stay here. And she respected that about him.

"I was never joking."

"But we wanted different things." She shook her head. "Oh my God, what are we talking about?" Her head was spinning. She leaned back on her barstool. "Okay. What is going on here?"

"Hell, Phoebe. For such a smart woman, you can be really obtuse sometimes."

"Hey! I take offense at that."

"I just miss you. A lot."

"Do you really expect me to believe that?" She laughed. "I never hear from you. You just show up and don't even tell me when you're coming. I see you about once a year at best, and now you pop up in a bar, and I'm supposed to buy what you're saying?"

But her pulse was racing at the thought. Deep down, this was what she'd always wanted. She'd wanted Bear to want her. To stay with her. If she thought deeply enough, she would probably even say that, on some subconscious level, the reason she'd been so antirelationship was because she held out a secret hope that Bear would one day settle down and come home to her.

And now he had just appeared and was making strange suggestions, and everything just seemed off.

He tilted his beer mug to his lips, took a slow swallow, and set it back on the bar. Then he casually glanced at her, his green eyes as serious as a heart attack. "No. I don't expect you to believe me."

Cue *Twilight Zone* theme song.

She shook her head. "Now I know you're messing with me. You're not making any sense."

"I'm making all kinds of sense. Listen, all I'm asking is if maybe you'll let me take you out sometime. Maybe we can catch up. Talk about the old days. I'll admit it,

Phoebe. I've never stopped thinking about you. And I've always wondered if I made the right decision when we broke off our engagement."

She was speechless. She flapped her mouth a few times, but no words came out.

"And every time I come back to Redbolt I flirt with you. I send you these signals that you never seem to pick up on."

"You are seriously tripping me out, Bear." Freezing, she narrowed her gaze at him. "Do you want a mistress or something when you come back to town?" She laughed. Loudly. "'Cause I'm *so* not down with that."

"No, I don't want a mistress."

"Then...then..." She didn't understand anything that was going on.

He shrugged, and his eyes held a glint of humor. "It's kinda fun to see you flustered. Adds to your charm."

"Shut up!"

"Make me."

"You are such a rascal, Bear. You really are."

"True. But I really do like you, Pheebs. Always have. In all my travels, I've never met anyone quite like you."

"I—I like you, too." But she wasn't sure in what capacity. If Bear had been talking to her like this a year or two ago, she'd probably have been throwing a party in her head. But for some reason, she was thinking about Nick.

Thinking about her surly, conceited, talented chef who was the exact opposite of Bear.

There was something seriously wrong with her.

If she was getting this right, Bear—her former fiancé and man of her dreams, a man she admired from the bottom of her core for his moral values, his work ethic, his adventurous personality, his honesty, and, let's face it, his amazing ass—was once more showing interest in her and all she could think about was Nick?

She needed a hole in the head. Stat.

Bear leaned in close to her ear. That earthy smell of his wafted into her nose. It wasn't a bad smell. She should have liked it.

But no. It wasn't Nick's scent.

Bear's words were warm and moist on her skin. "So what do you say, Pheebs? You wanna go make out in my truck?"

Luckily, she didn't have to answer. At that moment, a group of their old friends surrounded them, attacking Bear with questions and hugs.

Still, as he mingled with the group, his gaze kept flicking back to hers.

She ordered another beer.

Monday nights at Joe's were always busy. Because so many of the businesses were closed that particular day of the week, the locals tended to end up at the bar. The place had been crowded earlier. Now it was obvious word had spread that Bear was back in town. The locals tended to treat him like some sort of celebrity, and soon Joe's was packed, and Bear had a large group surrounding him, hammering him for more stories of his adventures.

Every time Phoebe looked at him, he met her gaze.

"I always thought you two would get back together."

Glancing beside her, she saw Steve had arrived. She gave him a startled look. "What are you doing here?"

He tried to look nonchalant. "Oh, I just thought I'd come out for a beer."

She crinkled her brow. "Really?"

"Why wouldn't I come out?"

"Um, because I haven't seen you step foot in this place since—" *Since Judy died.* The words stilled on her tongue. "You just don't normally come out here at night."

Shrugging, she watched him try to look casual as he scanned the crowded bar.

"Oh, for heaven's sake," she said.

"What?"

"By any chance are you looking for a certain blonde wine distributor?"

He jerked back as if she'd slammed him in the face. And he wasn't a good actor. "What? Me? Of course not!"

"Uh-huh."

But then his entire expression lit up. She followed his gaze to see Sherry walking in the front door. And trailing behind her was a very disagreeable-looking tall man with spiky black hair.

Great. What was *Nick* doing here?

And yet her body heated, and her heart skipped at the sight of him.

It hadn't done that when she'd seen Bear. Or even when he'd gotten close to her.

She stamped her foot. Damn, damn, *damn*. She *knew* she never should have started having sex with Nick. That's all this was. Her body was confused. It thought it should want Nick, when really, it should want the reliable choice. Bear.

Yeah, Bear the reliable one, who'd broken your engagement so he could plant seeds in Nigeria. Whatever. Any way you looked at it, it was still illogical. She shouldn't be excited to see Nick, whom she saw every day, when Bear had popped up and apparently wanted to take her on a date.

So what the fuck? Why did her heartbeat just jack up several notches because Nick had entered the room?

Of course, he immediately nailed her with his annoying blue-eyed stare.

Don't come over here, don't come over here, don't come over here...

But her silent mantra went unheeded. Of course, maneuvering through the crowd, he made a beeline straight for her.

She couldn't help it. Every step he took, every inch he came closer to her, her pulse went a little more crazy. And when he was there, standing right in front of her, she could barely contain her jittery hands.

Why? Why did he have this effect on her?

"What are you doing here?" she asked him.

He glanced disdainfully around the crowded bar. "Sherry dragged me here."

"Right. I'm sure you'd rather be at some trendy nightclub, but alas, this little pub is pretty much all we have here in Redbolt." She lifted her mug and took a deep gulp. "Mmm. Beer. I bet the bartender can make you something fancy if you like, though. Maybe an appletini?"

He gave her one last snarly look before ordering a shot of tequila.

"I see you like variety in what you drink," she said sarcastically.

His stare was chock-full of sex. "I like variety, baby. But I also like plain ol' tequila. Sometimes a guy likes something he can rely on."

"Yeah. So does a woman." And she gave him a good once-over to let him know he wasn't the kind of person to be relied upon.

But that wasn't quite true. In her entire life, she'd never been as able to rely on anyone as she had with Nick when it came to one thing. Sex.

It was good. So damn good just being close to him made her sex tingle. She wanted him. She wanted him like she'd never wanted another man in her entire life. Even with Bear—her dream man—standing a few feet away, her body responded to only Nick.

She hated that about Nick.

Sex. It seemed to pulse between them like an electric current. She wondered if he felt it as strongly as she did. She wondered if she was crazy. She wondered if she was the only one thinking about variety. Because in the short time she'd known Nick, she'd experienced nothing but variety. In the kitchen, in the stockroom, on the beach, in the restaurant, in the forest.

Yeah, he was all about variety. She wondered when he'd be tired of her and move on to the next flavor of the month.

"Pheebs. Your mug is empty. Can I buy you another one?" The offer came from Bear, who had approached them and taken the barstool next to Phoebe.

"I'd like that. Thank you, Bear."

Of course, Nick hadn't offered to buy her a drink. That was because he was a selfish, narcissistic, thoughtless prick. She had absolutely no idea why she was attracted to him.

Unlike Bear. Who was nice, handsome, and did his part to make the world a better place. Bear, who thought to buy a girl a drink. Bear, who, apparently, had been trying to hit on her earlier.

"So, Pheebs. Is this your new chef?"

She glanced to Bear and then to Nick. "Oh. I'm so sorry. Yes, Bear, this is Nick Avalon. He's our new chef. He's come all the way from L.A. to delight us with his superior knowledge. Nick, this is Bear. I've known him for twenty years, and he's just come back from a stint in South America. He's part of the Food Core. They help developing countries use their natural resources to end world hunger."

"I know who they are," Nick bit out.

Bear held out his hand, but Nick ignored it and took a sip from his glass of tequila. Instead he gave Bear a short nod. "Nice to make your acquaintance."

"You're British?" Bear asked.

"Nothing gets past you, mate."

Phoebe kicked Nick's knee. "Why are you being such a prick?"

He rubbed the spot on his leg where she'd just kicked him. "What? I'm being myself."

"Good point."

"Okay," Bear said, obviously trying to diffuse the tone of the conversation. "So. What part of England are you from?"

"You probably wouldn't know it."

"I might. I lived in the UK for almost five years."

"Oh?"

Bear nodded. "Sure did. I worked for UNICEF Europe awhile."

"Interesting." But Nick wasn't even looking at Bear. He was looking into his glass.

What was Nick's effing problem?

She looked at Bear and smiled. "How long are you in town for this time?"

"Just a few days. But actually, I'm going to be returning soon. Permanently."

"What?" Phoebe said. "Really?"

Bear nodded. "Yup. I've decided it's time to put some energy into my hometown. Get more involved in my local community."

When he said the phrase "get more involved in my local community," his gaze was pointed directly at her.

Phoebe jumped off her stool to give Bear a big hug. "Oh my God! I am so happy to hear you're moving home."

He hugged her back and said quietly into her hair, "I really missed you, Pheebs."

She swore she heard Nick whisper "*Pheebs*" under his breath in a sarcastic tone, but she ignored it.

Smiling at Bear, she said, "I missed you, too. And it's wonderful news that you're coming back."

"I hope we can spend some time together. You know, hang out sometime. I meant what I said earlier."

She pulled back and met his gaze. "I'd like that. Very much."

"Oh, why don't you two just get a room?"

They both turned to Nick, who was scowling at them.

"Why do you have such a bee in your bonnet tonight, Nick?" Phoebe asked.

"I told you. I'm just being me."

"Well, *you* need to not talk to your *boss* that way," Phoebe said. "Or anyone, for that matter."

"Oh, you're pulling out the boss card now? That's brilliant."

She met his gaze. A public fight with Nick was the last thing she needed. She grabbed her belongings and smiled at Bear. "Would you excuse me? I think it's time for me to head home."

"Sure thing. Call you later?"

She could have sworn she heard Nick mimic Bear under his breath again, but she ignored him.

"Please do." She gave him a kiss on the cheek. "I'll talk to you soon."

Then she turned and grabbed Nick's arm. "Come with me." She didn't give him a choice. Anger fueled her strength, and she yanked him along behind her.

Phoebe burst outside. They were meant to get some unseasonably heavy rain over the next few days, and the portending cold, damp breeze hit her in the face.

But she was too angry to care about the chilly air.

Still dragging Nick by the arm, she marched across the parking lot to her car. She needed some privacy, and, at the moment, there was no one outside.

She released him and crossed her arms over her chest. Staring at him, she said, "What is wrong with you?"

He pulled a pack of Marlboros out of his pocket. Using his teeth, he extracted a cigarette from the pack.

Everything he did was measured. Deliberate. Controlled. She hated it, but it mesmerized her. Even now, just watching the easy way he flipped his lighter closed and replaced it in his pocket caught her attention. Because she knew what it was like. Knew what it was like to have all those traits focused on her.

Her legs trembled at the thought.

"I have no idea what you're talking about," he said.

"You were a total jerk back there inside the bar."

"Was I?"

"You know damn well you were. Why?"

He shrugged nonchalantly. "I wasn't aware I did anything out of the ordinary."

"You didn't even shake Bear's hand."

"Sorry. Back in the UK, it's not that big of a deal. Just ask your friend. He should be able to tell you, considering he's such a cultural expert."

"You're full of shit." She was so angry that she was starting to shake. "You were being even more of an ass than usual."

"Sorry. I didn't mean to offend...what was his name again? Tiger? Horse?"

"You know what his name is."

"Want me to go back and apologize?"

"No. I want you to stop embarrassing me in front of my friends."

Now his expression tightened. He drew in a deep drag from his cigarette and exhaled. "I'm sorry. I guess I just don't know how to behave when I see the woman I'm fucking picking up some guy."

That froze her. She stood there, silent. Processing what he'd said.

Then she finally leaned back against her car just to stare at him. "That's what this is about? You're jealous?"

But he scoffed. "Jealous? No fucking way."

"Then what did you mean?"

He was smoking faster now. "Nothing. Forget I said anything."

"You are." She couldn't help it. She giggled. "You are so jealous."

"I'm not. I just think that guy looks like a fucking moron. I thought you had higher standards."

"Hey, don't you dare say anything negative about Bear. He's a wonderful person. I've known him my entire life."

"He wants to fuck you."

"That is not true." But hadn't Bear basically said the same thing? Still, she had doubts that he was serious. "You're wrong."

"Don't be an imbecile."

"I'm hardly an imbecile. That's more your style."

"Sometimes. But trust me on this one. That guy is all over you."

"If he is, so what? What does it matter to you?" Her heart was pounding in her throat. What did she want him to say? That he wanted her and only her?

Even if the sex was good—okay, *fine*, it was phenomenal—that was all there would ever be between Phoebe and Nick. Good sex was great, but it certainly wasn't something to base a relationship on.

And yet...she had to admit there was this really small part of her that was seeing glimpses of what it might be like if Nick could get rid of his major attitude problem. She couldn't help but remember those moments where there had been something perfect in their encounters. And each time that occurred, the more she speculated: What if?

But he was never going to be happy here. No matter what happened between the two of them, she loved where she lived and Nick hated it here. End of story.

So should she let herself keep falling for him? Or end things before her heart was broken?

This situation was just getting worse and worse. She took a deep breath and prepared to set things straight. "Nick. You work for me. We have sex. That's it."

"I know that. What? Do you think I'm asking you to marry me or something? That's the last fucking thing I need in my life. I don't want any sort of relationship. With anyone."

"Then why do you care if Bear has feelings for me?"

"So you admit he has feelings for you."

"No! I didn't say that. What I asked was why it would possibly matter to you." Her heart was speed-racing. What did she want him to say? She already knew what she wanted.

Right?

He threw down his cigarette and stomped on it. The sound of his shoe smashing the gravel was like a loud boom in the silence between them.

Finally he looked at her. "I can't help it. I want you."

"Don't sound so excited about it," she said, trying not to sound immature and girlish.

He came at her. "Fuck," he said just before grabbing her shoulders. "I *want* you."

And she felt it, pulsing between them. Magnetic. It was always like that.

"I want you, too." What the hell was she saying? All she knew was that her skin was tingling, her breasts were throbbing, and her pussy was aching. And it was because this man was touching her.

"I hate you," she said just before bringing his mouth to hers.

She kissed him. He pressed his body against hers, smashing her between his heart and the cold metal of the car.

"I hate you, too," he said.

But she had to smile against his lips. She'd heard the

expression before, but she'd never felt it to be so true as it was at that moment: There's a fine line between love and hate.

That had to be it. It was wrong, it was dangerous, and it was going to end badly. But there was no other explanation for any of it. No explanation for this intense, mind-blowing response she had whenever she was around Nick Avalon.

All those things she hated about him—none of them mattered. Yes, sometimes she hated him. But, she thought as she nuzzled her head against his chest and breathed in the unique scent that was him, she had to admit she was walking that line. Love and hate.

She loved Nick.

Chapter Twenty-Three

Jesse thought she'd hidden all the evidence.

Her dad was out at Joe's. Based on his recent behavior, she assumed he'd gone because Sherry was there. Her dad seemed smitten with the blonde. And Jesse had to admit, she'd become quite fond of the woman as well.

She didn't want to like her. After all, she knew Sherry was here only temporarily, and when the sophisticated woman returned to Southern California, Jesse's dad would go back to that dignified, quiet sadness she'd been living with for so long.

But none of that was Sherry's fault, was it? From what Jesse could tell, Sherry hadn't led her dad to believe for one minute that she was here for the long term. And Jesse's dad wasn't stupid; he was smart enough to make his own choices. And, right now, he was choosing to be happy, and Jesse could understand that.

More than anything, she wanted her dad to be happy.

And Phoebe, too. Chances were that one day Phoebe would actually find a man who could handle her, and she would get married and move out of the house.

And now that Sherry had dropped the idea of the

Green Leaf being eventually handed down to Jesse, she felt even more chained to this place.

Not that she didn't love the café—she did. It was just that, ideally, she wanted to experience what it would be like, if only for a little while, to cook in another environment. To see more of the world. To window-shop for fabulous shoes.

But for now, at least, she had her home kitchen.

So now she placed the Julia Child cookbook that Nick had given her in her backpack. It blended along with her junior college textbooks. And then she gave one last glance around the kitchen, making sure there was no evidence of what she'd been doing while she'd had the house to herself.

Filet de boeuf, or filet of beef. She could practically hear Julia's voice as she'd read the description of the dish, a description Jesse could recite by heart.

. . . a magnificent recipe for an important dinner, and it is not a difficult one despite the luxury of its details . . .

Jesse whispered the words aloud. The very way Julia described food was luscious, like a dish personified through words. To Jesse it was a type of poetry, and it inspired her as much as preparing the food itself.

But sometimes Julia was wrong. This was the fifth time Jesse had attempted to prepare filet de boeuf, and this was only the first time Jesse had felt she'd succeeded. Despite what Chef Child said, the beef recipe was a tad difficult, or at least it was for Jesse.

She wasn't exactly a meat connoisseur, so what did she know? All she knew was that she'd made something that was delicious, and she'd loved doing it.

But there was something missing. She'd eaten her

meal all alone. What she really wanted was to cook for her friends. She wanted to share this joy of cooking with them. Because that's exactly how she felt when she'd been sautéing the carrots, turnips, and leeks with the meat. She'd felt such joy, such satisfaction. It had bubbled up inside her. She'd wanted to share that feeling with her closest family and friends.

Only her family was busy, and her friends? Jesse hated to admit it, but she didn't have a big interest in hanging out with them.

Her friends, the kids she'd grown up with, were all nice individuals. But it was always the same. Talking about high school antics and who was dating whom. And while Jesse didn't want to cook for someone just to be appreciated, she did admit she wanted someone to share the enjoyment. And she didn't know anyone outside her own family who could experience that with her.

Instead she'd eaten alone. But that was okay.

Standing, she took a deep breath and put her hands on her hips. That was when she realized she was wearing a dirty apron over her loose dress. *Damn it!* Reaching behind her neck, she untied the apron strings, pulled it off her body, and stuffed it into her backpack. Then she zipped the bag and ran up to her room.

She threw herself on her bed and stared at the ceiling. *And wondered.*

If she were to actually go to cooking school, which she wasn't going to do, she would need to know everything there was to know about Paris. She'd been reading online about the city. She knew all the finest restaurants in every district, which neighborhoods had the best street markets, where to go for the most extensive array of cheese choices. Or *fromage*, as they say in French.

She wanted to taste *fromage* and even worse, foi gras.

Nick had slipped her a taste of the forbidden food one day. Jesse had thought she'd died and gone to heaven. It. Was. So. Good. Nick had made it himself, but he'd mentioned there was a place in Paris that had the most excellent foi gras in the entire world. A small place, he'd said. A place only a local would know.

Jesse wanted to visit that place.

She rolled her eyes at herself. Why was she torturing her brain this way? Why was she so obsessed with doing something she knew would never, ever happen?

It was one thing to be a tortured teenager. But she was eighteen, and this was ridiculous. She was an adult. She had responsibilities. She was happy, and her family needed her.

She could not run away.

She heard the sound of tires on the gravel driveway. Then the sound of the front door opening and hushed voices.

Her father's deep chuckle.

Sherry's tinkling laugh.

He was happy. Jesse loved seeing him happy. But it wouldn't last.

She listened to the footsteps coming up the stairs. More hushed voices. Then it was quiet, and she heard her father's door close. She heard Sherry in the bathroom, getting ready for bed.

And so Jesse put on her pajamas, shut off the lights, and went to bed herself.

Stupid, stupid, stupid.

Phoebe couldn't believe that she'd let Nick persuade

her to come back to his house. Of course, it hadn't been hard to do. A few more kisses, his hands on her body, his hot words in her ear...

Simply put, she couldn't resist him. Her body craved him. Everything in her craved him.

But now, more than ever, she wanted him. Yeah, she knew it was wrong, knew it was dangerous. And it still freaked her out. But obviously, for once, she was losing control. She couldn't resist Nick.

Scary? Yes. But she was also a realist, and she couldn't deny anymore how intense her feelings for the man actually were. Now, the smart thing to do would be to be strong and stay away. This whole relationship with Nick had "train wreck" written all over it.

Yeah, she thought to herself as she pulled up to his house. *Stop this train. Stay away.* And she couldn't help but laugh. Staying away didn't include getting out of her car and walking up to Nick's porch. Staying away didn't include knocking softly on his door and letting herself into his house. Staying away didn't include going into the kitchen, where she found him sitting at the kitchen table, holding an orange. In the center of the table was a bowl piled high with the fruit.

He was wearing only jeans. No shoes, no shirt. And there was that stupid tattoo on his chest. That stupid tattoo, which, for some reason she couldn't explain, sent a little thrill shooting through her. Maybe it was because it just emphasized all the things about Nick she needed to stay away from. His conceit, his danger. His tempting body.

Yeah. That whole staying-away thing really wasn't going so well for her.

"You came," he said, looking up.

Her palms were sweaty as she walked into the room. "I have no idea why."

"You do. You can't stay away from my overwhelming charm."

She sank into a chair across from him. "Something like that."

He stood and took a seat in the chair next to her. "You're shaking."

"Am I?" She took a deep breath and tried to calm her nerves.

"Yes." He raised a palm and cupped the side of her face. His hand was warm, gentle, and strong. She turned her head slightly and placed a kiss on the center of his palm.

"Oh, Phoebe."

When she turned back to him, his eyes were soft. He opened his mouth as if he was going to say something, but instead he slid his fingers down her face in one tender motion. Then he cupped her chin.

"Come here."

"I'm right here."

"I want you closer. I want you in front of me. I want you on your knees."

Immediately, her pussy dampened. She wanted to be close; she wanted to kneel in front of him. At this point, it was ridiculous to pretend she didn't want to let Nick do whatever he wanted. So she didn't resist when he lightly tugged her down.

The wood was hard on her knees, but she didn't care. She needed the solid surface beneath to lend her its strength. To ground her.

He picked up the orange and began peeling the outer layer from the piece of fruit.

"Sherry brought these back from a farm down south. There's nothing as good as a fresh, sweet orange sprinkled with a little cinnamon and tequila."

"Do you do anything without tequila?"

"Hush."

The word was soft. He'd dragged out the "*sh*" sound of the word and, for some reason, it was calming. But it was also a command, and that made her body thrum with erotic anticipation.

Maybe that was it. He had the ability to calm her, to own her, in just one word. She had no choice but to let go. So she did.

He was almost done peeling the orange. He broke it into two sections and rested the fruit on a small plate. Then he took a small glass of tequila from the table and splashed a bit of the liquor onto one of the orange pieces. Next he picked up a jar of cinnamon and sprinkled the glistening orange with a spattering of the red spice.

He picked up the orange half. "I'm going to do this to you later."

"W-what?"

"I'm going to treat your pussy like this piece of fruit." His tongue darted out, and he licked a drop of juice off the tip of the orange. "I'm going to spread you open, and I'm going to lick your delectable flesh. I'm going to lap up every last ounce of your juice."

Her pussy was pounding with lust. She could almost feel his face between her legs: licking, sucking, tugging...

"Yes, Nick. Do that to me. I want to feel your mouth on my pussy."

"I will. First, taste."

She knew the routine by now. Holding still, she watched as he brought the piece of fruit to her mouth. It was a large chunk, so when she opened her mouth she couldn't take the entire thing inside.

She bit down. Immediately she tasted the combination of tart tequila and sweet orange. And the touch of cinnamon tied the flavors together, heightening the contrasting taste and texture.

"Deeper." He pushed the orange against her mouth. She didn't know why, but it was erotic. The orange filled her mouth. The juice ran down her throat, coated her lips, and the skin all around her mouth. As she swallowed, she could feel the sticky juice on her chin. She felt a drop of fluid drip down onto her chest.

He continued to feed her until every last bit of the orange was gone. By the time she swallowed the last of it, her skin was burning with desire. Her thighs trembled and her pussy throbbed.

Her face was sticky with orange juice; she could feel it. She moved her arm in an attempt to wipe herself off, but Nick stopped her. Holding her arms at her sides, he moved her toward him.

He leaned in. Then his tongue was on her. He licked her lips, her skin. He licked every last drop of orange juice from her face. Her eyes drifted closed, and she tried not to moan aloud.

As he kissed and licked her, she felt his strong hands on her arms, and she felt his hot breath contrasting against the damp spots on her skin. She felt his energy coursing into her.

"Such a good girl," he said. "On your knees, letting

me feed you. Lick you. But I bet you're still thinking about my mouth on your pussy. Are you, Phoebe? Are you thinking about me licking your wet pussy like I just licked that orange juice off your face?"

"Yes," she managed. She was out of her head. She couldn't think about anything else except what he said. What he said he would do to her.

He unzipped his jeans.

She licked her lips.

"First I want to feel my cock in your mouth. I want you to show me what a good girl you are by sucking my cock. Taking me in your mouth like you took that orange. Licking, sucking, swallowing."

"I want to suck your cock, Nick. Please."

He stroked her head. "Such a good girl. I like it when you beg. I love hearing my Phoebe plead to suck my dick."

My Phoebe. The words sent a shudder through her. "Please, Nick. I want to taste you."

"You will, baby. You will." He tugged off his jeans and boxers and tossed them aside. Her gaze fell on his erection. His dick was long and strong, just like him, and Phoebe had to swallow because it made her mouth water.

He sliced open another orange and picked up half of it. Her eyes widened as she watched him squeeze it right over his cock. Orange liquid coated his skin, dripping down the shaft in tempting, lickable drops.

He set the orange aside. Then he took her head in his hand and coaxed her toward his shimmering flesh.

"Take me in your mouth, Phoebe. I want you to lick every last drop of juice off my cock."

"Mmm," was all she could manage. All she wanted

was to do what he said. Sucking the orange off him made her sex throb with want, her nipples pebble with the need to be touched. And pleasing him turned her on even more.

She licked the tip of him. Running her tongue around the head of his dick, she tasted his essence, his skin, and sweet juice from the orange.

It was a heady combination. At that moment, on her knees on a kitchen floor, sucking orange juice off Nick's erection, she needed nothing else.

Her lust was so strong that it made her entire body tremble. She took him deeper, wanting him as far in her mouth as she could, until he hit the back of her throat.

She felt his thighs clench as she swallowed. "Such a good girl," he said. His words sent a new wave of desire through her. By then, her pussy was as juicy as any orange, and she could feel herself dripping into her panties.

She was aching for him. And that ache somehow fed her. Fueled her. She could barely believe how deep she could take him in. He pulled out and entered again, playing with her mouth. She felt the entirety of his orange-flavored dick filling her mouth. She felt the tip of him on the roof of her mouth, sliding farther and farther and farther.

Again he hit the back of her throat.

His hands still on her head, he sank back into the chair. "Fuck, Phoebe. Fuck yeah, girl."

She wanted to please him. Pleasing him made her satisfied. It heightened her own pleasure. So she swallowed. He moaned. She opened her throat until she was afraid she might gag, but he held her firmly. Just far enough. As far as she could take.

"Oh, yeah, baby. Just like that. Suck my cock like a good girl."

She ran the tip of her tongue along the outside of his dick, back up to the tip. If it was possible, this time she thought she felt him even deeper than before.

He stilled. Then he pulled her off him. "Come here."

He guided her to her feet. Her legs were quivering. She could barely hold herself up.

He kissed her. She melted. He held her upright.

She barely felt him tugging off her shirt, her bra, her skirt, her damp panties.

Her naked skin was hot. Her entire body felt like there was a fire burning inside her. A fire of need and want and lust.

She was about to burst into flames.

"That's a good girl." Nick urged her back onto her knees. But this time he followed suit, getting onto the floor in front of her. Then he pushed her back so she was lying on the floor, her legs spread out in front of her.

He had another orange in his hand. This time he made quick work of peeling it, and he tossed the bits of orange peel onto the floor.

She closed her eyes. She heard him squeeze the orange and then sticky drops fell on her skin—her breasts, her abdomen, her stomach, her clit.

"Oh my God, Nick. I need you. I need you so badly . . ."

"Shhh."

Then he was licking her. Licking orange juice off the tips of her breasts, licking the liquid off her stomach . . .

"Yes!"

Finally, his mouth was on her clit. He parted her legs, opening her wide. His tongue was swirling, nibbling, tugging . . .

"Yes, Nick . . . ohhhh," she moaned.

"Feel good, baby?"

"Yes. Hell, yes."

He paused. Before she knew what he was doing, he was touching her lips with the piece of orange.

After running the orange section across her lips, he pushed it into her mouth. "Chew."

He climbed back down her body and buried his face between her legs. She couldn't cry out or moan or scream, not with the orange in her mouth. So she sucked it, drew every last piece of juice out of that piece of fruit. Tasted, sucked, swallowed.

And felt Nick doing exactly the same thing to her pussy.

He didn't stop. He lapped at her as if her very flesh were a delectable piece of fruit. He spread her pussy lips and licked her. Devoured her.

"Don't stop, please, Nick..."

"I got you, baby," he said, and she felt his breath on her wet sex.

Up and down. His tongue explored her from her entrance to her clit. Back and forth. He didn't let up.

She tossed her head from side to side, not caring about the hard floor beneath her. Nothing mattered except what Nick was doing to her. Making her crazy. Making her cry out for him. Making her beg.

"Oh, God! Oh my God!" She squirmed and twisted under him, but he held her steady.

"I need you, Nick. I need to feel you inside me."

"Yeah?" he asked, his voice casual. "You need my dick? Fucking you?"

"Yes! Please..."

"Beg me for it, baby."

"I'm begging you, Nick. Please, *please*, fuck me now."

But he didn't. Instead he continued the assault on her pussy. But this time, as he swirled his tongue around her clit, she felt his fingers probing at her entrance.

"Yes, Nick. Do it."

"You want to feel my fingers inside you, baby?"

"I want your dick inside me."

He made a "tsk" noise. "Sassy girls have to wait. But I will do this instead."

Then she felt his fingers. She didn't know how many, and she didn't care.

"Okay, that'll do." She arched beneath him.

He fucked her with his hand. He fucked her with his mouth. She bucked against his face.

The climax ripped her apart. All she could do was scream as her entire body convulsed in an orgasm that shattered her into a million pieces.

Her eyes popped open and she saw the ceiling, but she couldn't focus on it. Or do anything. She felt paralyzed. The climax had been so intense that she couldn't move so much as a little finger. She could barely breathe.

She wondered how he'd done that to her. He'd known exactly what button to push to turn her into a lifeless corpse.

"Oh, God," she breathed. "That was . . . Wow."

"Yeah?" he said.

He'd moved up beside her and was now looking her in the face. His blue eyes were bright, his spiky hair even messier than normal.

She traced the tattoo across his chest. "Yeah."

"Well, I hope you're not too worn out. Because I fully intend on carrying you to the bedroom and fucking you silly for a good two hours."

A fresh wave of desire crashed over her. How could she be aroused when she'd barely recovered from the most intense orgasm of her life?

And yet she was.

She gave him a look. "You think you can go for hours?"

"I know it, love."

The word made her heart constrict, and she ignored it. Instead she gave him what he would call a cheeky grin. "Prove it, then, love."

Chapter Twenty-Four

You're going to Los Angeles?" Jesse watched her father throw a pair of trousers into a suitcase.

He looked up. "Why do you sound so shocked?"

Jesse whipped her skirt around her legs and plopped onto her dad's big bed. "Um, maybe because you haven't left Redbolt since"—she put a finger to her temple and pretended to think about it—"I can't remember when?"

He continued folding clothes and putting them into the luggage. "Well, Sherry invited me, and I'd like to go."

"But what are you going to do there? How long will you be away?"

Looking at her, her dad sighed heavily. Then he walked over, sat on the bed beside her, and took her hand in his. He looked her in the eye.

"Dad? What's going on? You're freaking me out."

"Jesse, I know things have been hard on you since your mother passed."

"Well, yeah, but I thought you were doing okay."

"I am. But I worry about you."

She pushed a dread behind her ear. "Me? Why do you worry about me?"

"You were young when your mom died. I know it was hard. On all of us."

"Yes. But, Dad, what are you trying to say?"

"You're eighteen now. A woman."

She spoke slowly. "I am aware of that."

He ran a hand over his head. "This is hard for me."

"Dad, spit it out. What's up?"

"I just think it's time I started living again."

She was speechless. "You haven't been? H-have I done something wrong?"

"No, honey. Of course not. You've done everything right. I just wanted to make sure you felt secure and safe. I wanted to give you stability."

"I do feel safe. I do feel secure!"

"I see that. And I see how strong you are, how good you are at the café. And I know you're going to be okay."

"Of course I am. What are you saying?"

"I see the woman you're becoming. Strong and independent. Like your aunt."

"I don't understand. What does this have to do with you going to L.A.?"

"It's time to let you go."

"Let me go? Go from what?"

"Me. It's time I cut the strings, so to speak."

"Wait. Are you saying you...you don't need me?"

His grip on her hand tightened. "No. I'll always need you. You're my sunshine. But I also have a life, and now that you've grown up into a wonderful young woman, I've realized I can start living it."

Her mind was spinning. "So, what are you saying? That you haven't been living because of me?" She wasn't sure whether to laugh or cry.

"Of course not, sweetheart. But for so long my main priority has been you. And spending time with Sherry has made me realize I need to start thinking about myself again."

"Wow." She had no idea her father had those kinds of thoughts or feelings.

"You know, you'll always be the center of my world. But now that I see you can take care of yourself, I'm going to start doing more things for me. Things that make me—and only me—happy."

"I thought you were," she said in a whisper. Her throat was closing in a painful clench, and she felt tears stinging her eyes.

Her dad squeezed her hand. "This isn't coming out right. Honey, I love you."

"I know, Dad. I love you, too."

"I love you so much; all I've wanted was to make sure you knew you were safe after your mom died. That I was never going to leave you."

"I know that."

"And I'm glad. And I don't want you—" He squeezed her hand even tighter. "I never want you to think I didn't enjoy and love every single second we've spent together."

Through watery eyes, she just looked at him.

"But now it's time to start a new chapter."

"Because of Sherry."

"No. Not because of Sherry. I've just been waiting until I knew deep inside that you were independent enough to be safe on your own."

"But—"

"You are. And I also see that somehow, in my attempt to create this safe bubble for you, you've taken on the role of caretaker for me."

She stared, totally floored that her dad had picked up on how she was feeling. In fact, Jesse was floored because she wasn't even sure she'd seen it that way herself. She just wanted her dad to be happy.

As if reading her mind, he said, "I'm happy. It's taken a long time to move on past the sadness I felt when your mother died, but I'm happy now. And I want to keep going. And I want you to as well." Now he grabbed both her hands, leaned down a few inches, and looked her right in the eyes. "I want you to be happy. And that means following your dream. Whatever it may be."

"But"—she felt tears spill onto her cheeks and she felt silly, like a little girl—"I don't want you to leave."

"I'll always be there for you. You know that. And this is just a short trip."

"I know!" She wiped a tear off her face. "I mean, I know you're just going for a little while. But..." She didn't know what to think or feel.

"I just want us both to live. Actually *live*. It isn't because you mean any less to me. You know that, right, Jess?"

She nodded. For so long she'd been living her life under the assumption that her father depended on her. And, if she understood him correctly, he'd been living the exact same way. She'd been living her whole life around the thought that her father needed her. Here. And now he was saying none of that was true.

"So," she said. "This means you're going to L.A. with Sherry?"

Her father stood. "Yes. I hope that's okay with you. We're going to leave in the morning. There's a wine conference in Malibu, and I think it would be an amazing experience to go with Sherry."

"Of course that's okay with me." How strange to have her father asking her approval to go on a trip. Wasn't it supposed to be the opposite way around? But then, this entire conversation had her feeling as if she were on a roller coaster, the kind where you go upside down and around and everything just drops out from under you.

"Sherry brought this all out in you?"

He shook his head. "No. But she did make me remember what I was missing." He glanced at her. "*Life.*"

He kept saying that word, and every time he did images flashed through her mind: recipes she'd tried, courses from Le Cordon Bleu, those red shoes she'd "borrowed" from Sherry. Paris.

Life.

Jesse simply stared at her dad as he finished packing. The conversation had left her reeling. And she couldn't help it. There was one question that was niggling at her, and it wouldn't go away.

If your dad can live his own life, why can't you?

Phoebe pulled the tray of brownies out of the oven. She couldn't help the excited way her pulse raced. They were good. She knew they would be. It had been three months since she'd first started trying the recipe, and now she thought she had her aunt and uncle's formula down. The recipe hadn't really been exact, so she'd had to improvise.

Now she truly felt she had a chance of carrying on the tradition of winning the cook-off. She'd just kept making them, making small adjustments with melting the chocolate and the measurements of the butter and the sugar until finally she thought she had it down.

So now it was up to the judges. She placed a piece of foil over the baking tray and untied her apron.

"Ready?"

Phoebe looked up at the sound of her niece's voice. Then she caught sight of Jesse and Phoebe jerked back. "Jesse?"

Her niece blushed and ran a hand over her very short hair. "Is it bad?"

"N-no!" Phoebe could only stare.

Jesse looked like an entirely different person.

She'd always had remarkable features, but now her face was simply striking. Jesse had cut off her dreads into a stylish, short haircut that showed off the strong lines of her face, the symmetry of her features, and her almond-shaped eyes that were the color of fresh peas in summer.

And, for the first time since Phoebe had known her niece, Jesse was wearing makeup. It was subtle but just enough to bring out her natural beauty even more. A hint of shimmery eye shadow, a touch of eyeliner and mascara, and the barest smidge of blush highlighted the bone structure that was magazine-cover quality. Her lips shone with a natural shade of gloss.

Simply, Jesse looked astonishing.

"Do you like it?" Jesse asked, biting her lip.

"Oh, Jesse." Phoebe walked out from behind the counter. "You look beautiful."

Jesse ran a hand over her head. "It feels weird."

"I'm sure. You've had those dreadlocks for years."

"I know, but I was ready..."

"For a change?"

"Yeah."

"So, you just did this yourself?"

"No. Sherry did. She did my hair and my makeup."

Phoebe still had mixed feelings about Sherry, and she wasn't one hundred percent happy with the way Sherry seemed to be encroaching on her family, but Phoebe pushed those feelings aside. They were selfish. She was making Steve happy.

And Sherry was obviously trying to make Jesse happy, too. Recently Phoebe had sensed undertones of unrest in her niece. Jesse was only eighteen so she was still a teenager, although more and more Phoebe forgot that on account of how it seemed her niece was growing into a woman right before her eyes.

Phoebe wondered what had prompted her niece to make this change in her appearance. She hadn't just cut off her hair; she'd cut off her dreadlocks. Dreads were a statement. Like a tattoo, or a body piercing, they were a form of self-expression. Now, Phoebe had to wonder, what kind of statement was her niece trying to make?

Chapter Twenty-Five

The warm June sunshine, mixed with the scent of delicious flavors, flooded Phoebe's senses as soon as she stepped out of her truck. It was finally here. The day of the big cook-off. She smiled. Despite her many failed attempts at baking the brownies, she thought all her practice had paid off. Pulling the still-warm tray off the passenger seat, she inhaled the chocolaty aroma rising from the dish. The brownies smelled like home. Like her aunt. And, if Aunt Sally was watching from above, Phoebe wanted nothing more than to make her proud.

She thought she had a damn good chance.

Jesse had tasted the final batch and agreed that Phoebe's brownies were, in fact, as good as the original recipe. Remembering the day Nick had arrived and picked up the hard lump that was the result of one of her first attempts at the recipe, she just shook her head. Pathetic. Phoebe had seriously doubted she'd be able to pull it off.

She bumped her hip against the driver's-side door of her Land Cruiser and set off to enter the county park where the cook-off was held every year.

As her sandals hit the gravel parking lot, she gazed into the green expanse of lawn where dozens of tables were set up with a mishmash of tablecloths. The place was already filling up, and she greeted several locals on her way to the dessert competition area. This was one of the regional events very few people missed, and Phoebe knew practically everyone she ran into.

Her smile grew. This was what she loved. The bordering grass field, the fresh redwood-tree-scented air, and the hills that surrounded her. The turquoise water of the Eel River ran on the outer edge of the picnic area, winding its way next to the gathering. The banks of sand edging the river were filled with families on blankets. Toddlers splashed in the shallow banks and the older, more adventurous kids were jumping off large rocks and landing in the water with big splashes. The cook-off brought out the largest crowd, but the park would be full of picnicking families and kids on summer break all season long.

Phoebe loved the community, the free way of thinking, the simple things that made the locals happy. Trees and clean air and a fresh river. Being surrounded by the very people she'd grown up with. While she understood why people like Bear felt stifled here, Phoebe was the opposite. Sure, she'd enjoyed her time living in Berkeley. She'd taken advantage of the sophisticated culture, the cafés, the art, and the parties. But she'd always known she'd come back to Redbolt. She'd always known she wanted to spend her life here. Home.

It took awhile to make her way to the dessert section. She'd been so busy with the café and her farm that she hadn't seen a lot of her friends for some time. She'd forgotten how nice it was to actually socialize away from the Green Leaf, and she took her time chatting as she wandered toward her destination.

"Are those what I think they are?"

Phoebe turned to see Mary, her aunt Sally's best friend. The woman was aging gracefully, and her hair was only lightly streaked with gray. She wore it in a long braid that fell halfway down her back. She wore no makeup, but her smile was gorgeous. Her outfit consisted of a flowery summer dress and flip-flops.

Phoebe said, "Mary, so nice to see you."

Mary leaned forward to give Phoebe a hug. "I'm sorry, but I'm not a good hugger right now," Phoebe said with a smile as she glanced down at the tray of brownies in her hands.

"That's okay, honey." Carefully, Mary wrapped her arms around Phoebe's shoulders and gave her a kiss on the cheek. Then she stepped back. "How are you? I haven't seen you in ages."

"Good. And I apologize. I've been meaning to call you, but things have been so crazy lately."

"Oh, you don't need to apologize to me, honey. I completely understand. I know all too well how hard your aunt worked at that café."

Phoebe felt a twinge of guilt. She really hadn't been working as hard at the café as she probably should have been. But Nick had given her more and more reason to delegate additional responsibilities. And Jesse was blossoming under Nick's supervision, which made Phoebe happy but also a little disappointed in herself.

She'd started to wonder why Jesse's newfound confidence seemed to be emerging under the influence of Sherry and Nick. Why hadn't Phoebe been able to do that for her niece?

Either way, with Nick and Jesse working as a team,

Phoebe had more time to work on her first love. The farm.

So now, talking to Mary, Phoebe just shrugged. "Yes. The café definitely takes up a lot of time."

"I completely understand. Whenever you have a second, just stop by, and we'll catch up over coffee."

"I promise, I will." And Phoebe meant it. Mary was practically family, and Phoebe needed to be better about keeping in touch. Because at the end of the day, family was all anyone had.

Plus, Mary's garden had always been an inspiration to Phoebe. Sitting on the flagstone patio, surrounded by climbing roses, butterfly bushes, and lavender—it was impossible not to feel peaceful and tranquil. "I promise to stop by this week," Phoebe said, genuinely looking forward to it. When had she lost contact with anyone not related to work?

"But you never answered my question." Mary pointed a finger at the brownies Phoebe was carrying. "Are those what I think they are?"

Phoebe smiled. "What do you think they are?"

"Sally's brownies?" Mary said, and Phoebe didn't miss the flash of incredulity that flashed through the woman's sharp green eyes.

"They are." But now a bit of Phoebe's confidence had gone down. Was it really that ludicrous that she'd give this a try?

"Well, I'm glad you're carrying on the tradition."

"I didn't want the tradition to die just because…" Phoebe trailed off. Normally that expression would have been benign, but Phoebe had foot-in-mouth disease.

But Mary touched her shoulder gently. "I'm glad you made them. Your aunt would be proud of you."

Phoebe shifted in her sandals. Would she be proud? What if Phoebe was wrong and the brownies were horrible? What if her taste buds were off from eating so many mistakes? What if she lost?

Mary's grip on Phoebe's shoulder tightened as she repeated, "Sally would be proud of you."

Mary didn't say it, but Phoebe knew what she meant. *Even if you don't win.*

It was a nice sentiment, but Phoebe didn't care. She didn't take on challenges if she didn't think she could win. Furthermore, these brownies represented a lot more than continuing a recipe. She wanted to prove to herself that she had succeeded in carrying on the legacy of the Green Leaf. The café was a staple of the area, and the region a claim to fame, no matter how small. The café meant something.

Now, if she won, everyone would know that she wasn't going to let her community down.

"Okay," Phoebe said after taking a deep breath. "I better get these entered."

"Yes, off you go. And good luck."

"Thanks." *I think I might need it.*

"What are you doing here?" As Phoebe arrived at the table packed with luscious desserts, she narrowed her gaze on something even more mouthwatering. Nick Avalon.

"Why are you surprised?"

She placed her precious brownies on a clear spot on the table and grabbed an entry form. She leaned down to fill out the form but glanced up. "I don't know. It's just that this is all so local and probably seems very bumpkin to you. I would think you'd avoid it at all costs."

"You're right." He nodded a hello at one of their regular diners. "But how could I miss this chance to see the big cook-off everyone's been talking about for so long? Plus, I have nothing better to do."

She gave him a wary smile before turning back to fill out the entry form. He was lying. He was beginning to like it here. She could tell. His skin looked healthier, he actually smiled sometimes, and she'd noticed his tobacco use and tequila consumption had decreased dramatically. He had even stopped complaining about the music she chose for the restaurant. In fact, a couple of times she'd actually caught him humming the tune.

Sure, there were still moments when she wanted to smack him in the head with a frying pan, but those were becoming fewer and farther between every day. With a start, she realized that she'd gotten to the point where she actually looked forward to seeing him.

Bear had left after only five days of being home. Of course. He'd said he was here to stay, but less than a week had passed and he'd been called away to help the emergency crew during the aftermath of a hurricane in Bolivia. And at the end of the day, if Phoebe did get in a relationship (and that was a big if), she wanted someone who enjoyed the community as she did. She wanted someone who wanted to enjoy the small moments of life with her.

Like now. In the park, surrounded by her community at an event she'd been attending as long as she could remember. She'd never been happier.

And even more strange? She was having these thoughts while standing next to a man who seemed to embody all the things she didn't like.

But something had changed. She watched him make

small talk with Oscar, who owned the hemp clothing store on Main Street. Nick's stance was relaxed, his feet spread solidly apart, and his arms crossed over his chest. Oscar said something, and Nick laughed. A laugh that was sincere and that made the corners of his eyes crinkle. A laugh that was hearty and manly. A laugh that made her heart skip a beat.

These moments. This was what she wanted.

Pushing the thought away, she turned in her form and got a number for the brownies she'd entered. Number thirteen was a lucky number. That was a good sign, right? Right.

Chapter Twenty-Six

Out of the corner of his eye, Nick watched Phoebe. In her flowery dress, with her long curly hair spilling over her shoulders and her impish smile, he thought she looked like a fairy nymph.

Her dress was a bit low-cut, though. He didn't mind, not at all. He loved the way the V-cut gave him a glimpse of her phenomenal cleavage. However, he wasn't at all comfortable with the way he'd caught several male attendees catching a glimpse. Wasn't it a bit chilly? Perhaps he should get her a sweater.

You fool. It wasn't chilly at all. In fact, the sun and clear blue sky were creating the perfect weather to enjoy a day at the park. It was so warm, in fact, that a large portion of the crowd had taken advantage of the coolness of the river. No, Phoebe didn't need a sweater.

He just wanted her to cover herself up.

What is wrong with you? Why did he care if a bunch of perverts were ogling Phoebe's breasts? When he'd paraded hot little starlets around the trendiest clubs in L.A., he'd loved seeing the girl he was with get attention. In his old life, women were like cars. Nothing more than status symbols.

What do you mean, back in your old life?

Leaning against a tree and sipping from a plastic cup of beer, Nick reminded himself that where he'd been less than six months ago hadn't been his old life. *It is my life*, he told himself. As in present tense.

So what had him thinking like this? Why did he feel so possessive over a woman he didn't really like?

Ah, but there was the rub. He did like her. He liked her independence, her natural beauty, her wit, her drive to succeed.

Her body.

In fact, he liked her body so much, he didn't want to share it with anyone. Ever. The very thought of someone else smelling her neck, rubbing their hands across her nipples, tasting the special flavor of her pussy—the very idea actually made his stomach turn.

He didn't like it. Not one bit.

This place was getting to him. Now, as he watched people talk and laugh and eat from plates piled so high with food they could have fed small countries, he couldn't help but get a little twitchy. Because he wasn't used to it. He wasn't used to this feeling, and it made his nerves jerk.

He took another large swig from his cup of beer.

It didn't feel right. This... thing. This feeling of—*holy shit*—being content.

He liked chaos. He liked unpredictability. He liked the madness of the kitchens he'd worked in. That's where he felt safe and secure.

Right?

So why was he so... happy? Everything here was exactly the opposite of what he'd based his life around. Every day was predictable. For the most part, people were inevitably friendly. No one yelled in the kitchen at the Green Leaf. Well, no one except him, that was. And occasionally Phoebe, but he was beginning to find her outbursts endearing. The thought of all those things should make him uncomfortable. So why didn't it?

Why would he rather be here, right now? Surrounded by nature and hippies and home cooking. He should be shuddering at the very idea. Yet, there was nowhere else he'd rather be.

He sipped at his beer and said hello to yet another person attending the cook-off. Since when did he know so many of the locals? And why did they treat him like he was one of them? Like he was welcome? Nick was an outcast; he didn't belong here.

And he knew they still made fun of his Hummer behind his back.

Bumpkins.

But the idea of everybody around him being nothing more than new age, old-fashioned, unsophisticated rednecks just didn't ring true anymore.

And the fact that he didn't care for Phoebe didn't ring true either.

She was beautiful. As she brushed aside a lock of that wild hair, his chest tightened with want. He wanted to hear her voice, to listen to what she had to say. He wanted to touch every curve of her body, from the curve of her shoulder to the dip of her waist. He wanted to wake up next to her in the morning.

Emotions churned inside his gut, fighting with each other. He'd worked so hard to achieve the life he'd led back in L.A. He'd worked so fucking hard, and he'd had everything he'd ever dreamed of.

And yet, right here, right now, it all seemed so empty. Right here, right now, he had all he needed.

Except Phoebe in his arms.

You're getting daft, old boy. Daft.

Nick downed the rest of his beer just as an old man stepped onto a podium and leaned down to talk into a speaker that must have been circa 1970.

"Attention, please," the old man croaked out. Then he went on about how he'd been announcing the winner of the Redbolt cook-off for umpteen years, and he was honored to be announcing the winners and blah, blah, blah. Nick tuned the voice out.

Okay, so maybe some things about this place still bored the crap out of Nick.

Except when they got to the dessert category. He stood up straight, his eyes on Phoebe. He saw her brow furrow in worry, and he wanted nothing more than to go hold her tight. He knew this was important to her. He knew that if the Green Leaf didn't take first place, she'd see it as some kind of failure on her part. Which, he thought, was ridiculous. But he understood that everyone had their own ideas about success, and this was hers, so he was behind her one hundred percent.

He clenched his fists behind his back and leaned against the tree. What he didn't want anyone to know was that he was crossing his fingers for the Green Leaf Café.

Who'd have ever thought they'd see the day Nick Avalon would be standing in a forest a million miles away from civilization, secretly crossing his fingers that a tiny café he worked for would take first place in a bake-off?

It was official. Nick had gone crazy.

* * *

Thirteen, thirteen, thirteen.

Phoebe chanted the words silently in her own mind as she waited for the announcer to get to the dessert competition. *For fuck's sake, announce it already.* Did Nick have a cigarette? She wanted a cigarette so badly she nearly started sucking on her finger. Nice coping method. *You don't smoke, remember?*

In the past, she'd been only a taster, not a contestant. So this year, she wasn't enjoying listening to the results like usual. She just wanted to hear the winners, hear her number and her name and then go celebrate all she'd accomplished.

As old Tom droned on, Phoebe really wasn't surprised when she heard who the winners in the other categories were. The same people who'd been winning every year. Rick's Fed Gunny took the award for the best macaroni-and-cheese dish. Bola Julienne took first place for the category titled "Everything but the Kitchen Sink." Paul Carr won for the best PBR frittata. Chalice Stickler nailed the "Best Aphrodisia Salad" award (the cinnamon was, in Phoebe's opinion, the key to her success). Jar Jelly Nelson took the prize for his tamale pie. (Phoebe had to admit it was tasty—she especially liked the addition of Aji Pinguita peppers, but she may have been biased, considering the fresh peppers had come from her very own farm.) The fabulous duo of Roam Piecing and Sunlit Jewels took the trophy for "Most Creative Mycological Casserole."

So then it came down to the final category. Desserts. Phoebe bit her lip and wrung her hands. *Thirteen; come on, thirteen.*

She gazed up at old man Tom and held her breath.

He coughed.

The crowd was silent.

He squinted through his round glasses at the piece of paper before him.

"And the prize for best traditional brownie goes to..."

Thirteen! She was going to win; she could feel it!

Tom shouted into the speaker. "The winner is...number *three*!"

Everything inside Phoebe froze, even as she felt sweat break out on her brow. She felt a million eyes on her, like spiders crawling up her skin. There was a minute of absolute quiet, and she thought everyone was thinking the same thing.

She'd failed.

She hadn't been able to do something so simple as carry on a fucking recipe for brownies. And if she'd failed, who had beat her?

"Number three, with Nick Avalon as chef. Nick, please step up to the podium."

Everyone looked around, waiting to see who had been the first person in ten years to steal first prize from Phoebe's aunt and uncle.

Phoebe felt a chill go up her back. No. It couldn't be.

No, no, no.

Nick was walking toward the podium, a satisfied look on his face.

Her heart stopped. How could he? How could he do this to her?

With her heart pounding in her tightened throat, she attempted to keep her cool as he stepped up and received the trophy.

Nick nodded a humble thank-you that would have been believable if she didn't know what a conniving, manipulating prick he was.

Anger boiled inside her like an untended saucepan of béchamel sauce. How dare he?

He'd purposely gone behind her back and one-upped her. Just when she was starting to think he was a decent human being, he'd gone back to being Nick the Prick, the guy who had to be the best at everything. The guy who had been challenging her since the moment he'd walked through the door to her café.

The guy who'd had her fooled into thinking he was good.

Now, as he took the trophy (a porcelain sculpture of cake made by a local artist), he met her gaze. Clenching her fists, she felt ill as she saw the triumph in his eyes. And damn it to hell, she felt her own eyes well up at his betrayal.

Gazes locked, she continued to stare him down. Slowly, she noticed the look on his face change a bit. The winning glimmer flickered, and his forehead crinkled a bit. She had no idea what any of that meant. All she knew was the pounding of her heart, her hands starting to shake, her throat growing tight.

Leaning down to speak in the microphone, he said, "This is for the Green Leaf Café. May the legend live on."

But it was too little, too late.

Betrayal. It coursed through her and landed in her stomach, swirling as if in a blender. Her entire chest thought it might collapse from sadness.

"Pheebs, can you believe it?"

She turned to see Jesse looking back and forth from her to Nick. "We won!"

"What are you talking about?" Phoebe spit, and held out her number. "I was number thirteen. Not three."

"But the prize goes to the café, not a number."

"Jesse, don't you understand?" An even greater sense of frustration coursed through her. "Nick entered to beat me. To prove he's better. And I lost. This is *our* family tradition, not his. He knew how important this was to me."

Jesse's gaze didn't falter. "Nick knew how important it was to you for the café to win."

"And he knew how hard I'd been working."

"I know. But he also thought two entries were better than one."

Gasping, Phoebe pulled back. "You knew what he was up to?"

Slowly, Jesse nodded. "Um, yeah. So?"

Phoebe had to bite the inside of her lip to keep from screaming. "So? So you were in on this! Neither of you had enough faith in me to think, for just one second, that I could win this?"

"Actually, we both thought you would win. But we both knew how important it was to you to have the café succeed, and, like I just said, we were only trying to help our chances."

"Why didn't you tell me?"

"We wanted it to be a surprise."

"Well, you failed," Phoebe said.

Jesse looked shocked. "I don't understand."

"I'm not surprised that Nick is a selfish asshole who refuses to think a woman might—just might—be better at something than him. I'm not surprised that Nick took something he knew was important to *me*"—she pointed at her chest—"and claimed it for himself. I'm not at all surprised that he wants credit for a family tradition that I wanted more than anything to continue."

Gazing at Phoebe, Jesse was silent for a few moments. "So is that what's bothering you?"

"What?"

"Credit. Is that why you did this whole thing? To get the credit for it? To have your name announced?"

"N-no." Phoebe angrily shook her head. "Of course not."

"Then why did you enter? Why is winning so important to you?"

"Because I . . . I wanted to make Sally and Dan proud."

"And don't you think they are?"

Phoebe was starting to think she really liked the old days when her niece was a lot less mature. "I don't know," she said, and tried to compose herself. "All I know is I want to rip Nick's head off for taking this away from me."

"But, Phoebe, what exactly did he take?"

"The trophy!"

"Exactly."

"That trophy was meant for me—I mean the café!"

Jesse spoke softly. "And isn't that who won?"

It took Phoebe a minute to answer. "No. I mean, yes, but only because Nick made sure everyone knows he's better than I am."

"Phoebe, everyone already knows that. That's why you hired him, remember?"

It was true, but it didn't stop the words from stinging. "That's not the point here."

"Then what is the point?"

Phoebe glanced over Jesse's shoulder to see Nick approaching, holding the winning trophy in his hands.

Flee. It was all too much; she couldn't deal with any of it right now.

But Jesse wasn't letting up. "Phoebe. What is the point? What does it matter if it's your name or Nick's on that award? It's for the café, right? And we won. You should be happy."

Confusion. Nick coming at her. Her niece saying things that were making her question her own motivation.

Turning on her heel, she did something she'd never done in her life. She ran away.

Chapter Twenty-Seven

Well, that was fast." Mary held open the porch door, and Phoebe stepped inside the house. It was just as she'd always remembered it inside. It was an old Victorian that had been updated but still held its original charm. Bright light shone through large windows covered in lace curtains. Old worn carpets were placed sporadically over the original wood flooring. Framed pictures, filled with images of familiar faces, were scattered on nearly every available surface space.

"I hope you don't mind," Phoebe said.

"Of course not! In fact, I was thinking it would be a lovely time for an afternoon glass of wine. What do you think?" Mary's eyes glittered. "Care to join me on the porch?"

"I'd like nothing more."

Moments later they were relaxing under an arbor covered in fragrant climbing jasmine. Mary had set two comfortable chairs in the shade and brought out a bottle of wine and two glasses. Silently, the women sat there sipping wine. Listening to the hummingbirds, the bees buzzing around the lavender, the tinkle of the wind chime when a slight breeze tickled the air.

Suddenly Phoebe turned to Mary. "Do you think I entered the contest for selfish reasons?"

Mary sipped her wine. "I don't know, honey. Did you?"

"I didn't think so..."

"But?"

"I really wanted to prove something. To prove that I was capable of carrying on the legacy of the restaurant."

"And you think winning a cook-off proves that?"

Phoebe sheepishly brought her wineglass to her lips. "Um...well, I kinda did."

"So why are you questioning yourself?"

"Because I was so pissed when Nick won!" Phoebe lowered her voice. "I'm sorry. I didn't mean to say that."

Mary laughed. "Honey, you never have to censor yourself around me."

"Thanks." Phoebe pushed a curl behind her ear. "It's just that I wanted to win this so badly, and Nick knew that. And he entered anyway."

"And beat you."

"Yes, and beat me." It played like a movie in her mind. She kept watching him go up to that podium and take the trophy. The trophy that should have been hers.

"You're so like your mother," Mary said.

Phoebe's heart skipped. It always did when the subject of her mom came up. "What do you mean?"

Mary gently smiled. "She was so independent and a perfectionist. Just like you."

"Thank you," Phoebe mumbled. She didn't know if Mary was giving her a compliment or not.

"She'd be proud of you, dear."

Phoebe glanced at Mary. "I highly doubt it. I just lost the contest for the first time in over a decade!"

"Do you really think she'd care about any of that?"

Phoebe opened her mouth, but no words came out. Instead she took a sip of wine. Would her mother have truly cared? Would her aunt and uncle have shunned her for losing?

Of course they wouldn't have.

"They'd all be proud of how hard you work, and the successes you've accomplished."

For some reason Phoebe's eyes stung, and she simply nodded.

"Phoebe, let me ask you this. Why does it matter who actually cooked the damn brownies?"

"Because it's my family recipe!"

"But the café's always entered them."

"I know, but..."

"This has nothing to do with any brownies, Phoebe."

"It doesn't?" Phoebe sipped more of the fruity red wine. As usual, Mary had selected an excellent bottle from a local winery.

"No, it has to do with you being in control."

"But I am."

"That's your choice. Furthermore, caring what people think about you is your choice, too."

"Wow. Is this Beat Up Phoebe Day?"

"I don't know, honey. Is it? Or is it Phoebe's self-realization day?"

"I only care what people think because our family has been such a big part of this community for so long."

"That's respectable, Phoebe. But sometimes you have to remember that you have your own life to lead as well. And spending all your time trying to control everyone else's isn't going to help you at all."

"Why does everyone call me a control freak?" With a harrumph, Phoebe lifted the wine bottle and refilled her glass.

"You've been through a lot of loss in your life, Phoebe, and survived with a smile."

Phoebe felt her cheeks warm. "Th-thank you." She hadn't been given such a nice compliment in a long time.

"But just make sure you don't use it as a crutch to forget about yourself. And your own wants and needs."

"But what about Nick? You don't think I should be mad at him for taking the trophy away from me?"

"I think he should have told you. But don't just assume his intentions were all bad. At least try talking to him about it."

"Ha! Trying to talk to him is like trying to talk to...to...I don't know, but it's not easy."

"Who ever gave you the impression that men were good at communication?"

"Cheers to that!" Phoebe raised her wineglass and toasted Mary.

The next day, Phoebe needed to be at the farm. Her soul was craving the dirt and her plants. Kneeling, she felt a cold breeze raise gooseflesh on her arms and suppressed a shiver. She hoped the chilly air wasn't an indication of frost. Although it was early June, late spring storms weren't unheard of. So Phoebe prayed to the gods of farming that the warm weather would continue.

Funny how one day could change so much. Yesterday the sun had been promising the warmth of summer; today she wished she'd brought a windbreaker out with her.

And, of course, she didn't know what to think about

Nick. And the things Jesse and Mary had said. Phoebe hadn't spoken with Nick since she'd run away from him yesterday, and she was glad she'd taken the time to think. Why did it matter if it wasn't her own name on that stupid trophy? Why did she need the credit? The more she thought about it, the more she believed Jesse, and she wanted to trust Nick. Hadn't she just been thinking about how far he'd come since that day he'd arrived? The more she thought about it, the more she doubted his plan had been a nefarious one.

What if he had done it just out of the goodness of his heart? What if he had truly changed into a good person? What if the happiness she felt when she was with him could actually be something...more?

She wanted to be less of a control freak, but when it came to her feelings for Nick, she simply couldn't help it; she just couldn't free-fall with Nick any longer. Not after the past day when she'd had so many revelations about herself.

She didn't need to be a control freak.

She could trust other people.

Nick had continued the cook-off legacy on behalf of the café.

Did she mention she could trust other people?

Just the thought made her shoulders feel lighter. The café, obviously, needed her less and less. She was delegating, and now her farming business could receive even more of her attention.

And this was where she really wanted to be. In the dirt.

Her plots were already showcasing their first crops. She pulled a piece of asparagus from the dirt and tossed it into an already-full basket. Every vegetable she pulled from the earth added to the sense of satisfaction settling deep within her. The sun was warm on her back; her hands were dirty. The crops were doing well.

Perfection.

Except for that chilly breeze. She glanced to the north. The wind was just a bit too cold, a bit too sharp. Maybe she was being overly sensitive, but someone had told her a long time ago that she'd developed a farmer's intuition when it came to the weather, and so Phoebe gazed at her crops and once more said a little prayer.

All her newly found free time had allowed her to focus the majority of her attention on her organic farming business, and it seemed every day her business grew a bit more. It seemed every day she had a new customer placing an order. She would need to hire more help.

Even now, despite the enjoyment she obtained from pulling the vegetables out of the ground, she felt the pressure of filling an order. The restaurant in Berkeley had been requesting more and more of her produce, and she needed to get a box ready for shipment by 5:00, which was only an hour away.

"Hey, Pheebs. Need a hand?"

She looked up to see Bear standing a few feet away. She hadn't seen him since that night at the bar. Typically, here he was again. No warning, no notification. It was like he had a transport machine.

"Bear. How are you?" She felt her neck turning red. Oddly, she wanted to tell him about her feelings for Nick. She wasn't sure why, but if Bear wanted to make another advance at her, it would feel like she was betraying Nick if she didn't say anything to Bear.

He walked inside the garden and crouched next to her. "Good. It's good to be home, and to see you."

She smiled uncertainly. "Yes, it is."

"You look like you could use a hand."

Her first instinct was to say no, but she realized she could, in fact, use a bit of help. She nodded. "That would be great. Thank you."

As an agricultural specialist for the Food Core, Bear didn't need any lessons on the basics of pulling vegetables. They settled into a rhythm that was easy and efficient.

He glanced at her. "So, how are things? Really?"

Pulling weeds with Bear, Phoebe realized they'd always been friends more than anything. She'd idealized him into some sort of perfect man and was happy while they were engaged. But when they called it off, she really hadn't been that upset. And now that she could compare her feelings about Nick, she realized what she'd felt during their engagement really hadn't been love at all.

She smiled at Bear. "Really good, actually."

"And Nick? He's still working out as your chef?"

"Yeah. About that. I'm so sorry he was rude to you that night."

"No biggie. The guy obviously has some anger-management issues."

She laughed. "Yes. Sometimes he does."

Bear's voice turned serious. "But he treats you well?"

She threw a spear of asparagus into the basket. "What do you mean?"

"You know. Does he treat you well? I was a bit worried about you after that night. I wouldn't want to see you dating some asshole. You deserve better."

"Oh. I-I'm not dating Nick. He just works for me." But the words faltered on her tongue.

He cocked a brow. "Really?"

"You don't believe me?"

"It just seemed like you two have something going on."

"We don't. We do—I mean, I don't know." Other than the cook-off incident (which Phoebe was now realizing she was going to have to eat crow and apologize about), things with Nick had been going well since that night at the bar. They'd certainly wasted no opportunities to have sex. But that was as far as it went. Now, she wanted to bring it up. To discuss things with him. But just the thought—the fear of being rejected by him—made her heart clench with pain.

"Honestly, Bear. I'm not sure what to think."

"Do you like him?"

She paused. "I really don't know anymore. Sometimes, yes. Sometimes I want to punch him in the nose."

He laughed. "I know what you mean. Okay, let's switch subjects then. How are things working out at the café? He's doing a good job?"

"He is. I had a lot of doubts at first, but he seems to have settled in. Settled down."

"Wow."

"What?"

"It's just that I never thought I'd see the day Phoebe Mayle would give up control over anything."

"Shut up! I'm not that bad. Am I?"

"Sometimes."

She shrugged. "Well, I guess I'm learning. Hiring Nick was a good thing."

"I'm glad, Phoebe. You know I've always cared about you. You're one of my favorite people in the world. I want to see you happy."

"Thanks, Bear. That means a lot." Just then she felt her cell phone vibrate in her pocket. She pulled it out and flipped it open.

"Hi, Jess. What's up?"

Her niece's tone of voice was frantic. "Nick hasn't shown up."

Phoebe's blood went cold. "What? It's past four."

"I know," Jesse said. "He's not here. I've tried his phone like a million times, and he's not answering."

Phoebe pushed herself to her feet. "Damn him."

"What do I do?"

"Start prepping. I'll be there as soon as I can."

Bear stood next to her. "What's wrong?"

"I guess I spoke too soon. Looks like I have a missing chef on my hands."

Bear immediately assumed the take-charge attitude that made him so successful in his travels. "What can I do?"

She bit her lip. "I hate to ask . . ."

"Then don't ask. Tell me."

She hesitated only a second. She didn't really have a choice.

See what happens when you depend on others?

She couldn't think about that now. Instead she took an invoice out of her pocket. "Thank God you're here, Bear."

"I'm glad I can help."

She handed him the invoice. "I just need this order filled. Everything's listed. I have almost all the vegetables pulled; they just have to be boxed and shipped. UPS will be here at five."

He took the piece of paper and gave it a glance. "No problem. I promise to take care of it. Go deal with the café."

She gave him a quick hug and a kiss on the cheek. But she frowned as she jogged to her car. Where was Nick? She didn't want to think he'd bailed on them, not now, when she'd just started to trust him.

But tidbits of conversation came floating back to her...*He's here to get his life back in order*...Was that what he'd done? Had all her conclusions about how Nick had changed, had become so much better than when he'd first arrived, actually meant he'd only accomplished what he needed to do?

The thought made her stomach turn.

That couldn't be true. She was jumping to conclusions again, being nonsensical. Just like when Nick had won the cook-off. She'd assumed his plan had been diabolical, to show her up and beat her, but he'd really just been playing on her team.

So he was late. For the first time ever. That didn't mean he'd ditched them. In fact, the more she thought about it, she started to worry about him. She hoped he was okay.

Just as she was starting her car, her cell phone rang again. It was Jesse, probably calling to tell her Nick had shown up.

"Hi, Jesse."

Her niece's voice sounded strained. "Um..."

"What?" Phoebe's heart stopped for a minute. "Is Nick okay?"

"I think so."

"Then what's up?"

"I just got a call from some guy in Hollywood. He was

looking for Nick, said he couldn't reach him on his cell."

Phoebe's blood went cold as she turned the key in the ignition. "Is that all he said?"

"No, he was also wondering if we knew what time Nick had left here. Apparently they want him at some party tonight." Jesse's tone of voice sounded defeated and let down.

"Listen, Jesse. I'm sure this is all one big mistake. Nick wouldn't just up and leave us. We'll figure it out."

"I hope you're right, Pheebs."

Me, too, she thought as she peeled out of the driveway.

Chapter Twenty-Eight

For the millionth time, Nick glanced at his phone. Still no fucking cell service. He'd been driving three hours. He'd been trying to reach the café the entire time, but as soon as he'd left Redbolt, his service had dropped. And in his haste to leave, he'd forgotten his phone charger.

"Fuck." Now the battery had died, leaving him no access to any of his phone numbers. "Damn it." He tossed his phone onto the seat next to him. His palms were so sweaty he could barely keep a grip on the steering wheel. He'd have to find a pay phone somewhere and look up the number of the café.

Yeah, the café you just up and abandoned?

What the fuck are you doing, Avalon?

Exactly what he needed to be doing. Exactly what he'd wanted to do since the second he'd left Los Angeles. He was going back.

Or was he running away?

He couldn't help it. He kept recalling that hurt look of betrayal in Phoebe's eyes when she'd stared up at him from the crowd during the cook-off. He'd been so happy to have won. He'd hoped his attempt would show that he did care about her winning, and about the café.

But she'd taken it all the wrong way. He could see it in her face. She hadn't changed her mind. She thought he was a selfish prick. That hadn't changed.

And he'd allowed it. It had made his plans to leave so much easier.

And that's what felt like a knife stabbing him in the gut.

He'd let himself think, just for a second, that she saw something in him no one else had. She'd made him feel like more than some shallow status-oriented stair-climber out for nothing more than his own pleasure.

She'd made him want more from life.

Sometime during the last few months in Redbolt, he'd found he wanted so much more than to cater to the whims of the current Hollywood celebs. Nothing came close to the satisfaction he'd begun to feel at taking something Phoebe had grown in her own garden and turning it into a meal that he could share with the community. Friends. People he actually *liked*.

He'd begun to feel like they were a team.

He punched the steering wheel. How could he be so stupid? How could he so quickly forget what he really wanted? He'd let himself be fooled. He'd let himself feel. He'd let himself love.

But Phoebe's opinion of him had never changed.

Timing was a crazy thing, but just that morning, a call had come in that made it pretty fucking obvious what he was supposed to do. Some studio exec and his cronies were opening up a new restaurant, and the buzz was that it would be the next hot spot in Beverly Hills. They'd called Nick to see if he was interested in interviewing for the position of chef.

Yes, he was.

But he knew how these things worked. If you didn't pounce on an opportunity, someone else would. This was a cutthroat business, which was why he'd done so well so far.

As soon as he'd hung up the phone that morning, he'd jumped into his Hummer and started driving. He hadn't even thought about it. He'd simply gone. For about thirty minutes, he hadn't looked back.

But now it was hitting him. Even if the experience yesterday had left a foul taste in his mouth, it was still irresponsible to up and ditch the café.

And he couldn't help it. Even if it was all bullshit, he'd come to actually like the Green Leaf. He'd become very fond of the people he'd worked with—especially Jesse—and the patrons were becoming more like friends. He'd even started to not hate the mismatched decor and rustic tables and chairs.

But. The experience yesterday had been like a sucker punch back to reality. That wasn't what he wanted. What he wanted was to go home. To Hollywood.

Still, he should have let them know what was going on.

To his surprise, he was scared to. He didn't like the idea of letting them down; in fact, it made his teeth clench. But he dismissed it. Obviously, they expected nothing else from him. So what did he care? They wouldn't be surprised. Not one bit.

He glanced at his phone. If he had cell service, he'd call Phoebe.

But it was dead. The battery had run down searching for a signal. So no calling Phoebe.

He could only imagine what she was doing right then.

Hating him.

But that was okay, because he was Nick the Prick. Selfish, driven, focused. Nothing else mattered except achieving his own goals.

So why was his gut churning with guilt? Why did he have the incredible urge to flip a U-turn and drive right back to Redbolt?

Why did he even care?

Six months ago, he wouldn't have cared one bit. Six months ago, he probably wouldn't have even bothered to call Phoebe. He would have just disappeared.

What had changed?

He'd gotten soft; that was it. All that time in hippieland had made his head turn into mush.

Nick pushed his foot down on the gas pedal. This was what he wanted; this was what he needed. He'd gotten so used to the low-key café that he'd forgotten the adrenaline rush of working in a real kitchen.

He'd forgotten what he'd worked for his entire life. And now he had the opportunity to get back on track, and he was feeling guilty about it?

Fuck that. He wanted this job. He wanted his life back.

He didn't go to culinary school in Paris to make bowl after bowl of vegetarian pasta salad. Although Phoebe's tomatoes were, by far, the best he'd ever tasted.

He hit the steering wheel. *Don't think about Phoebe's tomatoes. Or her. Or oranges. Or chocolate or oysters or whisks...*

Or her eyes, or her smile, or her wit.

Don't think about it. Just drive.

He turned on his iPod and blasted some electronic music. The first song had a strong, pounding beat that made the entire car vibrate and thump. Yes. This was one of his favorite songs. He hadn't listened to it in...months.

Yes. He needed his old life back. He could be at a club that night. Surrounded by beautiful women who didn't make him think. Who demanded nothing. Who wouldn't ever argue with him.

Yeah, he could probably have that tonight if he wanted it. He did want it. He really did.

"I can't believe him." Phoebe pulled her hair into a ponytail and yanked on an apron. "I really can't believe him."

Jesse looked up from the pile of onions she was currently slicing. Phoebe couldn't help but notice she was becoming incredibly efficient with her chopping skills.

"Maybe something's wrong. Just because we got that call doesn't mean he left for L.A. I'm worried."

A bitter laugh escaped Phoebe's mouth. "Don't give him that much credit. Lester at the gas station saw his Hummer speeding by on the freeway. And Nick was headed south at quite the clip, according to Lester."

"What are you saying? That Nick just up and went to L.A. without telling us?"

"That is exactly what I'm saying. I knew I never should have trusted him."

Jesse shook her head. "We don't know that yet."

"Oh, I know all right. I know exactly what that man is capable of."

Jesse's eyes were sad. "I'm sorry, Phoebe."

"Don't be. We don't need him." Phoebe glanced at the fixed-price menu for that evening. Because Saturday night had become so popular, they'd started doing the set menu on Friday as well.

"Oh, hell." Phoebe read over the menu. "I can't cook any of these things."

"Let me see." Jesse took the menu and gave it a quick scan. "Hmm. I don't see anything on here that looks too difficult."

"Really? Really?" Phoebe realized her voice was starting to sound hysterical. But she couldn't help it. "We're booked solid with reservations, people are expecting the fixed-price menu, and we don't have a chef. I'd say everything right now looks pretty damn difficult!"

Jesse came over and put a calming hand on her shoulder. "Seriously, Phoebe. You haven't been at the café as much lately."

"Great. Now you're going to make me feel guilty?"

"No," Jesse said firmly. "You finally learned how to delegate."

"Yeah, and look how well that turned out for me."

Jesse's grip on Phoebe's arm tightened. "Phoebe. Calm down."

"But—"

Jesse gave her aunt another squeeze. "Seriously. We—*I* can do this."

Phoebe paused and looked at her niece. "How?"

"Listen. Nick's been giving me cooking lessons. I've learned a lot from him. And…"

Phoebe saw two light red patches stain her niece's cheeks. What was going on here?

"And what, Jesse?"

"I've been practicing a lot at home. When you and Dad aren't around."

"What? Why have you been hiding this from us?"

Jesse's cheeks turned the color of two ripe tomatoes.

"Because I've been cooking meat. Lots of it."

"Really?"

"Yes. And I feel guilty. You know, about Dad."

"But we've already discussed that. He would never tell you how to live your life."

"I know, but . . . I still feel bad."

Phoebe rested her backside against the counter. "Wow. I've been so wrapped up in my own life, I didn't even know I had a secret chef living under the same roof."

"Please don't tell my dad."

"I won't. You know that."

"Thank you."

"Well, I'll be damned." Phoebe couldn't help but smile at her niece. "When did you get so grown up?"

"I don't know. Did I?"

"I think so."

Jesse shrugged sheepishly. "I just like cooking. That's all."

"Well, I hope you like it as much as you think you do."

"Why do you say that?"

Phoebe glanced at the menu in Jesse's hand. "Because you're the head chef tonight. Now let's get going. You just tell me what to do."

Jesse's smile was blinding. "Okay. We'll start with the truffle oil sauce . . ."

An hour later, Phoebe found herself in the storage room. She'd gone in looking for . . . what had she been looking for?

Looking around the room, her heart hurt. Nick's presence was everywhere. She saw him perched on the crate, lighting a cigarette. She saw him leading her around with a whisk in his hand. It was overwhelming to be in that room and know he'd abandoned her the way he had.

She'd been feeding off her anger all afternoon. It was better than the other emotions bubbling inside her.

Betrayal. She felt utterly betrayed by him. She couldn't believe she'd allowed herself to trust him. To rely on him. To like him.

To love him.

It hurt. It hurt so much, right in her heart.

How could he do this to her? Did she mean nothing to him? Nothing at all?

Obviously, that was exactly what she meant to him. He didn't care about her, her feelings, or about anything except himself.

She wouldn't cry. She did not want to cry.

Fuck. She was crying.

She hadn't cried since her aunt and uncle had died. But now big, stinging tears welled up in her eyes and spilled over. She couldn't stop them.

She was shaking, and her legs were threatening to give out. She leaned back against the storage room door. The very door Nick had held her against as he'd used her.

Because that's exactly what he'd done. *Used* her, in every possible sense of the word. Used her business, used her heart. Used her body.

And now, he was done.

If only it would be that easy for her to be done with him.

Sinking to the ground, she let the tears escape. Wrapping her arms around her legs, she let her head fall to her knees. She cried. She felt her heart actually ache. She nearly let the sadness take over.

But she didn't. She had a job to do. She had a business

to run. Two of them. And she didn't have time to wallow in self-pity because she'd been stupid enough to fall for Nick the Prick Avalon.

It was her own damn fault.

She pushed herself up and wiped off her face. So this was what it felt like to have your heart broken. Suddenly all those stupid songs about love and heartbreak made perfect sense.

Chapter Twenty-Nine

What the fuck are you doing?"

Nick glanced at Sherry, who was sitting on a plush leather sofa beside him. They were at one of Hollywood's most trendy bars, and Nick was sipping a glass of fine tequila.

The entire place was filled with beautiful women. Trancelike ambience music played from a sound system, and the modern decor was trendy and hip.

He'd gotten the job.

Life was good.

Or at least that's what he kept telling himself.

"What are you blathering about now, Sherry?"

"You and your stupidity." She sipped daintily at a glass of red wine.

"Are you referring to wearing the wrong shoes with the wrong belt again?"

"Don't be an ass. I swear, I am on the edge with you right now."

"The edge of what?"

"Liking you."

He shrugged. "Do what you want, Sherry. I can't control how you feel."

"Did you really just up and ditch Phoebe?"

"I left a message on her cell phone."

"A message. And what did this message say?"

"That I had an emergency in L.A., and I needed to come down here ASAP." He drained his tequila.

"So you just up and vanished on her?"

"Hey." His voice was harder than he intended. "I did what I had to do. I got the most coveted restaurant job in this town. We should be celebrating, and you're giving me shit. Not cool."

"No. What's not cool is your behavior." She shook her head, and he saw pity in her eyes.

It made his gut twist. He could handle anything except someone's pity.

"Don't judge me," he said. "And don't look at me like that."

"I'm sorry, Nick. I guess I just thought better of you."

"Well, I would have thought you'd know what a mistake that could be. You know what they say, Expect the worst and you won't be disappointed."

She emptied what was left of her wine and stood. "The only people who say stupid shit like that are idiots who want an excuse to fail."

Leaning forward, Nick placed his elbows on his knees. "Fail? Fail? What don't you understand here? I never wanted to leave Los Angeles. I never wanted to cook in some ass-backward hippie town. I want my old life back."

"Yeah. Well, it looks like now you have it back. Have fun with it. Expect the worst while you're at it. Then you won't be disappointed."

"Fuck," he muttered, sinking back into the sofa. What didn't Sherry get about this?

He watched as a tall man in an Armani suit attempted to pick up Sherry. She smiled sweetly at him, and Nick saw her mouth the word *no*. The guy kept trying, and again she said *no*. Finally he went away.

She came back carrying a tequila for Nick and a glass of cabernet for herself. After placing the drinks on the round table in front of them, she took her place on the sofa.

"You're judging me?" Nick asked.

"No. I'm calling you on your shit."

He laughed. "What about you? You're done with your hippie boy and you just left him?" He sarcastically shook his head. "Sounds like you ditched him. How very not cool you are."

Her smile was sickly sweet. "As usual, you're totally wrong."

"Pray tell."

"Steve is moving here."

Nick froze. "What?"

"Yup. But it's a secret at the moment. He's waiting for the right time to tell Jesse."

"Wait. So you got Steve to move to L.A.?"

"It wasn't hard. Frankly, I think he's been wanting out of that town for a while. And he can still visit all he wants. I'll be traveling up there a lot for work, anyway."

"But I'd think he would hate this town."

She shrugged. "We had a blast when he was down here. He especially loved Venice Beach. He and my son really hit it off. I think Redbolt has too many memories for him. He seemed like an entirely different person when he was away."

"So you like this guy?"

As if he had to ask. She was positively glowing. "I do. Yes, very much. So, you're wrong. I didn't ditch anyone. That's more your style."

"For fuck's sake, Sherry. Give it a rest, will you?"

She just shrugged in a know-it-all way that was highly irritating.

One thing. He'd wanted one thing ever since that day he'd been fired six months ago. And now he'd achieved it, and for some reason, Sherry was giving him all kinds of shit about it.

He didn't care. He'd lived his entire life not caring what anyone thought. Nick Avalon looked out for himself. That was something he'd never made any qualms about hiding. Hell, how many times had Phoebe herself said as much to him? How many times had she called him a self-absorbed, thoughtless prick?

Yeah, earlier it had bugged him that he was proving her right. But then he realized he didn't care. Let her be right. He hadn't changed in the four months he'd been away from Los Angeles.

This was where he belonged. It was home. This was his life. Everyone else could fuck off.

Across the room, a familiar-looking blonde smiled at him. Maybe he'd fucked her; he couldn't recall. He smiled back.

He beckoned a waitress for another tequila. His gaze roamed the room and landed back on the blonde.

Yup. He finally had it back. He had all he needed. City life, decent music, beautiful women who didn't argue with him all day long.

It was good to be home.

And that's what he was going to keep telling himself.

* * *

Fourteen days later, Nick was in the kitchen of his new restaurant. Things were going swimmingly. His staff was already intimidated by his surly demeanor. He'd planned an amazing menu. The kitchen was a top chef's dream.

They were opening that night.

The entire place buzzed with anticipation and energy. This was exactly what Nick got off on. High-stress, fast-paced—and he was the leader. The manager knew enough to back the fuck away and let him do his job.

Everything was perfect.

Waitstaff scurried around him, preparing for the first customers. And they weren't a bunch of hippie teenagers. He'd forgotten that out here, a server at a high-end trendy restaurant needed to actually know what they were doing. They needed to be savvy on things like gourmet food and wine. A job at a place like this was hard to come by, and most of the staff were actors, which translated into career waiters. Unlike some places that he refused to think about, here the industry was taken seriously.

Nick looked around the restaurant and crossed his arms over his chest. He was in his element. He had regained what he'd lost.

And everything inside him felt empty.

Yes. He'd pulled off what he'd set out to do. He'd burned bridges, hurt people, and been exactly what Phoebe had always called him: a fucking prick.

He was back.

But back where? He'd thought he was coming home. But everything here felt wrong. He realized that he missed sitting on the porch of the cabin, sipping tequila and listening to the crickets. He missed teaching Jesse how to cook. He had to admit that he missed the challenge of creating a menu out of whatever random produce Phoebe tossed at him.

And, most of all, he missed Phoebe. He missed her so much his chest felt like it had a boa constrictor in it. Squeezing and squeezing him until he thought his ribs were going to implode.

He couldn't even look at another woman; the thought of touching anyone but her made him feel sick. Even that blonde from the other night. Everything about her had been wrong. Wrong hair, wrong eyes, wrong skin. But, obviously, Phoebe was never going to change her opinion about him. She was never going to actually *like* him.

Unless you change her mind.

Yeah, right. Even *if* he wanted to, how was he supposed to do that now?

He'd already totally fucked that up.

Nick looked around the busy restaurant. Sometimes things just felt wrong, even though you knew they should feel right. Sometimes you started out making an omelet but had to settle for scrambled eggs because you fucked up.

He was living in a big old mess of overcooked scrambled eggs.

"Fuck." He threw his white hat to the sous-chef. "Have at it."

Manuel, who'd been second in line for Nick's job, just stared at him. "What are you doing, man?"

Nick was already headed for the door. Over his shoulder, he said, "Making a fucking omelet."

Chapter Thirty

Phoebe. It's pouring outside. We don't need quail eggs that badly."

Phoebe swung her bag over her shoulder and pulled out the keys to the Toyota. "It's on the menu."

Jesse stared at her. "So. What. That doesn't mean you need to go out driving in a freak rainstorm to get them!"

"It's not raining that badly. Really, Jesse. It's just a drive. I don't understand why you're freaking out."

"Well, maybe because my aunt has gone off her rocker and is driving to some tiny farm out in the middle of nowhere when it's pouring rain? For quail eggs?"

"Pshaw. I'll be fine. You know I can drive my Land Cruiser through anything."

"Just because you can doesn't mean you should."

Phoebe narrowed her gaze at her niece. "I'm not so sure I like this grown-up side of you."

"Too bad. It's here to stay."

"I don't know if hiring you as my head chef was such a good idea. It's gone to your head."

"Well, at least I'm using my head! Unlike some people I know. *Auntie*."

"It's Saturday. Remember? Nick made the tradition of

having poached quail-egg salad with watercress and tarragon sauce?"

"Yes. So?"

"So. Some people come in now just for that salad. I'm not going to say we don't have it just because Nick left."

"We won't have it because we can't get the eggs!"

"Same difference."

"Phoebe. You're acting crazy. You can't do everything. When are you going to learn that?"

Never. "I'll be fine. Seriously. It's just a little rain."

Jesse inhaled a breath, and Phoebe was taken with how much, at that moment, her niece looked like Phoebe's sister when she'd been about to give a lecture.

"You get everything ready for tonight. I'll be back with those eggs before you know it."

"What if something happens out there? You know there's no cell service in the hills!"

"Jesse. I'm going."

"Fine. But I don't like it."

"I'm still your boss."

Jesse grunted but said, "Just be careful."

"I will. Back in a jiffy."

Phoebe pulled out of the lot and headed toward the winding, two-lane road that led to the small farm where she got most of her eggs. The rain had caused a small mudslide in the farm's driveway, which was keeping their deliveries from being executed. But they'd agreed to meet Phoebe at the end of the driveway so she could pick up supplies for the restaurant.

Ah, the joys of living in the backwoods. Mudslides, falling trees, bad cell phone service. No wonder Nick had hated it there so much.

Damn it. She punched the steering wheel. She was trying really, really hard not to think about that bastard. Because when she did, her heart hurt and that really sucked.

And she got really pissed off at herself for allowing him to get to her. He didn't deserve an ounce of her energy. He was all the things she'd pegged him as from the start. He'd driven that point home like a samurai drives a sword into a person's chest.

She wouldn't think about it. Instead she concentrated on driving. It really was raining hard, much harder than she'd predicted. Even with her windshield wipers on high, she still had a hard time seeing the road.

As she drove deeper into the forest, the road became littered with broken tree limbs and rocks. She had to slow to a crawl. Maybe Jesse had been right. Perhaps driving out here in this weather hadn't been the brightest of ideas.

But she really hadn't been able to think right since Nick left. She'd go from being incredibly sad to blindingly angry. It was affecting her judgment, and it had to stop.

She would stop.

She needed a distraction. Distraction was good. She'd kept busy with the farm and the café, but it was still hard when she was alone. In her own head.

It was too quiet in the car.

Reaching down, she turned on the radio, but there were barely any stations that transmitted out here, so she had to fuss with the dial before she found anything decent.

She found a station that was playing an old Crosby, Stills, and Nash song. And that was when the three-hundred-foot redwood tree fell to the ground, landing on the road directly in front of her.

Nick skidded to a stop in front of the café. The rain had become downright torrential the closer he'd got to Redbolt, and now he sprinted from his Hummer to the door of the Green Leaf. He'd left last night, right after he'd walked out on his dream job. And even just breathing the Northern California air seemed refreshing and welcoming.

Inside the café was a different story.

Dinner was just getting started, and the place was filling up. Except the minute he walked in, the place went silent.

Yeah. So he probably should have expected a reception like this.

Ignoring the angry glares of his previous customers, he stalked to the kitchen.

Jessie stared at him. "What the hell are you doing here?"

"Where's Phoebe?"

"Why?"

"Jesse. Just tell me where she is. Is she at home?"

Jesse stared at him a moment before pulling him into a corner. She spoke in a hushed voice. "She insisted on going out for eggs at this farm about twenty miles into the mountains. I told her it was a bad idea. She should have been back over an hour ago. I'm getting really worried."

"Have you called her?"

"No cell service out there."

His blood went cold. "Give me the address and directions."

"What are you going to do?"

"What do you think I'm going to do? I'm going to go find her."

"Any word from Phoebe?"

Nick turned to see his very best friend, Bear, standing a few feet away.

Jesse shook her head. "No. Nick's going to go look for her."

It was then that Bear's gaze landed on him. He scowled. "Is he now? What, did you get fired again and want Phoebe to give you your old job back? I really don't think that's gonna happen, not the way you treated her."

Nick tensed but tried to keep his cool. "Just get out of my way. I'm going out to look for Phoebe."

Bear stepped in front of him. "That's ridiculous. If anyone goes out looking for her, it's not going to be some unreliable flake who probably can barely even drive his big expensive car."

"Move aside."

"Go back to L.A. We don't need you here."

Nick's blood went from ice cold to boiling hot in one second. He got right up in Bear's face. "Listen, you dickwad. Step the fuck back."

"Phoebe doesn't want anything to do with you. She's seeing me now."

Nick didn't plan on punching the guy; he really didn't. His fist just shot out and punched Bear in the nose. Big Bear reeled back, trying to stop the blood streaming from his nostrils.

"Boys! This is totally not cool. We're in a restaurant, for God's sake," Jesse said. Then she turned to Bear. "And you are full of shit. You're not dating Phoebe."

"I know. I just said that to keep this dog off her tail."

"Right," Nick said, shaking his throbbing hand. "I'll see you later. I'm going to get Phoebe." And with that he walked out the door, jogged through the pouring rain, and hopped into his Hummer. Bear was dead wrong. Nick knew how to drive his car incredibly well. And now he was going to use it to go find Phoebe.

She could have crashed her car.

She could be hurt, lying in a ditch.

She could be unconscious.

He didn't need directions. He realized he knew exactly what farm Phoebe had been headed to. He'd gone there himself on several occasions.

The road was winding, narrow, and treacherous in the best of conditions.

Damn it, Phoebe—what were you thinking?

She'd better be okay. She *would* be okay. She had to be. Nick realized he needed her like a good roux needs flour. He just hoped that she'd give him a second chance.

Now Phoebe was getting really cold. The rain hadn't stopped, and heavy streams of water were rushing down the side of the mountain in muddy torrents. Her head was pounding, and her neck was sore.

So stupid. Such a stupid thing to prove she could do.

Surely Jesse would have sent out a search party by now. But if she had, could they even reach her?

The rain was pounding so hard on her car she thought it might dent the metal. She could barely see the mountain she currently faced. No one was going to find her. Not anytime soon, anyway.

Yup. You've really done it now.

She'd been staring out the window for more than an hour. It was gray. Wet and gray. She could barely see more than five feet beyond her window.

Except... What was that? Something huge... and yellow... was crawling toward her.

No effing way.

She knew only one person with a car like that. One person who would be stupid enough to come get her. One person who would be stupid and arrogant enough to even think about coming back to town.

Nick Avalon. Yup. He pulled to a stop near her, jumped out of his Hummer, and ran through the mud to her car. He yanked open the door and assessed her in one fell swoop.

"Are you okay, baby?"

She just glared at him. "Yes, I am. And don't call me baby."

He smiled at her. "Oh, bloody hell. I fucking love you."

"Did you crash? Do you have a concussion, too?"

"No."

"You came for me," she said.

He just nodded.

"But you left."

"I know. It was stupid... I was stupid. I was so stupid I want to shoot myself."

"I want to shoot you, too. And you're soaking wet and now so am I."

With the door open, rain was pouring onto both of them and drenching the car inside. "I'm sorry." He leaned in to pick her up. "Are you hurt?"

"No, not really."

Gently, he lifted her out of the car and shut the door

with the heel of his boot. Then he walked to his Hummer and opened the passenger door. After he'd placed her on the seat, he shut the door and got in on the other side.

He turned to face her.

"You're bleeding." With the hem of his jacket he wiped the rain and blood off her face.

"I'm fine. Nick?"

"Yes?"

"Why are you here?"

"I told you. I love you."

"And what do you want me to do with this informa tion?"

"Give me another chance? Please, Phoebe. Listen. I've just left everything I've ever worked for behind: my job, my life in Hollywood, recognition. None of it matters anymore. Because I'd take a day in the forest, or collecting oysters on the coast, or anything that involved a moment with you, over anything else in the world."

Her heart was beating like a jungle drum. "What are you saying? That you want to move here? Permanently?"

His voice sounded gravelly and hoarse. "Yes, but only if you want to be with me."

"Nick. Are you asking me to be your girlfriend?"

"Yes."

"You're saying you just left Hollywood and want to move here and be with me? For good?"

He nodded. "I know you don't trust me, and that you think I tried to one-up you with the whole brownie thing, but—"

She held up her hand. "Nick, I'm the one who needs to apologize about that."

"What do you mean?"

"I jumped to the wrong conclusions. I didn't trust you. But I know you had good intentions, and I'm sorry I didn't recognize them right away."

For just one second, she actually thought she saw his eyes go just a tad watery at her words.

She stared at him. "Goddamn you, Nick."

He slanted one of those grins at her, the kind that made her heart skip a beat. He took her head in his hands and kissed the wound on her forehead. "Thank you, Phoebe. Your words mean a lot to me."

"It still doesn't negate the fact you up and ditched us!"

"I know, baby. I behaved horribly. I promise to never do it again."

"How can I trust you?"

"Would it help if I told you that on the way here, I got a phone call with an offer to host my own show, and I turned it down?"

She jerked back. "You did? Why didn't you take it?"

"Because I want to be here. In the middle of freakin' nowhere. With you. That's what makes me happy."

"How can I believe you? Trust you? How do I know you're telling the truth?"

"I'll do anything to make you believe me. To trust me. To understand that deep down"—he pounded his chest—"this is what I want. You. The café. The forest, the beach. And did I say you?"

He held her to his chest. He was so warm, her shivering body soaked up his heat. She buried her nose in his shoulder. That scent. She couldn't help it. It got her every time; it was home and sex and connection and earth. And Nick.

She paused. "Cardamom."

He glanced down at her. "Um, pardon me? I kinda thought we were having a moment."

"We are. Have I told you I love the way you smell?"

"No, you haven't."

"But there's something about your scent I never could quite identify. Some spice."

"I take it it's cardamom?"

Inhaling again, she nodded. "I like it."

"I use it every morning to make chai tea."

"I like chai tea."

He tilted her head up. "Good. Can I make it for you to-morrow morning?"

Slowly, and biting back a goofy smile, she nodded.

He kissed her nose. "And the morning after that?"

"Yes, Nick. And if you're lucky, the morning after that."

His blue eyes sparkled with that thing called happiness he seemed to have developed. "I'm a pretty lucky guy," he said.

She tried to look serious. "Well, since you're going to have me as your girlfriend, you are a pretty lucky guy."

He kissed her then. It was a slow kiss, a kiss of prom-ises. Of forests and beaches and redwood trees and chocolate and oysters. It was a kiss of hope. Of trust. Of security.

Then the kiss deepened, and her body responded. Her breasts ached for his touch, and between her legs a pulse began to beat.

He held her face to his, and as he explored more of her mouth, as he tasted her and licked her, she wanted to fall into him. Become one.

When they pulled apart, she was panting.

"I love you, Phoebe."

"You must," she said, looking around. "After all, we're here, stranded *in the middle of nowhere*, and I think I just heard another tree fall. That might keep us from getting back, even in your Hummer."

"Nope," he said, starting the car. "We're going to make it back safe and sound." He glanced at her. "Ready?"

"Yes," she said with a smile. "Let's go home."

Ruby Scott is a beautiful, quiet event planner who leads an oh-so-respectable life. Yet the things that go on in her secret fantasies are anything but...

Bound to Please

Turn this page for an excerpt.

Chapter Two

Ruby, meet Mark St. Crow. He's the head of the Dark Riders." Emmett gave her a look that she knew meant *Kiss his ass*.

And her first thought was, *Okay! If you insist*. Because the man standing before her made her heart race. Made her feel all tingly and they hadn't even spoken yet.

His head was shaved and gleamed in the dim light, clean and shiny. She'd never been with a bald man; she wondered how the skin would feel beneath her fingers, if she'd be able to trace the bones of his skull. Her fingers curled at the thought.

She uncurled them and held out her hand. "Nice to meet you." Their palms met and her pulse jumped.

She took her hand back.

Young. He looked so very young. But, at thirty-seven, it seemed everyone got younger every day.

He gazed at her through black-rimmed glasses. *Damn*. She'd always had a thing for glasses on a man. She'd had a serious crush on an art history professor in college who wore them. At night, she'd study nineteenth-century Italian paintings, then go to bed and think of him as she used her hot-pink bullet vibrator.

For fuck's sake, don't think about that*!*

"Ruby. Do you know there are at least forty songs with your name in the title?" Mark asked.

"Um, actually I didn't. So you get points for an original twist on an old line." She cringed. Why had she said that? She could almost feel Emmett's censure, but when she turned she discovered he, along with Meg, had vanished.

She looked back to see Mark raising a brow over those bloody glasses. "So are you saying I'm not original?"

"I don't know yet. Can you name all the songs?" Was she flirting? That sounded like flirting.

"Probably. But I want to get paid for my talents. Fortunately, I work cheap. A beer ought to cover it. I'll even get it myself."

She raised a hand to protest. "That's really not necces—"

"Be right back."

She watched him walk away. Tall and sinewy, his black T-shirt showed off a solid torso, and the short sleeves gave her a nice view of well-defined, tattoo-covered arms. Faded, low-slung jeans—not too tight—wrapped around long legs that carried his form with a confidence that drew her attention. He looked too young for that kind of confidence. So young he could get away with leather bands circling both his wrists and make it look hot.

In fact, he had a lot of leather on his body. Bracelets, belt, boots. All black, all worn. The sight of all that leather sent a thrill through her, which she quickly stomped down.

Now he was walking back across the room with his gaze fixed on her. Like she was some kind of target, like he was some kind of predator. Hell, he probably was. Young, gorgeous, talented. She'd go down like a gazelle under a lion's attack.

He handed her a chocolate martini, and she could swear she smelled the leather from his bracelets. Which made her remember the wall of leather at the sex shop. There was a specific smell to this type of leather. Woodsy, freshly cut. Sexy.

No, no. Don't think about that . . .

But of course she did. She thought about the time she'd gone with Ash to the fetish store to purchase suspension equipment. Ruby had been drawn to the wall of floggers and paddles and other mysterious implements; her palms had dampened as she approached all that leather. Nervous and excited just to see the tools, all lined up in neat, erotic rows. She'd wondered how the leather would feel striking her skin. Would it sting a lot? Or a little? Would she like it? Her hand had trembled as she ran her finger over the soft strands of a buckskin flogger.

"You like them?"

"W-what?"

Mark shook his wrist. "These. You were staring at them."

"No. I mean yes. They're lovely." *Lovely?*

That damn brow of his went higher.

She felt hot. All over. Which compelled her to take a calming sip of the drink he'd handed her. As a rule, she didn't drink at her own events, but so far she'd broken her own rule twice in one night. First with Meg, now with Mark. *Mark something St. Crow.*

"Do you have a middle name?" she asked.

He tilted his head. "Why?"

"Um. Just wondering." Seriously, her legs were trembling.

"Let's sit." Was he reading her mind now?

He led her to a table in a corner. And the only reason she took the seat he offered was because of Emmett. Really, it was. Emmett wanted to record this band, and, as his wife's best friend, she felt an obligation to do whatever she could to help out. And if that meant making small talk with a young man who wore black glasses and smelled like leather and looked at her like she was the only woman in the room, so be it.

She stifled a shiver.

"You cold?"

"Nope. Uh-uh. Not at all." In fact, she was burning up. *Conversation. Make conversation.* "So. You're in a band." *Real clever.*

"Yup. Sure am." Why did he always seem to be holding back a smile?

She went on. "What do you play?"

"Everything. Piano, guitar. The Bazantar—"

"You play the Bazantar?" she said, her eyes wide.

"On occasion. You know what it is?"

"It's a five-string double bass, invented by Mark Deutsch."

He stared a second too long. "Wow. I'm impressed."

"So am I. That you play it, I mean." She cleared her throat. "Anyway, what else do you do?"

"I sing. I'm a bit of a control freak about performing, actually."

She couldn't help but find that interesting. Mark St. Crow was a control freak. He seemed the opposite of her, and yet she often referred to herself with that same exact phrase. Well, everyone referred to her that way, didn't they? "What kind of music does your band play?" she asked.

"Rock and roll. Punk. Electronic. Everything." Now he did smile before he tilted his beer bottle to his lips. She surmised that, by now, he must have realized she had no idea who his band was. It didn't seem to bother him.

Which was even more interesting. But she shook the thoughts out of her head. She really should be checking in with the caterer, mingling. So she had no idea why she asked: "Didn't we have a deal? Were you going to name forty songs with the name Ruby in the title?" So now she was asking him to serenade her. *Niiiice.* Not flirting at all.

"This might not be in chronological order; I'm a bit rusty."

"I understand."

He coughed into his hand, cleared his throat. Made a show of it. She bit her lip, trying not to laugh at his silliness. With all this charm, no doubt he had girls falling over him every night. The thought sobered her up, and she straightened in her seat.

Suddenly she had the distinct feeling that she was being watched and she looked up to find the woman Mark had arrived with staring at her. Tall, with a supermodel's figure and sparkling green eyes, the redhead was stunning. And, judging from the intense expression on her face, she disapproved of Mark talking to Ruby.

"What's up?" Mark asked.

Ruby tried to shrug indifferently. "Your girlfriend doesn't look too happy."

"That's Yvette, my singer. She's not my girlfriend."

"Are you sure she knows that?"

"Yeah. I already ventured down that road, and it didn't work out so well. Hit a dead end, so to speak." He chuckled; his laugh was deep and husky and made her soften even more.

So, he'd been with Yvette. Who cared? Ruby had no idea why it mattered that Mark's gorgeous, talented, soon-to-be-famous ex-girlfriend was staring at them like she would be perfectly happy if a hole opened up and swallowed Ruby alive.

"Don't mind Yvette. She's just overprotective. We go way back."

"I don't mind," Ruby said as Yvette turned away. "Not at all. It's great to have good friends. Anyway, I should be going. I have to check on . . . things." As if she didn't have every detail, down to the exact number of hand towels in the bathroom, under control.

His hand on her knee made her pause. "But I haven't finished my side of the deal yet. So sit back and listen, my darling Ruby."

She flicked his hand away. "I'm not your darling anything."

"I know. It's a song. By Mossa."

"Oh."

"House music."

"I don't listen to house."

"Understood. It's not nearly as good as the hair-band music you have going on here."

She bristled. "Eighties rock is *back*."

"Sadly."

She agreed but didn't say it. And she really wished he would stop smiling like that. It did funny things to her stomach.

He opened his mouth to speak, but she interrupted. "So you're on. List every song with Ruby in the title. And, just for fun, how about you do it by genre?" She smiled innocently.

"A bit of a challenge, but I'll give it a try. What should I start with? Not house. Rock? Alternative? Jazz—"

"Jazz." Ruby loved jazz and was quite sure this young rock star would be stumped. Which, bizarrely, would please her.

"Jazz it is. Okay, then. *A-hem.* Of course we have 'Ruby, My Dear' by Thelonious Monk; 'Ruby, I Need You' by the Steel Brothers; 'Ruby' by Ambrose Akinmusire; 'Ruby' by Art Farmer; 'Ruby' by Jimmy Smith; 'Ruby' by Benny Carter—"

She froze. "You've heard of Benny Carter?"

"You seem surprised."

"I am. Not many people know jazz."

"How do you know so much about jazz, Ruby So Sweet?"

"My dad turned me on to it." She just stopped herself from adding, *before he left.* "When I was a little girl. Not many people have heard of Benny Carter."

"My father was a jazz musician. Upright bass. I'll never forget the first time he caught me listening to the Ramones. I thought he'd have a heart attack right there in my bedroom."

Ah, yes, the Ramones. Their album had come out when Mark was what? Ten?

She asked, "Was he a successful musician? Your father, I mean."

"In his time. Played with some of the greats. Monk, Brubeck, Hancock."

She leaned back, studying the way he coolly listed some of the greatest names in jazz. "Impressive."

He shrugged, and for just a second his eyes flashed with an emotion she couldn't place. "At the time. He gave it up when I came along."

"Really? Why?"

His laugh was wry. "The usual. Mom didn't like the late nights, the travel. The unpredictable income."

"That's understandable."

He eyed her over his beer. "Maybe. Anyway, he taught me everything I know about music. So, Ruby baby. Shall I continue?"

Nodding, she settled into her chair and listened. And listened. And listened. Finally, she waved him to stop. "Fine! I get it. There are a lot of songs with the name Ruby in the title!"

"As there should be."

She rolled her eyes and bit back a grin. Yeah, he was a charmer, all right. And she'd fallen right into his trap. But why her? Why had he picked her to flirt with? Glancing around the room, she saw half a dozen gorgeous young things, some of whom she'd hired herself as eye candy. And that they were. In her vintage suit and high-buttoned shirt, Ruby felt downright dowdy in comparison. At least her red peep-toe pumps were sexy.

Straightening her blazer, Ruby took a deep, calming breath. But then she looked up and her heart stopped. Because Mark wasn't just looking at her; he was scrutinizing her. She found herself pinned under his gaze as if he'd tied her to the chair.

He took a slow swig from his beer. "I noticed the tattoo on the back of your neck. It's nice work."

She wore her hair in a high ponytail, and her hand

went to the cherry blossom tattoo at the top of her spine. "Thank you."

If possible, his gaze became even more intense. "It looks familiar. In fact, it looks exactly like something on a piece of art I bought recently. Here, in San Francisco."

She felt the blood drain from her face. No. It couldn't be. Ash had promised to never sell any of the photographs he'd taken of her. He was a narcissistic, chronically late, tortured artist who, on occasion, cheated on his girlfriend. But he wasn't evil.

Was he?

Mark went on. "The thing is, this piece I bought? It's of a woman, bound in rope. It was one of the sexiest things I'd ever seen." Still watching her, he took another casual swig from his beer. "Until now."

She met his gaze, silent for a minute. Then she started laughing. High-pitched hysterical giggles that had him looking at her with an expression of confusion.

Finally, her laugh died out. "So that's what this is about."

"What 'what' is about?"

She flapped her hand between them. "*This*. You talking to me. You think I'm easy because I posed—*past tense*—naked in erotic photographs. You think I'll tie you up, let you worship my shoes or something." She pushed herself to her feet. "And this is exactly why I didn't want anyone to know it was me in those pictures. You let someone take a few nude photographs, and the next thing you know, guys are begging you to spank them—"

A firm grip on her wrist stopped her midturn, midsentence. He was standing now and she jerked her chin up, confronting his stare.

"Ruby, I'm never the one begging to be spanked. Trust me on that."

He used two fingers to tilt her chin up just a fraction, and the scent of his leather bracelets assaulted her. His brown eyes told her everything: There was nothing submissive about Mark St. Crow.

He said, "You're vibrating."

She shook her head. "I'm not."

That smile again. "You are." He slid his free hand into her blazer pocket like he had every right to do so, and the heat from his arm made her shiver more than she already was. Releasing her wrist, he placed her phone in her palm. The phone that was, in fact, vibrating.

"You might want to get that. Could be important."

"Right. Thanks." Without looking at the caller ID, she turned away and flipped the cell open. "This is Ruby."

"Are you okay?"

Glancing over her shoulder at a grinning Mark, Ruby took a few more steps away from him and scanned the room. "Meg? Where are you?"

"Hiding behind a palm tree. Did you know these things are fakes? Anyway, I saw the way Mark was holding your arm. Is everything all right?"

She looked behind her to find Mark still watching her. She turned away. "Yes. Fine. Turns out Ash sold one of those photographs, and guess who happened to buy one?"

"No way!"

"Way."

"So why was he holding on to your wrist? Does he think you're easy or something 'cause of those pictures? Fuck the recording contract. I'm gonna kick his ass."

"No! No. It's fine, really." Ruby didn't know how she

knew this; she just did. And she couldn't help the fact that a part of her was enjoying their banter. Enjoying him. Yeah, as a musician he was a sworn-off species, but that didn't mean she couldn't enjoy a little flirting, did it? She was thirty-seven. Even if the lighting was soft, it felt good to have a hot young guy hitting on her. Not to mention her wrist still burned from where he'd held her. And that excited her even as it freaked her out.

"Really, Meg. It's fine. Thanks for checking, though." She flipped her phone shut and faced Mark. He was, of course, still staring at her. But now he was sitting again, sipping his beer. Looking innocent. But there was nothing innocent about him. And there was something in his eyes that made her go liquid inside. Made her heart flutter. *Flutter.*

Shit.

Stiffly, she sat back down, picked up her drink, and took a sip. She wasn't stupid. She knew what was being offered. A one-off with a gorgeous young man who made her pulse race. A fast fuck with a man who purchased erotic art and probably thought she had more experience than she had with BDSM. A man who'd said he was never the one begging to be spanked, worded in such a way to imply there was, in fact, someone who had begged for such a thing.

She couldn't get that smell of leather out of her nose.

His gaze darted to the patio door and back to her. "Have a cigarette with me," he said, and she looked up to find those intense brown eyes of his boring into hers.

"I don't smoke."

"Neither do I."

A heartbeat later, she nodded.

Mark placed his beer bottle on the table, and then he took her hand. She loved the feel of his dry, strong fingers laced with hers. Loved the way he confidently led her through the crowd. Even as she broke rule number two—never leave your own event—she loved the way her heart hammered as she followed him onto the terrace. Besides, if anyone needed anything, she was just outside the door.

On this empty patio. All alone. With Mark St. Crow. Her heart started to race in a way it hadn't in a long time, in an anxious pace that made her palms moist.

But then his hand was on her arm, stroking softly. The feeling passed.

She met his gaze and her heart quickened, but in a much more pleasant manner than it had just a moment ago. Were they going to do it now? Have sex? Here?

It suddenly dawned on her that she was about to have a quickie on the patio with a man she'd just met. Why else would he have led her out here?

Why else would she have let him?

Just do it and get it out of your system!

Hell, they were halfway there anyway, right? He'd already seen her at her most vulnerable. The man possessed pictures of her, not just nude, but in bondage. Rope wrapped around her breasts, her arms, between her legs. Totally bound. God, he'd seen more of her than any man had in over a year.

Turning, she smiled shyly at Mark. "You've seen me naked."

"Don't think I'm not thinking about that." The corners of his mouth lifted in a mischievous smile as he took a step closer to her.

She lifted her chin a fraction, then jumped into the unknown. "Do you just admire the art you buy, or do you play?" Her entire body seemed to shake as she waited for him to answer.

His hand went to his belt buckle, where he lightly stroked the brass. "I'm interested in all aspects of power exchange."

And she wanted to give him that power over her.

How had he brought out this side of her so fast? Because she wanted to sink to her knees before him, give herself to him right then. She'd forgotten what that craving was like, how encompassing it could be.

She shook her head. All this talk about leather and bondage and spanking had her head spinning, had her acting crazy.

Instinct told her to run, but then he pulled her to him and cupped her face between his hands. "I'm going to kiss you, but only if you promise to come to my show and then wait for me afterward."

"What if I hate the way you kiss?"

"You won't."

"You're so sure of yourself?"

He lightly stroked the top of her ear. "Yes."

She had no intention of going to his show, but he didn't need to know that. She pulled him down toward her. She loved the way a man's neck felt in her palm, and she closed her eyes and savored the seconds before their first kiss. Then his lips touched hers briefly and she opened her mouth, slid her tongue gently toward his. She tasted him. Took pleasure in the easy way they connected.

She'd forgotten what a kiss could be like. How it could make her legs tingle. How it set loose butterflies in her belly. How it melted her.

His hands were roaming her back, pressing her body against his. Desire hit her like lightning, shooting through her veins in a hot bolt. Their kiss became harder, more intense. His hands held her steady as he explored her mouth, and she groaned against his lips.

Slowly, he moved his fingertips from her shoulder to graze the outside of her breast, down her rib cage and over her hip bone until his hand clenched around her upper thigh. With two steps he had her backed up against the wall. She went limp as he covered her, until she was sandwiched between his hot body and the hard concrete, still warm from the day's muted sun.

His hands were in her hair, loosening the strands. Stroking and pulling, pulling until she gasped from the sharp sting. Her legs quivered and he brought her closer, tilting her head so he could run his tongue across her teeth in just such a way it sent little quivers shooting through her. When he brought her hands together and stretched her arms to hold them high above her head, she allowed it.

How easily she followed his lead. How easy it was to let him direct her. *How could this be happening so fast?* The feeling was too intense, and it was exactly what she was afraid of. Letting go, craving something she couldn't control. Craving the *need* to let go.

So why did it feel so good?

He released her arms, but she kept them over her head and she felt his hands at her chest, steady as he undid the first few buttons of her blouse. Still he kissed her. His knuckles were warm on her skin as he spread the fabric and then his fingertips found her nipple. She gasped into his mouth as he pinched, twisted. The pain shot through her, straight to her sex.

Ash, the others, had always been gentle.

She realized she did not want Mark to be gentle.

She was getting wet. Wet between her legs, but she didn't want him to touch her there, not yet. She wanted to feel the void, feel the want. The journey was as good as the destination, and she wanted to enjoy every moment of the ride, make it last.

Which was bad. Very bad. This was supposed to be a quickie, nothing more. She pulled back. "Do you have a condom?"

He stepped between her legs and yanked up her skirt, lifted her up and she wrapped her legs around his hips. She held him between her thighs as he pushed his denim-clad erection against her panties, which were now moist and damp. "Mark. Please tell me you have a condom."

"Yeah, I have one in my pocket." He sounded so calm. How could he be so calm when she was so quickly becoming undone?

"Thank God." She rubbed her pulsing sex against him, sliding against the buttons of his jeans, letting them grate at her swollen flesh through her underwear. The muscles in his shoulders bunched beneath her hands, thrilling her. She could come, just like this, with a stranger.

He continued to kiss her, stroke her, wrap her hair in his fist. Grind his cock between her legs until she was begging him. "Please, Mark. Condom."

"Come, Ruby."

"I will, I promise. As soon as you put on the condom and we . . . you know. *Do it.*" She whispered the last two words.

He shook his head, and—*damn him*—he seemed to

be biting back a smile. Again. "No, I mean come to the show. You obviously like the way I kiss."

She was panting as if she'd been running, and she had to fight to catch her breath. "Why do you care if I go later?"

By now her neat ponytail was practically nonexistent, and he wrapped a lock of hair around his finger. "Because then I can see you afterward."

"But—"

He gave her hair a gentle tug, and fuck it, her sex clenched from the sharp pain. Like a puppet, she responded to his every touch.

"Listen, Ruby. I want you."

"Here I am. Take me!" She wiggled a bit against his body as a prompt.

His eyes searched hers, darting back and forth. "I want more than a quickie against a wall. I want the night with you. And I have a feeling you want more, too."

Everything in her froze. "Like what? What do you think I could possibly want?"

Leaning in, he kissed her earlobe. "I think you want to give yourself over to me. I think you want to feel my hand on your ass. I think you want to know what it would be like to be owned by me. Just for one night."

Speechless, she stared over his shoulder at the jasmine growing in a pot in the corner. She bit the inside of her cheek. He was wrong, so wrong. She *so* did not want those things.

So why was she trembling? Why was her pussy throbbing just from those simple words? Why were her nipples tingling beneath her satin bra?

And, most important, why were her insides melting

into a puddle of lust with each passing second he breathed against her ear?

This was such a bad idea.

But the alternative was going home to her vibrator, which sounded much less appealing.

"Fine. I'll go," she said.

Her reward was another kiss that blew away any reasonable thoughts left in her head.

He slid her down his body and put her on her feet. Then he straightened her skirt and fastened one button between her breasts. How could he look so controlled when she felt anything but?

And then, with his hand, he encircled her throat, his palm pressing against her clavicle, and something calmed inside her. His eyes were dark as they drilled into hers. "I'll leave a pass at the door. There will be a spot reserved for you near the stage. Where I can see you."

"Yes," she breathed, loving the way his hand enclosed her neck. Loving *everything*.

"I'll tell the bartender to have a drink waiting for you. If any men approach you tonight, I want you to ignore them. Do you understand?"

She nodded. She couldn't help herself. She liked the feelings Mark had set off inside her too much to say anything at all, especially the word *no*.

Pinned to the wall, his large hand on her throat, she sank into him as he kissed her again. His mouth gently belied the rough grip he had on her body, and the juxtaposition of sensation nearly killed her.

How could she deny herself this? After all, it was just one night.

Art gallery curator Joy Montgomery has never liked her body's generous curves, and she's always been too shy to explore her wild side. But when bad-boy artist Ash Hunter asks her to pose as his model, Joy finds her life is about to change.

Dare to Surrender

Turn this page for an excerpt.

Chapter Four

She saw the corded muscles of his arms loosen, the only sign that he'd been anxious she might say no.

It took only a couple of minutes, and just the process of him binding her, the feeling of the corded material wrapping around her skin, made her pussy go wet, made her entire body hum with lust. When she felt him tie her off, she tested the rope, and while it wasn't uncomfortable, it was secure. Her wrists were bound, like she was his prisoner.

"You all right?"

"Yes." She was more than all right. The act of submission made her pussy ache in a way she'd never experienced and, surprisingly, calmed her.

Smiling, he pulled her arms tight above her, his body stretched against hers, something she was quite sure he did on purpose. Against her hips, she felt his erection through his jeans and her dress; goose bumps erupted over her arms.

He stepped back, and when she tugged her arms, she realized she couldn't move; he'd secured her to the wall.

"Ash?" She was hovering on the edge of being anxious and thrilled, the two emotions mingling until she couldn't tell them apart.

He took her face between his palms again and kissed her, gently, for the longest time, until she was calm, until the ropes around her wrists felt almost comforting, like they were part of her. Submitting to him, she stopped fighting, and then he got on his knees before her, moving slowly to kiss her body as he made his way down. When he nuzzled his face against her hip, kissed her hip bone through the fabric of her dress, she lost it, lost all control.

"Ash...I need you." Between her legs there was a want; she was pounding with need—for him. She'd never felt a need like this. Ever. The bonds heightened every sensation coursing through her, and she welcomed, claimed, each one.

He lifted the hem of her dress until it was pushed up around her waist. For a second, she thought she must be out of her head, because normally she felt very self-conscious when she was exposed. And she'd never been so vulnerable with someone she barely knew.

But now, that sense of anonymity seemed to entice her, and she stretched her body, arched, let his hands move under her dress to feel her skin. She saw desire in his eyes, and it made her feel sexy, feminine. Maybe it was the ropes, being bound and helpless, giving herself to him; she felt a bit as if she were floating. She felt her own smile on her face as she waited for him, watching Ash's gaze, which was now focused on her panties, her swollen clit.

He glanced up. "Do you like being tied, Joy?"

She nodded.

"Tell me you like it." He placed a soft, warm kiss in that spot he'd been staring at, his breath muffled through the lace of her panties.

"I like it, Ash. I like being tied by you."

"I don't know what it is about you, baby. You make me so fucking turned on." With one hand, he yanked her panties down her legs, still holding her dress up with his other hand. "You always look so..."

"What?" she whispered. How did he see her?

"Ready for me. Like you want me to take you."

"I do. Take me." She couldn't believe the words coming out of her mouth. She'd never talked like this, never been so demanding. But with Ash she felt safe. *Maybe too safe,* a little voice whispered in the back of her head, and she ignored it.

"Spread your legs."

She stepped her legs farther apart, as wide as she could go. With both his hands, he kept her dress up around her hips and pushed her ass back against the wall. Rope hung to her left and to her right, above her. Binding her. Surrounding her. She shuddered.

"Taste me, Ash. Fuck me."

"How did you know dirty talk turns me on?" he asked with a wicked grin.

"I want to feel your mouth on my pussy."

"That's my girl," he said, and then he was licking her, spreading her with his thumbs, spreading her wide so he could use his mouth to sweetly torment her, and she heard herself moaning, pleading.

"Oh, God," she said, pressing hard against him, pulling at her bindings. "Yes, oh my God. I'm going to come, Ash...."

He looked up. "Do it. Come for me, right here against my face. And then I'm going to fuck you, and you're going to come again."

"Yes," was all she managed. "I want that...."

Slowly, tortuously, he licked her, from as deep as he could reach to her throbbing clit: licking, sucking, tugging. She threw her head back against the wall, feeling her hair tangle as she thrashed her head from side to side. When she came against his face, it was like lightning shooting through her, and she screamed his name, crying out over and over as he sucked every last tremble out of her body.

Finally, when she stilled, he stood. His gaze raked over her, and she imagined what she must look like. Arms tied overhead, her dress wrinkled and hanging around her waist. Her hair a rat's nest. In total disarray, the exact opposite of everything she'd come to know about Ash.

But he smiled at her and brushed a strand of hair off her face. "You're a mess."

She felt the blush starting at her neck.

"I like it. I don't know why, but I do. You're so different, Joy. Different from any woman I've been with."

She lifted her chin. "Is that good or bad?"

"Good." He kissed her, and she tasted herself on his lips, acidic and erotic. "Right now it feels really good."

"You know what would feel even better?" she asked against his mouth, licking at his lips and tasting herself and him, while a fresh wave of lust washed over her.

"What's that, baby?"

"If you did as you promised and fucked me."

THE DISH

Where authors give you the inside scoop!

♥ ♥

From the desk of Jill Shalvis

Dear Reader,

I've received many, many letters regarding the leads in my latest book, HEAD OVER HEELS. Sawyer and Chloe—what a combo. We start off with a bit of a wild heroine. Add to the mix a reformed bad boy hero who now wears a gun and is on the right side of the law as the town sheriff. Explosive chemistry.

The thing about Sawyer is that he thinks his life is just right. A job. A house. Two best buds. The occasional woman warming his bed ... Yeah, he thinks life is good.

But then Chloe blows into Lucky Harbor like a good-time girl. A one-time girl. Only problem, one time isn't enough. And Sawyer starts to understand that he might never be able to get enough of her.

Problem. A big one.

It was for me too. I like it when people get along, when there's no tension and friction. But I'm telling you, these two have tension and friction in spades. It was an interesting book to write. To practice keeping that tension high, I pretended I was a wild child. The research was lots of fun.

I'm back to being myself now, and that's fun too. Because now I get to present you with HEAD OVER HEELS.

Happy reading!

Jill Shalvis

www.jillshalvis.com

♥ ♥

From the desk of Lilli Feisty

Dear Reader,

If you've read any of my books, you might have noticed I have a thing for food. Eating is one of my favorite pastimes, and I don't think I've ever written a book without at least one food scene. I am a person who strongly believes a person should live to eat, not the other way around. Food can define culture, history, relationships, and family.

So I tend to write scenes that involve food and eating. To this day, I still get emails from readers about the infamous strawberry scene in my book *Bound to Please*. It seems anyone who read that book can't ever look at strawberries the same way again. And in *Dare to Surrender*, I had a lot of fun writing about my heroine's best friend, a culinary student in San Francisco. They had all kinds of fun in the kitchen.

It seems no matter what story I write, I need to include scenes involving eating. Sometimes they're sexy scenes, sometimes not. Food inspires me on a lot of levels. I once hopped on a plane to Madrid because I wanted to eat tapas. I got more than little plates of food—I experienced an entirely different culture that inspired me to have more fun in life. While on a trip to France, I stayed with families so I could eat home-cooked, seven-course meals. I always eat street-food in Mexico—and my next vacation destination is Vietnam because I love spring rolls.

Obviously, I really like to eat!

I got the idea for Phoebe and Nick while staying in a small town in Northern California. While driving from San Francisco to Portland, I stopped at a small café that served only organic, natural food. Most of the cuisine was vegetarian. It was a small café, but the dishes were mouth-watering. There was something so satisfying about eating locally grown, organic, earthy food that I wanted to try everything on the menu. Obviously, the food was scrumptious, so scrumptious it inspired me to create a story revolving around my delicious experience.

Some of my fondest childhood memories come from our dining table. While writing DELICIOUSLY SINFUL, I dug out my grandmother's copy of Julia Child's *Mastering the Art of French Cooking*. Published in 1966, it has my grandmother's notes penciled in the margins and little squares of cutout recipes tucked in between pages. That cookbook sat on my desk the entire time I wrote DELICIOUSLY SINFUL. It is the one thing I inherited when my grandmother passed away. I cherish it.

I've always thought that food has many meanings. It creates and brings back memories, it writes stories, it brings people together. Every week while I was writing DELICIOUSLY SINFUL, I tried out a new recipe. It reminded me of my mother, my grandmother, and dinners of the past. And every week, I would pick out a recipe, shop for ingredients, cook, and invite my friends over for dinner. I'll admit some of my culinary attempts were...not so good. But it didn't matter. I put love into those meals, just as I put love into this book. I hope you enjoy DELICIOUSLY SINFUL as much as I enjoyed writing it.

Love,

Lilli Feisty